Carl Weber's Kingpins:

The Ultimate Hustle 2

Carl Weber's Kingpins:

The Ultimate Hustle 2

T. Friday

www.urbanbooks.net

Urban Books, LLC
300 Farmingdale Road, N.Y.-Route 109
Farmingdale, NY 11735

Carl Weber's Kingpins: The Ultimate Hustle 2

ISBN 13: 978-1-64556-687-8
EBOOK ISBN: 978-1-64556-697-7

First Trade Paperback Printing May 2025
Printed in the United States of America

10 9 8 7 6 5 4 3 2 1

Distributed by Kensington Publishing Corp.
Submit Orders to:
Customer Service
400 Hahn Road
Westminster, MD 21157-4627
Phone: 1-800-733-3000
Fax: 1-800-659-2436

The authorized representative in the EU for product
safety and compliance
Is eucomply OÜ, Parnu mnt 139b-14, Apt 123
Tallinn, Berlin 11317, hello@eucompliancepartner.com

Dedication

This book is dedicated to the five most important people in my life: my babies, Jordin, Jacob, Jacory, Jakayla, and Jalisa. Please understand that everything I do and every struggle I've overcome is so that you guys don't have to worry about a thing. I love you guys and never forget it. Also, to my heartbeat and headache, Blunt. Thank you so much for always believing in me and having my back.

Acknowledgments

To my publisher, Racquel Williams, RWP, you rock, Boss Lady! People always say to make your first choice your best one, and I can say that making you my first and only publisher was the best decision that I could have ever made. I have learned so much about this industry over the last few years of getting to know you. No matter what the situation was, you have always had my back every time. You have shown me nothing but love, and for that, I really love and appreciate you.

To my pen sister, Christine Davis, it's because of you that I'm doing something I love. I really appreciate you and your grind.

To the wonderful ladies of RWP, I really love and appreciate all the support you guys have given me.

To my wonderful readers and my supporters, I'm nothing without you. For the last five years and thirty books later, you guys have read and reviewed all my books, and I appreciate each and every one of you guys. I want to say thank you from the bottom of my heart. It really touches my heart when I hear some of you say I have become one of your favorite authors. You all make me keep going stronger.

To my baby sister, Amanda Jordin Hollis, I love and miss you so much. I swear fifteen years wasn't long enough to have you here with us.

To my mom, Lisa, and dad, David, I wish you guys were here to see that I'm finally doing something I love. I love and miss you guys so much. Please continue to watch over the family.

Chapter 1

Pierre left the store with his usual: some blunts. He was addicted to smoking but knew he was gonna have to stop once the baby came. He had already stopped smoking around Erica. He wanted her to carry his seed without a care in the world. He knew she had been a little stressed out about falling out with Nicole, so the fact that they had made up really made him happy.

"Damn, my bad," Pierre said as he walked out of the store door and bumped into an older woman.

"It's OK, but do you have a dollar so I can get a sandwich from McDonald's?" she asked, not having no shame in begging.

Her voice sounded familiar, and that made Pierre quickly turn around. There stood the woman who had given birth to him but let drugs get the best of her before she ran out on him, leaving his grandma to raise him.

Pierre looked her up and down. He couldn't help but frown at her appearance. She wore a dingy gray tee shirt that was two sizes too small and some little black shorts that were clearly too damn tight, and, by the way, they weren't black anymore. They were ashy-looking. He looked down at her shoes, then quickly looked back up at her face. It was too much to deal with. Her face told him that she was still out doing her thing with drugs.

"Do you know who the fuck I am?" he asked the lady.

"I'm just trying to get something to eat. Are you gonna help me or not?"

Taking a step closer, he got loud with her. "Look at me!" he ordered.

The lady looked up and stared into the face of the son who she abandoned years ago. She couldn't help but get teary-eyed. Little Pierre looked just like her first love, his dad. Minus all the tattoos, he was his father's twin. Pierre looked at her like she was crazy. He had so much anger built up about her that he couldn't understand why she was so emotional.

"Little PJ," she mumbled.

She tried to reach out and touch his face, but he quickly smacked her hand away.

"I'm sorry. I just got a little carried away. PJ, I'm so happy to see you."

"What the fuck you so happy for? You wasn't fucking with me back then. Keep that same energy now."

"I see you got the same attitude as your father. You know, most people would be happy to see their mama," she said, hoping to get on his good side.

Pierre let out a little laugh before responding. "Yeah, well, most people don't run out on their child. And as far as you being my mother, my grandma was my mother up until she died. She was all I had while you were out chasing that high."

Kim put her head down in shame. She knew back in the day she was never what you would call "mother of the year." "Look, PJ, I was fucked up back then, but I swear I'm trying to get my life back on track. I'm off them drugs now."

Pierre stood there silently for a moment. He had so much hate in his heart for her that it took everything in him not to walk away from her. He actually was thinking about paying her back and abandoning her ass right there at the liquor store. All of a sudden, Kim started to cry. The sound of her crying brought back some childhood memories of when his dad used to whip her ass.

He then thought about how he would tell everyone how he didn't have a family, and now, here was his opportunity to give his mom another chance.

Thinking about his promise to his grandma that he would make sure she was okay made him show her a lot of love.

"Ma, stop crying. I promise everything will be OK."

Kim and her son hugged each other for the first time in years. Kim was happy and surprised that he didn't go off on her and leave her exactly where she stood.

"I'm sorry, son. I wish I could change things, but I can't. The only thing I can do is be your mom now."

Releasing her from the hug, Pierre looked down at his phone and saw that Erica was calling him. He placed the phone back in his pocket. He had a feeling that she really didn't want anything important. He planned on calling her back a little later.

"Come ride with me. I'll get you something to eat and shit," Pierre said as he started walking toward his ride.

Kim followed behind her son with a smile on her face. She was happy that he was well off. It was clear that he was following his father and uncles' footsteps. She just hoped that he wouldn't pick up any of their other habits.

Pierre pulled into Applebee's. He was gonna treat her to a meal and probably take her shopping. She was never a mom to him, but he felt good knowing she was at least clean and alive.

They sat at their table and looked over the menu. Pierre stared at his mom, wishing that even for a second, he could go back in time when she wasn't on drugs and actually took care of him and showed him just how much she loved him. He then thought about how he told Erica that they had to get things right with her dad so their baby could have a family. Now, it was his chance to make things right as long as his mom wanted a real relationship with him.

"Ma, how long you been clean 'cause you were outside of a liquor store begging for money?"

"Look, it's only been four months and some change. I've been staying at this stupid-ass shelter. They have a dumb rule that from 8:00 a.m. until 6:00 p.m., we have to be out finding work. So, I use that time to panhandle. Ain't nobody gonna hire me. I'm too old to be working anyway," Kim explained.

Pierre ate his food while listening to her talk. She went on and on like she really could have used a friend throughout the years.

"Damn, excuse me. I'm just running my mouth. What's been going on with you, baby boy?" Kim asked Pierre.

"I just got out of jail a few months ago on a drug charge. I have a fiancée and a baby on the way," he quickly said.

"Hold up. Wait a fucking minute. You telling me I'm gonna be a grandma and you getting married? Goddamn, PJ. Boy, I always knew these fast girls was gonna be after my baby."

Pierre laughed at his mom. She was talking like he was a teenage boy.

"Ma, she not fast at all. To be honest, she a good girl, and I went through a lot to get her to finally give me a chance. Her dad is the pastor at a church."

Kim smiled at the information she was taking in. She was proud of her son. He seemed so happy with his life.

"I know I wasn't shit back then, but can I please be in my grandchild's life?" Kim asked.

"Yeah, Ma, and I want you to meet Erica. She a sweet girl, and I think you would love her. Plus, she can cook her ass off," Pierre said, bragging about the love of his life.

"Is that why you so thick? That girl been fatting you up, son?"

They both laughed before returning their attention to their plates.

Pierre always put in his mind that if he ever saw his mom again that he was gonna act like he didn't even know her ass. He was gonna play the same game she had been playing for years. It was crazy how when he finally saw her, he was able to push all that shit behind him and show her some love.

"Look, Ma, I don't hate you anymore. To be honest, I'm glad we bumped into each other after all this time. Plus, I'm glad that you're clean now. You looking a lot better from the last time I saw you."

"I'm sorry for not being there and everything. I wish I could change things, but since I can't, is there a way that I can make up for the past?" Kim said as the tears began to flow down her cheeks.

"Ma, stop crying. We good, OK?"

Pierre looked down and saw that Erica was calling again. And again, he told himself that he was gonna call her later.

Pierre and Kim caught up on old times. He even took her on a little shopping spree. He wanted to make her feel loved, and by the look on her face, it was working.

Mekco climbed into the bed and cuddled up under Nicole. The smell of fresh soap woke Nicole up from her sleep.

"Hey, baby, everything OK?" she asked.

"Yeah, ma. If not, I wouldn't be in bed. I'd be still out handling shit."

Nicole sat up in the bed. "Baby, have you heard from P today?"

"Now that you said something, I haven't heard from him. I wonder what he been up to. Anyway, what you asking about him for?"

"Well, you know Erica been tripping since this afternoon. And she bugging out 'cause she hadn't heard from him all day," Nicole answered.

"Man, that girl gotta learn to chill the hell out. My nigga probably was busy handling business and shit. He'll hit her up in the morning."

Nicole lay back down, taking his word for it.

They cuddled up until they both fell asleep in each other's arms.

***

The sun shining through the apartment window woke Erica from her sleep. She looked over to her left and picked up her phone. She had no missed calls from Pierre, and that pissed her off.

After taking a shower and getting dressed, she decided to leave Nicole's house. She could hear that she was busy with Mekco anyway. The last thing she wanted to do was hear them having wild sex while she couldn't even get a phone call back.

Erica got into her car and got ready to pull off. That's when she was cut off by Pierre's car.

He jumped out of the car like everything was all good between them. He had no idea that she was mad at him.

"What's up, baby? Where you on your way to?"

Erica rolled her eyes, which told him that she was clearly pissed off. "Damn, baby, what the fuck wrong with you?"

Erica turned her attention toward Pierre. "So, you don't know how to answer your phone? I called you all day yesterday."

"Damn, baby, calm down. I got caught up with something yesterday before losing my phone."

"Whatever, Pierre. Your day wasn't as busy as mine. Now, move your car. You're in my way," she demanded.

"Let's go to breakfast, and I can tell you about my day," he said, trying to calm her down with the promise of food.

"I don't care about how your day was, not after my day. Now, move!"

Pierre walked back to his car and backed off her car. Erica took that moment to drive off. After being chased down by a man with a gun, she told herself that she wasn't gonna drive that car anymore, but she wanted to get away from everyone.

Looking through her rearview mirror, she saw that another man was once again following her, but this time, it was Pierre. She laughed 'cause he looked pissed off.

"I'll teach you to ignore me," she mumbled before turning down her dad's block.

Pierre shook his head. He really didn't know what trip Erica was on, but seeing her dad wasn't in his plans for the day.

"Fuck," he said as he made the same turn as she did.

He knew she saw him following her, so her pulling up to her dad's house was pure bullshit.

Erica parked her car in front of her father's house. His car was parked in the driveway, right along with Nicole's mother's car.

"What the fuck is your problem?" Pierre yelled as he jumped right out of his car.

"Just leave me alone, Pierre. Go finish doing whatever you were doing yesterday when you were too busy to talk to me."

Her attitude was on a hundred, and Pierre had no idea what the fuck he did wrong. He snatched Erica by the arm and lightly pushed her up against her car. He needed her to talk to him and not run into the house with an attitude.

He then positioned his body in front of hers and held her close. The smell of his cologne almost made her forget that she was even mad at him in the first place. But she quickly returned to her senses.

"I needed you yesterday, and you wasn't there to help me," she cried out.

Pierre hated to see her cry, but at the same time, he knew she could be a spoiled crybaby at times.

"What's going on, baby? I'm here now. What the hell happened?"

Before Erica could say anything, her father came out of the house with a bat, screaming, "I know I didn't see you put your hands on my daughter."

Erica and Pierre both turned their attention toward the pastor. Pierre saw the bat and instantly got heated.

He stepped toward Eric, but before he could defend himself, Erica started talking first.

"Daddy, go back inside the house. Why are you out here causing a scene for these nosy neighbors? He didn't do anything to hurt me."

Without taking his eyes off Pierre, the pastor continued to yell, "I know what I saw."

"Man, go back in the house with that shit," Pierre yelled.

"Pierre, chill out and let me deal with this. Just get in the car, please," Erica begged.

Pierre gave her dad an evil smirk as he climbed back into his car.

"You better listen, boy, before I have your ass locked up," Pastor Collins yelled.

Erica gave her dad a look before telling him that he needed to chill out. "Dad, I'm about to leave. I'll call you later."

Pastor Collins shook his head before speaking his mind. "You need to stop chasing behind that thug and get your life back on track. Sometimes, you can be so simple-minded, just a straight-up dummy."

"Really, Dad? Well, since that's the way you *really* feel, you don't have to worry about me ever again. And you can forget about being in my child's life as well."

Erica let her feelings get the best of her, and before she knew it, she was crying. Pierre was about to hop right back out of his ride when she hurriedly wiped her eyes. She was tired of crying because of her dad's judgmental ways.

Before she could get into her car, Pastor Collins yelled, "Go ahead and be with your drug-dealer boyfriend and raise that bastard you carrying around."

That was the last straw for Pierre. He jumped out of the car and headed straight toward him. Pastor Collins proved that he was more bark than bite. He was so scared that he dropped his bat and took off running into the house.

"Pierre, get back in the car and drive off. You *know* he calling the police," Erica ordered.

Pierre stood there for a minute. He was pissed and wanted to beat that man's ass. He debated on whether to listen to Erica or kick that muthafucka's door in and whip his ass. Erica could tell he was plotting to do damage.

"Baby, the police is coming. Let's go now," she ordered and grabbed his hand.

Pierre wasn't a dummy and knew he only had one more strike against him, so he did what was best for him, Erica, and his unborn child. He jumped into his ride and got the fuck on. Erica was right behind him in her car.

"Eric Collins, what in the world is your problem?" Theresa yelled as she followed him out of the living room and into his bedroom.

"Listen, lady, that is *my* daughter, and I don't want her with that thug," he yelled back.

"I just think you're going overboard and doing too much. You gonna run that girl away for good," Theresa tried to explain.

"You might think it's cute that your daughter is running around trying to kill herself over that thug, but that will not be *my* child."

If looks could kill, Eric would have been dead.

"You're a coldhearted bastard. I don't know why, after all these years, I allowed myself to get mixed up with you and your dirty ways," she yelled as she grabbed her purse off the dresser.

She had officially had enough of his shit.

"*My dirty ways*? Are *you* serious? Did you forget about *your* dirty, slutty, and sneaky ways?"

"Eric, don't even go there with me. I'm so done with you."

By this time, she was headed toward the living room. But before she could hit the door, the pastor yelled for her not to move.

"I'm about to go all the way there since you wanted to call me out on my bullshit. I'm gonna remind your dirty ass of all the times my wife was in the hospital sick, and you was begging to take her place. You made sure to suck my dick every chance that you could. Now, what you got to say?"

"You're an evil bastard, and I can't wait for the church to find out about the true you."

With that being said, Theresa stormed out of the house, slamming the door behind her with the promise of never returning.

Pierre parked his ride, hopped out of the car, and walked to Erica's car, which was parked right behind him. He opened her door. "Come on, get out. We need to talk."

Erica took his hand and allowed him to walk her toward the bench facing the water. The riverwalk had become their go-to place whenever they needed to clear their mind. And right now was the perfect time to get some things together.

"So, tell me what pissed your little ass off yesterday 'cause I swear I would never just ignore you on purpose."

"Yesterday, when me and Nicole were out eating, some guy had a gun and chased us."

"Are you fucking serious? What nigga was this? Who the fuck do I have to kill?" he yelled.

Erica placed her hand on his hands. "Baby, calm down. Mekco took care of everything. I was scared, but I'm all right, I promise."

Pierre sat there rubbing his face with his hands. "Man, baby, I'm so sorry. I should have been there to kill that muthafucka for you."

Usually, Erica would look at him like he was crazy, but she couldn't help but laugh for some reason. "Oh my God, boy, you're so silly. You can get the next one."

They both laughed before kissing.

"Baby, do you remember me talking to you about making things right with your dad and being a family for the baby?" he asked.

"Yeah, I remember, baby."

"Well, I bumped into my mom after all these years. At first, I didn't know how I wanted to handle her, but I thought about you and the baby and decided to give her a chance. Can you believe after all this time, she was clean and had been trying to get her life back on track? I spent the whole day chilling with my mom. I must have lost my phone when I took her shopping."

Erica listened to his story and knew he wasn't lying to her. For one, he had never lied to her since day one.

"Baby, I'm happy for you. I can't wait to meet her."

"Hey, Pierre," a skinny, light-skinned girl said while standing in front of the couple.

Pierre stared at the girl like she was crazy. "What's up? What can I help you with?"

"I just came over to see what was up," she said like she didn't notice the deadly look Erica was giving her.

"Aye, you don't see me chilling with my wife?"

"My bad. You ain't got to get smart," she yelled before walking off.

"That's right. Get the fuck on, bitch," Erica yelled toward the girl.

The girl turned around and put her middle finger up at Erica. Erica did it back in return.

"Baby, don't be out here acting up. Fuck that bitch. Let's just chill."

Erica laughed. "I just hate females like that."

"I feel you, but still, don't start all that cursing, either. Don't change on me, baby," he said with a little laugh.

"All right, baby, but she was out of line. What she thought you was gonna do? Get up and leave with her or something?"

"Man, I don't know. Just let that shit go. I came with you and gonna leave with your sexy ass."

Pierre leaned forward and gave Erica another kiss on her lips. "Don't let that bullshit bother you. You all that I want and need. Please believe that."

Erica couldn't help but blush. Pierre held her heart just like she held his.

Pierre and Erica made their way back to his crib. She claimed to be tired and in need of a nap. Pierre made sure she got into bed because he was ready to hit the streets. His not having his phone the day before made him miss out on a lot, and he was pissed about it.

Even though Mekco handled the situation, he really wished that he could have had his hands in whatever took place.

Erica was being a big-ass baby, so he had to chill with her until she fell asleep.

"Damn, baby, you really holding a nigga hostage and shit. I told you I'm about to go get me another phone. That way, we won't have any more problems like earlier today when you were ready to cut a nigga dick off."

Erica fell out laughing. "You so silly, boy, and I would never do nothing like that."

"So, I wasn't gonna bring this up, but what the fuck we gonna do about your evil-ass daddy?"

Being honest, she gave him her best answer. "I really don't wanna be bothered with him anymore. I lived by his rules my whole life, and now that I'm grown and making decisions on my own, he wanna trip. What type of pastor would call their unborn grandchild a bastard?"

"Well, you know, at first, I was on that 'family need to be together' shit, but if that's how you want it, then that's how it's gonna be."

Erica lay there, lost in her thoughts. She really was sleepy, but having Pierre hold her felt so good that she didn't want him to leave, so she kept fighting her sleep. Once Pierre thought she was asleep, he tried to climb out of the bed.

"No, baby, not yet," she whined.

He lay his head back down on the pillow. "Erica, it was cute at first, but this spoiled shit getting on my nerves. Do you understand that once you have that baby, you are gonna be a parent, and that spoiled shit ain't gonna work with me anymore."

Even though he tried to talk with a little firmness in his voice, Erica still looked at him and laughed.

"Girl, I'm serious as hell."

"Pierre, I don't want that car anymore, baby," she said, changing the subject.

"What's wrong with your car, Erica?" he asked, thinking she was about to be on some spoiled shit.

"Since you were so kind to buy me my first car, all kinds of bad things have happened to me. I'm not being a brat and just trying to get a new car 'cause, truthfully, I don't even wanna drive right now."

Pierre understood exactly where she was coming from. "OK, baby, I guess you about to get fat and have me drive you around until you ready to drive again."

He waited for her to respond, but after a minute of nothing, he looked down and saw that she was knocked out. He slid out of bed quietly and got the fuck on.

His first stop was to the store to get another phone, and then he was off to see Mekco. It always pissed him off when he couldn't be the one to put in work.

Mekco and Pierre sat in Mekco's driveway, discussing what had occurred the day before. Pierre was heated that

them punk-ass brothers were back in town and on some
bullshit.

"Man, I wish that nigga wasn't dead 'cause I'll kill him
my muthafucking self."

Mekco laughed. "Damn, nigga, you always wanna be
the killer. When we find Brian, you can off that nigga."

"Good. As long as we got that shit understood, now,
pass that fucking blunt."

The next day, when Pierre walked through the door,
he could smell that Erica must have been in the kitchen
cooking. As he approached the kitchen, he could hear
her talking to someone and laughing. Walking into the
kitchen, he saw that his mom was there with Erica.

"Hey, Ma, I see you finally got the chance to meet my
baby."

Kim turned around with a broad smile on her face,
"Yes, and she is so beautiful. I can tell she also have a
beautiful soul as well."

Erica blushed. "Thank you, ma'am."

"Girl, I told you to call me by my name, Kim. I'm not
old enough to be called no damn ma'am yet."

Everyone laughed at her.

Erica could tell she was silly, just like Pierre, which she
liked about her.

"How long have you been here, Ma?" Pierre asked.

"Long enough to taste this girl cooking. She is a keeper
for sure," Kim said right before biting another piece of
her fried chicken.

Chapter 2

Erica stood in line to get her class schedule for the first semester. She was finally able to eat whatever she wanted without worrying about her baby making her sick. She was happy about that 'cause she would have been mad if she got sick during class.

It had been a minute since she talked to her dad, which made her sad. He would act like she wasn't even there at church or Bible study. She knew he was acting out because he felt like she had chosen Pierre over him, but truth be told, she loved them both and didn't see why she couldn't have both of them in her life.

It was finally Erica's turn, and she stepped up to the desk.

"Good morning," Ms. Brown said right before asking for her name.

"Good morning. My name is Erica Collins."

Ms. Brown typed her name into the computer and waited for her info to pop up.

"OK, Erica, it looks like your semester hasn't been paid yet. Now, you have until tomorrow to get it paid, or you won't be able to start your fall classes."

"Wait a minute, are you sure?" Erica asked, completely caught off guard.

"Yes, ma'am," Ms. Brown said before pressing a button on her computer. She then rolled her chair toward the printer and grabbed the paper that had just come out. Once back at her desk in front of Erica, she handed her the paper that showed her that all her classes were still unpaid.

"Like I said before, we need all classes paid in full by tomorrow in order for you to start school."

On top of being pissed off, Erica was embarrassed as she walked away from the long line of students. She stormed back to the student parking lot and jumped into her car. She said she didn't want to drive that car anymore, but since Pierre was caught up in some stuff with Mekco, she had no other choice.

She was on a mission and knew what person she had to confront about her classes not being paid for.

Erica pulled up to her dad's house twenty minutes later. Her attitude was on a hundred, and he was about to hear what she had to say. She pulled out her keys and tried to unlock the door, but for some reason, her key didn't work anymore.

"This man is beyond petty," she mumbled to herself.

Erica knocked on the door and waited for her dad to answer. She got even more pissed when he peeked through the window, smiling. He knew he was being an ass.

"What can I do for you?" he asked her as he opened the door.

He blocked the doorway as if she were no longer allowed in his house.

"Can I come in, Dad?" she asked.

"What can I do for you?" he asked again.

"Dad, I went to the school today and was told that my classes weren't paid for yet, and I only have until tomorrow to pay, or I can't start school this semester."

"Girl, I swear you're a little slow. Did you think I was gonna pay for your class when you have a whole nigga at home? You better make that nigga cough up some of that drug money and pay for your classes."

"Daddy, why do things have to be like this between us? I mean, why can't I have both of you guys in my life?"

Pastor Collins took a second to think about how he was gonna answer her question. "I already graduated from college and got myself together. I suggest you get your shit together too. Now, if we're done here, get the hell off my doorstep."

His words hurt her, but when he slammed the door in her face, it broke her heart.

Nicole smiled as she looked down at the pregnancy test. Her dreams had come true. She was finally gonna give Mekco a baby. She was so happy that she began crying as she entered his bedroom.

Nicole wished he was there to share the good news with him, but he had left earlier.

After getting herself together, she picked up her phone to call Erica but quickly remembered she had to go to her school and handle her business.

Feeling good about the news, she couldn't wait to be known as Mekco's baby mama. Just the thought of having hoes hating on her and her baby tickled her. She also loved knowing she was about to be taken care of for life.

Whenever Mekco wasn't with her, Nicole always found herself bored to death. She had no life without him because she had allowed him to be her everything. Instead of overthinking everything, she decided to take a nap.

Her mother had warned her about being so caught up in a guy at an early age. She told her that you slowly lose yourself when you get caught up with a guy. And once you're so deep in, there's no turning back. Theresa gave her this advice, stating that she once chased behind a man that she thought she loved, only to get her feelings hurt repeatedly. Nicole had no idea that her mom was giving her advice that still, to this day, she didn't follow. She was deeply in love with the pastor.

***

Mekco and Pierre sat at the desk in Mekco's basement. They both emptied the bags of money that they had collected earlier that day. They took turns placing the money on the counter and smiling as the dollar amount increased.

"Damn, somebody always calling when I'm fucking working," Mekco said as he picked up his phone from the desk.

"What's up?" he asked Toya.

It had been a minute since he last talked to her because Nicole was back in the picture. So, this call shocked him.

"Hey, Mekco, are you busy?" she asked.

"You already know what I be into. What's up?"

"Look, I'm not sure how to tell you this, so I'm just gonna say it. I'm pregnant. And yes, I'm sure it's yours."

"Man, what the fuck? Are you fucking serious?"

"Yes, I took two tests at home before I went to the doctor's office."

There was a silent moment between the two. Mekco wasn't sure how to feel about this. He always pictured his first baby would be by Nicole, not some damn jumpoff.

"Hello, Mekco, you still there?" she asked, hoping he didn't hang up on her.

"Yeah, man, I'm still here. Just give me a minute. I'll swing by there a little later."

"OK, see you later," Toya said before hanging up the phone.

Mekco placed his phone back down on the desk.

Laughing, P jokingly said, "Aye, nigga, what the fuck wrong with you? You over there looking like your dog just ran away."

"Nothing, man, just got some shit on my mind."

P had grown up with Mekco and knew that his homeboy was lying, but he didn't pressure him for the truth. Knowing Mekco, it was gonna come out sooner than later.

After the money was counted and placed into the safe, P let Mekco know that he was about to head home and that he was gonna hit him up later.

Once P left, Mekco sat back in his chair and thought about the bullshit that he had gotten himself into. He knew Nicole was gonna kill him. Another bitch having his baby while she had been trying for so long . . . He was a dead man walking.

Pierre walked through the door and went straight into the kitchen. He was surprised his mother was cooking in the kitchen and not Erica.

"Hey, Ma, what you doing over here?" he asked.

"Shit, boy, didn't I tell you the shelter be putting my ass out during the day? So, I came over, and Erica let me in. Something was bothering her 'cause she looked like she had been crying, but she asleep now."

"Ma, what the hell you still doing at the shelter? Didn't I give you enough money to stay at the room until we could find you an apartment?"

"Yeah, but I kept some of the money for my pocket and stayed at the shelter for free."

Pierre looked at his mother like she was crazy but didn't say anything.

"Don't look at me like that, boy, and I swear you ain't got nothing to worry about 'cause I'm not on that shit anymore," Kim said, trying to convince him she was still drug free.

"Yeah, OK, Ma. Let me go check on Erica."

Pierre walked out of the kitchen and made his way to his bedroom. He stood in the doorway and watched Erica sleep for a minute.

The way the sun shined through the window and hit her brown skin made her look even more beautiful in his eyes. A smile formed on his face as he realized that she was all his and wasn't going anywhere.

Erica barely opened her eyes but could see Pierre walking toward the bed. The smell of his cologne was what woke her up in the first place. She smiled as he climbed into bed and held her in his tatted arms. For that very moment, she forgot about her terrible morning dealing with the school and her dad.

"Hey, baby."

Pierre gave her a peck on the lips before replying. "What's up with you, girl? My mama said you were pissed off when she got here."

"Man, where do I start? First, I went to school and couldn't get my classes because they weren't paid for yet. Then I go to talk to my dad about him not paying for my classes, and he basically said fuck me. If my classes not paid for by tomorrow, I can't start school this semester."

Pierre lay there listening to her story and couldn't help but wonder why she didn't ask him for the money in the first place. She should have known her father wasn't fucking with her like that anymore. It was fucked up, but hey, that was life. People come and go. It was that simple.

Pierre placed another kiss on her lips. "I got you."

"For real, Pierre? You don't even know how much my classes are."

"It don't fucking matter. I got you. You wanna go pay for it now or wait until the morning?" he asked.

"If I wait until the morning, my classes might be filled up already."

Pierre got out of bed, then dug into his pants pocket, pulling out a knot of money.

"Here, count that and make sure it's enough before you leave. But let me go check on this lady and make sure she not burning down my crib."

He walked out of the room, leaving Erica speechless. She knew he had money, but damn, who really walks around holding that large amount in their pocket?

She picked up half the stack and started counting all the bills. Once she was done, she separated the money she needed and what was left over.

"Pierre," she yelled for him to return to the room.

"What's up? Was that enough?" he asked as he walked back into the room.

Erica looked at him like he was silly. "That was more than enough crazy. I'm only paying for the first semester."

Pierre took a seat on the bed. "Why don't you go ahead and pay for the whole year and get that shit over with?"

"It don't work like that, baby. I don't have my classes for next semester, so I can't pay for them yet. Anyway, here you go," she said, handing him the extra money.

"What's this, Erica?"

"That's yours. That's the extra money. This pile is what I need for my classes."

Pierre didn't even reach for the money, confusing Erica. "Here, Pierre," she said again.

"That's yours. Put it up," he said as if it were just a few bucks, not several thousand dollars.

Confused, Erica asked, "What am I supposed to do with all this money, Pierre?"

"Spend it, silly ass," he said, laughing.

Erica laughed right along with him. She wasn't used to someone just giving her money like that. Her dad made sure she had everything that she needed, but he never was too big on putting the money into her hand.

"Thanks, baby."

"What you thanking me for? I'm your man. I'm just doing what I supposed to be doing."

Erica jumped up from the bed and hugged Pierre, followed by a kiss. "I love you, baby. I swear, you're so good to me."

Pierre took this opportunity to grab a handful of her ass. "I love you too, but let's not start nothing that we can't finish right now."

Erica looked confused. "Huh?"

"Did you forget that quick that you had let my mama in before you took a nap?"

Erica started laughing again. "I guess I did."

Mekco drove to Toya's house in complete silence. He couldn't even listen to the radio because the news that Toya had shared was just too heavy on his mind. He couldn't believe that he got Toya pregnant. Out of every bitch that he done fucked, she was gonna be the first to carry his seed.

"Aye, I'm outside. Come on out so we can talk," Mekco said into the phone.

Toya was downstairs and in Mekco's car in no time.

Mekco stared at her sundress, which fit tightly on her body. Truth be told, her shape was what he first noticed and fell in love with. He really didn't have feelings for her, but her sex was everything to him.

Mekco couldn't lie. Baby girl was the best that he had sampled in a while. He had trained and molded Nicole to how he wanted her, but something new was always gonna be on top.

"Hey, baby, what's up?" Toya asked once she was comfortable.

"So, man, what's this shit you talking about?" he asked, blowing out the smoke from his blunt.

He was pissed, and it was clear to tell because of his facial expression. Toya wanted to cry herself. This was her first time being pregnant, and her baby daddy was acting like he didn't take part in making the baby.

"It's what I said on the phone. I'm pregnant with your child."

"This is a bunch of bullshit," he yelled before punching the steering wheel.

"Mekco, you tripping like I lay down and fucked myself. I didn't do this by myself. You know that, right?"

"What the fuck is it that you don't understand? I have a girl, so this shit right here isn't gonna work," he said coldly.

Toya started to cry. His words had hit her hard, and she couldn't control her emotions. She felt stupid for even listening to her girls. *"Fuck with a Brick Boy; they got money. You'll be set for life. Fuck'em raw, have a baby by a member of the Brick Boyz, and you and your baby will be paid."*

Now she was pregnant by a Brick Boy and wasn't shit going her way. He still had Nicole in his heart, and she could never compete with that, even with a baby.

"Look, your girl ain't got shit to do with me or our baby. If anything, you knew what you were doing when you were busting all inside of this pussy."

Mekco didn't say a word as she took his hand and slid it up her dress. Just like always, her freaky ass didn't have on panties. She was the freak he liked to have by his side, but then there was Nicole, the freak who held his heart. Nicole was the one that he could see himself being with in the future and having his kids.

"Fuck whatever you talking about. We are bringing a child into this world together, and that's that."

Mekco could tell that she was trying to be hard and stand her ground, but he still wasn't for her bullshit. "I'm sorry, but you can't keep this fucking baby."

"What the fuck you mean?" Toya yelled.

Mekco dug in his shorts pocket. "Look, I got the bread right here. You gonna have to get an abortion."

Toya started crying again. "I'm not killing my baby, not for you, and definitely not for your bitch."

"Just take the money and call the clinic. I'm paying for the shit, and I'll drive you there. Stop making shit harder for yourself."

Toya sat back in her seat, crying. She couldn't believe how he was trying to play her. Mekco tried not to look her way. He was trying not to get caught up in her emotions 'cause he knew he was wrong.

After a good ten minutes of listening to her cry continuously, Mekco pushed his seat back, then turned her way. "I'm sorry, Toya. Come over here with me."

Just like any other time before, Toya slid off her sandals and then climbed onto his lap. It wasn't a surprised that his dick was already hard, out in his right hand, and ready to enter her wetness. Without a second thought, she slid down on his dick.

She loudly moaned, letting him know he was the man and still in control.

Toya allowed her body to fall on his as she wrapped her arms around his neck. While fucking in the front seat of Mekco's truck, she whispered in his ear, "I want to have your baby."

Mekco shook his head no as he held her waist and pounded her a little harder.

"Please, daddy. I wanna keep my baby," she begged.

Mekco didn't say a word. He just pounded a little faster this time. The quicker he busted his nut, the quicker he could leave.

"Please, Mekco," she begged in his ear.

Mekco felt himself about to release inside of Toya. Between how wet and tight her pussy was and her moaning out his name, he knew he wasn't gonna last too much longer. He wrapped his left arm around her waist and held a handful of her box braids as his pace picked up.

"Damn, baby, I'm coming," he moaned out.

Toya tightened her pussy muscles around his dick while riding him to the best of her ability. This was the type of shit that had her in the situation that she was in now.

Toya took Mekco's moment of weakness to her advantage. She was gonna make sure that night was gonna be the last night that she cried to him about their baby. "I want my baby, daddy."

As Mekco busted his nut, he whispered back in her ear, "OK, baby, I got y'all."

Toya smiled from ear to ear as they shared a long, passionate kiss.

"You got us, baby?" she asked while getting off his lap.

"Yeah, Toya. Ain't that what the fuck I said?" he said with a slight attitude. Once again, he had let pussy take over.

"You gonna spend the night with me tonight or what?"

"Nah, I got some shit to take care of, but here you go."

Toya grabbed the knot of money that he was handing her. "Thanks, baby."

"Yeah, whatever. I'm gonna call you tomorrow once I'm done handling some business."

Toya leaned over to kiss him again, but he wasn't interested, so he didn't even budge. She caught on and just opened the door to walk away.

"Wait a minute, Toya."

She sat back down in the passenger seat. "What, Mekco?"

"I need you to do me a favor. Can you try to keep this between us?"

"Are you fucking serious right now? Do it look like I give a fuck about your girl's feelings when it comes to *my* baby? Matter of fact, fuck you and her," she yelled before getting back out of the car and slamming the door.

"Stupid, bitch!" he yelled back at her before driving off.

"Baby, where are you? Are you on your way?" Nicole said into the phone.

Mekco had gone home and jumped in the shower. He knew Nicole was waiting for him to pull up, but after the long hot shower, he fell asleep. He didn't even get a chance to put on anything besides some clean boxers.

Nicole, blowing up his phone, awakened him.

"My bad, Nicole. I had fallen asleep, but I'll be there in a minute."

Nicole looked at the time on her phone. It read 11:27 p.m. It was late, but she really wanted to see him. She couldn't wait to surprise him with the news about their baby. It had taken them long enough to make a baby.

"OK, baby, I'll be waiting. I love you."

Mekco didn't mean to, but he mumbled, "I love you too."

Usually, he would say it like he meant it, but with everything on his mind, it just came out dry, without any emotion. He hurried and hung up before she started to question him.

Half an hour later, Mekco was walking through Nicole's apartment door. She had grown tired of waiting for him and climbed back into bed.

"Nicole. Nicole, I'm here, baby," Mekco said, slapping her on the ass.

"Damn, baby, that hurt. Now come lie down with me and make it feel better."

Mekco stripped down to his boxers and lay on his side of the bed. Nicole smiled as his warm hands traveled over her body before landing on her ass cheeks.

Other than sex, she loved a nice booty rub from her man.

"Baby, I really wanted you to come over because I have some exciting news, and I couldn't wait until the morning."

Mekco couldn't wait to hear what she had to say because that bullshit Toya was on had him fucked up. He just knew Nicole was about to come through and make his night great.

"What's up, baby? What you gotta tell me?" he asked.

Nicola sat up in the bed with a huge smile before yelling, "I'm pregnant!"

"Oh my fucking God," slipped out of his mouth before he realized it.

Nicole punched him in the chest. "What the fuck you mean, 'oh my fucking God'? I know you not mad, nigga."

Mekco was now sitting up in bed. "Man, keep your fucking hands to yourself. I told you that shit before."

"I asked you a fucking question, Mekco. So, are you mad?"

"Nah, man, I'm not mad. I'm just a little surprised, that's it."

Nicole could tell that Mekco was bothered. She thought he would be happy about the baby 'cause he was the one who came to her and said he was ready for this.

Mekco sat there looking spaced out, and Nicole's heart broke into pieces every second that went by. He was killing her and didn't even know it.

She stormed out of the room with a face full of tears.

This night was not going how it played out in her mind. She thought he was gonna drown her with hugs, kisses, and lots of love, maybe even a ring.

Mekco sat there for a minute. He was really happy for Nicole. He just wished he had heard her news before he went to Toya's house.

After getting his thoughts together, he got out of bed and went into the living room. Nicole was standing up, looking out the window. Mekco walked up behind her and held her from the back.

While placing sweet kisses on her neck, he told her repeatedly how he was sorry and was really happy that she was pregnant.

"Mekco, you don't have to lie to me. The way you reacted when I told you about the baby was how you really felt. So don't worry about it, Mekco. I'll make an appointment tomorrow to get an abortion. The last thing I wanna do is make you feel like I'm trapping your sorry ass."

With that being said, she pushed him off her and went back into the room. Mekco was right behind her. "Nicole, don't fucking play with me. If you kill my baby, you might as well leave town 'cause I'm gonna kill your ass, so fuck with me if you want to."

"How the fuck you making threats when you don't even give a fuck? It was written all over your face that you weren't happy."

"I told you I was happy. You tripping for no fucking reason."

"Whatever, Mekco. I'm not stupid, muthafucka. But like I said before, don't even worry about it. I'll take care of it."

Without warning, Mekco snatched Nicole up and had her pinned up on the wall. "Stop fucking playing with me, girl. I'll hate to have to do you dirty, but I will."

The look in Nicole's eyes let Mekco know that he had her scared. He needed her to understand that he wanted his baby.

"Listen to me, Nicole. I love your ass. But that's something that you should already know by now. You just caught me on a fucked-up day. You know how business be sometimes."

Nicole stopped crying. "So. you OK with this?" she asked.

"Yeah, crazy ass. Ain't I been saying that shit since I got here? I love you, and I'm ready to be a daddy."

The two shared a long, passionate kiss before he picked her up and carried her to the bed.

Chapter 3

"Pierre, your future wife got good taste. I love the way she decorated this apartment," Kim said in disbelief at how beautiful her new apartment was.

"Yeah, Ma, I told you she was gonna make you fall in love with your new place. She was the one who decorated my place."

Kim got teary-eyed. "Thanks again, baby; thanks for everything. You just don't know how much I appreciate you. I mean, you didn't have to forgive me for the stuff that I had done, but you did."

Pierre gave his mom a hug. "Ma, stop all that crying. I told you I'm a changed man. All that shit was in the past. Let's just let it go."

Kim was still crying. "You have made me so happy since I've been back in your life. You have blessed me with a new apartment, a beautiful daughter-in-law who's carrying my first grandbaby, and most importantly, your love."

"Damn, Ma, you really trying to fuck with a nigga's emotions right now," Pierre said, laughing, trying to keep himself from getting too caught up in his feelings.

He then looked down at his phone, "OK, Ma, you got my number and Erica's. Just call if you need anything. I gotta go handle some business."

"All right, boy, and thanks again, Pierre. I love you, son."

"Love you too, Ma."

Pierre jumped into his car and made his way back to the house. Erica had a doctor's appointment, and he was driving them there. As he drove, he thought about his mom. He was happier than he thought he would be to have her back in his life.

See, before his grandma passed away, she had a long talk with him and basically made him promise that if he ever saw his mom again, he was gonna accept her back into his life. He remembered that day as if it were yesterday.

"PJ, come here, boy. Let me talk to you for a minute," *Grandma Rose yelled from her bedroom.*

"What's up, Grandma? I was about to go outside and play ball with Mekco."

"You play with that boy all the time. Come sit your ass down and give me a few minutes of your time."

Pierre took a seat next to his grandma on the flower-printed love seat. "Yes, ma'am."

"Look, you know I'm getting up in age and not gonna be here forever."

Just hearing her say that made the young man get emotional. All he had was his grandma, and he couldn't imagine living without her. She was his rock through it all.

"Grandma, stop talking like that. God not ready for you yet. He knows that I need you with me forever," *Pierre said, holding her small, wrinkled hand.*

"I need you to make me a promise, baby."

"Anything you want, Grandma; whatever you need."

"Listen to me, PJ. One day, your mama is gonna come back, and she is gonna need you, baby. I know you're mad at her for walking out on you, but when she come back to you, please don't dog her out. Please take her in and show her the love you have bottled up inside you."

"Man, Granny, fuck her. She left me to chase some fucking rocks," Pierre yelled.

"I don't give a damn that you mad, but you better watch your mouth before I pop you in it. Your mother messed up and allowed that drug to be more important than everything else in this world, but she is still your mother, and remember that."

Pierre let a single tear fall from his eye before quickly wiping it away. "I just hate her so much, Granny. I know she don't love me 'cause otherwise, she would be here with me right now."

Grandma Rose hugged her grandson and whispered in his ear, "Don't cry, son. Get that hate out of your heart, and the Lord will bring her back home. Just promise me that when she do come home, you'll have your arms wide open for her."

The young boy let the last tear fall before saying, "I promise, Granny."

"What time was your appointment again?" Pierre asked Erica.

"It's 1:30 p.m., baby. Chill. It's only 2:04 p.m. They will call me to the back in a minute," Erica answered.

He hated coming to doctor appointments. He felt like if the appointment time was at 1:30 p.m., then that was the fucking time they should see you. Erica sat there praying that they would hurry up and call her before he started acting a damn fool.

"Erica Collins, please come to the blue door," they heard over the speaker.

Pierre stood up, then helped her up from the chair. He smiled at the little stomach his baby was creating.

He couldn't wait to meet his li'l man. Yeah, he had already told himself that it was a boy. He really didn't want a girl; he knew that having a girl was gonna make him catch a case because she was gonna be just as beautiful as her mother, and he wasn't trying to get locked up 'cause a stupid nigga broke his daughter's heart.

Erica got up on the exam table like she did before and rolled her shirt up to right under her breasts.

Pierre stood there and watched the doctor squeeze some blue gel-looking stuff on her belly.

"OK, Mom and Dad, today I'll be doing some measurements, and if the baby allows me, I'll be able to tell you the sex if you wanna know," the doctor told them.

They both looked at each other and smiled. Pierre spoke up first. "Go ahead and tell her I was right, and it's a boy."

Erica giggled. "Whatever. It's a girl. This is mommy's little princess."

Dr. Thomas laughed with the couple. She was so used to couples coming in wanting a different sex than their partner.

Dr. Thomas looked into her screen. "Oh, OK."

"What does that mean? I was right?" Pierre asked, too excited to hear Erica was carrying a boy.

"Mom and Dad, are you guys ready for the sex?"

At the same time, both Pierre and Erica answered, "Yes."

Dr. Thomas turned her screen toward them so they could see their baby. "OK, I need you guys to pay close attention as I explain this. Right over here, you can see the baby's legs, and right here, in between, you can see that in the private area, something is hanging between his legs."

"Hell yeah. I *knew* I was right," Pierre said too excited.

"One minute, Dad, let me finish," Dr. Thomas said, interrupting his celebration. "OK, right over here is another set of legs, and as you can see, nothing is hanging between her legs. So, it looks like Baby A is a boy and Baby B is a girl. It looks like you both were right."

Erica and Pierre looked at each other, confused. Never in a million years did they expect their doctor to say twins were growing inside Erica's belly.

"Oh my God, are you serious? We're having twins?" Pierre knew he heard what she said, but he still had to ask.

Dr. Thomas pointed to the screen again. "Yes, Dad, here's Baby A and Baby B. Congratulations to you both."

Erica was shocked and couldn't do anything but cry, but it was only tears of joy. She was thrilled, and the fact that she could tell how happy Pierre was about the news made her day even better.

Dr. Thomas printed out pictures for the couple before she scheduled their next appointment for two weeks later.

Once in the parking lot, Pierre opened the door for Erica, but before she could climb into the car, Pierre grabbed her and pulled her closer to him. He hugged her tightly, showing nothing but love.

"Baby, I swear you have really come into my life and made it better. I love the fuck out of you."

Before she could even respond, they were kissing in the parking lot for what seemed like forever. After some time, they pulled apart, and Erica gazed into his eyes.

"I love you too, baby."

As they drove away, Erica turned her attention off the baby pictures and to Pierre. "Today was a good day, baby, but you wanna know what would make it better?"

"What's that, baby?" he asked, knowing she was about to bring up food.

Now knowing that she was carrying twins helped him understand how she could eat all fucking day long.

"Let's go out to eat. I'm starving. You know food always makes the day go better."

"You just greedy, baby," Pierre said, laughing.

Erica smacked her lips, acting like she had an attitude.

"I'm just playing, baby. I'm gonna take you to go feed my babies," he said, rubbing on her thigh.

He knew she liked that and was gonna calm down.

"Baby, can you go get your mama? I wanna share the news with her," Erica asked.

Pierre thought about it for a second and felt like that was a good idea. "You know what, baby? I like that plan. I'm gonna swing by her place right now."

Pierre liked how Erica and his mom got along. He never had a chance to let his mom meet any other female that he used to fuck with because he was too young when she took off. So he was glad that the only female she ever got a chance to know was the only one he ever really gave a fuck about.

Once in front of her apartment, Pierre pulled out his phone and dialed her number. She answered on the third ring.

"Hey, son, what's up?"

"Ma, you wanna go get something to eat with me and Erica?"

"Boy, you know I don't care about that restaurant food. I just got done cooking and was about to call you. Why don't y'all come over and eat with me?" Kim said.

Pierre quickly said OK before hanging up. He then ran down the plan to Erica. At first, he thought she was gonna be mad that he told his mom yeah before asking her, but she was cool with it. As long as she was eating, she was straight with whatever.

Kim had hooked up some lasagna, fried chicken wings, and a nice tossed salad. Erica smiled from ear to ear as she stuffed her mouth.

"Ma, we have some news to tell you," Pierre said, getting Kim's full attention.

"What's up, PJ?"

"First, please stop calling me that. I always hated every-one calling me that growing up."

"OK, I can respect that, Pierre. Is that better?"

"Yeah, Ma, much better," he said, laughing.

"Now, forget all that. Tell me the news," she said excitedly.

"Erica pregnant with twins."

Kim covered her mouth. "Are you guys serious? Please, don't play with me right now."

Erica stood up and walked over to her chair. She then placed Kim's hand on her stomach. "Yes, it's twins. A boy and a little girl."

Kim stood up and hugged Erica. "Thank you so much."

"Aye, Ma, why you thanking her? *I'm* the one who did all the work. I made them babies."

Everyone looked at Pierre and laughed. He could be so silly at times. Erica returned to her seat and continued to eat her food.

At this time, Kim was crying, "Boy, I tell you, God is so good. He helped me get clean and brought my son back into my life. Now, I'm being blessed with two grandbabies at once. I'm a blessed soul."

Erica had just left her last class of the day and was on her way to meet Nicole at the mall. Both had been busy and needed to catch up on each other's life. They both had big news to share with each other.

They linked up in the food court just like always.

"So, I'll go first with what's been going on with me," Nicole said, wearing a huge Kool-Aid smile.

"OK, I'm ready to hear everything."

Still smiling, Nicole blurted out, "Bitch, I'm pregnant."

Erica did a little dance in her seat, "Oh my God, boo, I'm so happy for you and Mekco."

"Thanks, girl. I'm so happy. Every time I think about it, I just can't help but smile. This has been a dream of mine since forever."

Erica swallowed her food before she continued the conversation. "So, how did Mekco take the news? I just know he was happy."

Nicole couldn't let the truth out and have Erica looking at her funny, so she lied. "Girl, I never saw that man happier. I swear, since we found out I was pregnant, he can't keep his hands off me. Just the other night, he was rubbing my stomach, singing to the baby, and it ain't even developed yet."

They both laughed.

"It's crazy how guys' whole attitude change when a baby is involved," Erica added.

"OK, bitch, my business is out there, now, what's been going on with you?"

"OK, so the other day, Pierre came to my doctor's appointment with me, and we found out that we're having a boy *and* a girl," Erica said with a smile.

"Wait a fucking minute. Are you telling me y'all having twins?

"Yes, girl, I'm having twins. Can you believe it?"

Nicole played everything off. She wanted to be happy for her friend so badly, but she secretly was jealous. She wanted her news to be better than Erica's, but her pregnancy couldn't top twins. Once again, Erica won. It's sad that she was in a challenge and didn't even know it.

The girls spent their afternoon talking and shopping. Erica had fun picking out clothes for her babies. She was so happy that she finally knew the sex.

After three hours of shopping and eating, the girls went their separate ways. They were both tired and so full that their beds were calling their names for a nap.

Since Erica had been kidnapped, she had made it her business to call Pierre when she was on her way. That way, he could meet her in the parking lot. So, as she pulled into the parking lot, Pierre stood there waiting.

"Hey, baby, I have a couple of bags in the trunk."

"What the hell you telling me for? You better get them. I'm off duty," he said, joking with her.

After laughing, she responded, "Don't play with me. I'm carrying two babies. I'm not carrying *any* bags."

She popped the trunk for him, and he grabbed every bag back there. "I know you didn't carry all these bags around the mall."

"I need all that stuff, baby," she whined.

When they walked into the house, Erica's mouth dropped open. While she was at school and out shopping, Pierre had done a little shopping of his own. Erica looked around and saw that he had bought the babies cases of diapers and wipes. They had cribs, walkers, swings, and everything else they would need.

Her couple of bags of clothes weren't shit compared to the dozens of bags that were sitting on the couch.

Erica couldn't help but cry. "Wow, Pierre."

"Baby, why are you over there crying?" he asked as he wrapped her in his arms.

"I swear you get better each and every day. I feel so lucky to have you, and I know you're gonna be a great daddy," she said, wiping her eyes.

"I told your ass from jump, just because I'm a street nigga, that don't mean I'm a ho-ass nigga. I'm gonna always make sure you and my babies straight for life."

Erica tried to stop crying, but her emotions were getting the best of her. Pierre held her tighter and allowed her to cry. He knew she was crying tears of joy, and there wasn't nothing wrong with that.

***

After a hot shower and a long overdue lovemaking session, Erica lay in Pierre's arms.

He held her, patiently waiting for her to fall asleep. He had to meet up with Cross and see what was popping in these streets.

Erica knew he was gonna leave, so she did what she always did. She fought her sleep and started a conversation with him.

"Baby, when I get up, I'm gonna start hanging up their clothes and putting some of that stuff in the dresser."

"Nah, don't worry about that shit right now. I'm gonna have someone come paint the room when you at school so the smell won't bother you. I'm gonna have this guy draw out all the Sesame Street characters all over the room to match all the shit I just brought them."

"Sesame Street?"

"Yeah, ma. You told me when we first started talking that you loved that show. I can't count how many times I caught your grown ass watching that shit," he said, laughing.

"I wasn't saying it like that. I was just surprised, that's it. And I hope you don't be telling nobody my business."

They both laughed before Pierre kissed her lips. She always talked to him when they were just chilling, and he would listen even when she wasn't sure if he really was paying attention.

"Hey, did Mekco tell you that Nicole is pregnant too?"

The thing was, Mekco did tell him about both of his bitches being pregnant. He also told him how he begged Toya to get an abortion, but she refused to do it, and how he almost fucked everything up with Nicole and ended up making her think she needed to end her pregnancy until he threatened to kill her ass. Pierre was pretty sure Nicole didn't share everything with Erica, and it wasn't his job to report her business either, so to keep the peace, he gave Erica another kiss before saying, "Yeah, he told me. That's cute our babies will be almost five months apart."

"Yeah, and Nicole was so happy. She couldn't stop smiling when she was telling me. I'm so happy for them."

She fell right to sleep, and just like clockwork, Pierre gave her another kiss and climbed out of bed. He needed to see what the fuck was up with Cross.

P arrived at Cross's house in no time. For it to be a nice day out, no one was really out, and he could fly through the streets. Once inside, he saw that Mekco was already there with some of the other members of the Brick Boyz.

"OK, now that everyone is here, I can let you all know what's going on. We have a problem that needs to be addressed now."

At once, many of the guys started asking what was going on.

"Chill the fuck out and let me talk," Cross yelled.

The room got quiet, and once again, he had everyone's attention.

"Word on the street is that Brian ho ass is back with a little crew, and they've been playing tough, robbing the young boys on the streets. We all know that I don't give them that much to work with at once 'cause they still young, but at the same time, they are still part of this family, and we gotta show these muthafuckas who's the boss around here."

Mekco stood up to speak to his crew. "Brian and Brandon crossed me before and came back into the city like it wasn't shit, but I'm proud to say that Brandon is dead, and Brian is next. Fuck him and his whole crew. I want y'all to watch the young niggas' backs. And if you gotta murk a muthafucka, do that shit, just don't get caught. If there's any problems, call me or my bro, P."

P stood up next to speak to the crew. "I want everyone here to make it home to their family every night, so with that being said, watch your back. We all know who Brian is and what he looks like, but right now, we don't know who his crew is. I'm just asking y'all to pay attention to your surroundings and have each other's backs."

Cross got back out of his seat. "Well said, now, y'all can get the hell out of my house before my girl get home."

Everyone laughed as they walked out the door. Mekco and P stayed behind to talk to Cross.

"Man, Cross, these niggas are fucking retarded. Brandon already dead, and now, his brother gonna follow in his footsteps," P said to his boys.

"Yeah, I just hope we find that nigga before he touch somebody on this team. After losing Face, we saw how that shit had hit us. We can't let that shit happen to nobody else," Mekco added.

Cross looked down at his watch. "All right, y'all my niggas, but y'all got to go. My girl will be here in a minute."

Mekco laughed, then asked, "What happened to all that talk about not cuffing a chick, only fucking them?"

Everyone laughed until Cross said, "Muthafucka, get your mophead ass out of my house. Don't be trying to quote me, nigga."

Mekco and P laughed until they were out the door. Cross talked a good game, but he was whipped just like the rest of the fellas.

P drove home thinking about what Cross said. He was right. They didn't know who was rolling with Brian and needed to watch their backs.

It was crazy how them niggas went out of town and formed a crew just to come to Detroit to fuck with them.

He cruised home with Erica on his mind. She had really come into his life and made him use his heart again. It was funny how shit worked 'cause, at first, he tried his hardest to stay away from her and just let her live her life. He was thankful he went against what he thought was right and stayed in her life. She had secretly become the best thing that came into his life. If it weren't for her, he probably would have been back in jail or something. Yeah, he still did his dirty, but her love kept him from being a hothead.

Pierre climbed right back into the bed with the future Mrs. Miller. She must have smelled him because even before he could wrap her up in his arms, she was moving over to rest her head on his chest. Holding her had become his favorite thing to do when she was around him.

Mekco went straight home. Since he learned about Toya and Nicole being pregnant, he had been chilling by himself.

Nicole called him all day, every day. He tried to tell her that it wasn't her, it was him, but she was acting like she didn't understand that.

Truthfully, he was so pissed at Toya that he couldn't even enjoy the fact that Nicole was also carrying his baby.

Mekco lay in his bed feeling like shit. Since he had been home, Nicole called him three times and texted him. The only reason that she stopped was because he finally answered and told her that he was in the streets handling shit and would be there later.

Trying to doze off, Mekco got pissed all over again, hearing his phone ring. He had put in his mind that he was about to go off on Nicole. He grabbed the phone off the nightstand and saw that it was Toya.

"Man, what the fuck you want? I hope you ain't calling me just to be on that bullshit."

Toya smacked her lips. "Mekco, I'm not on no bullshit, baby daddy. I was calling to see if you wanted to go to my doctor's appointment next week."

"Nah, I'm good on that, Toya," he replied coldly.

"Oh, so you really just gonna say fuck me and our baby? I swear, I thought fucking with a Brick Boy was the best thing that could happen to me, but I see the leader of the Brick Boyz ain't shit but a bitch boy," Toya teased.

"Man, bitch, watch your fucking mouth. You knew you wasn't shit but a fucking jumpoff."

Toya laughed. "Really, Mekco? Most niggas don't fuck their jumpoffs raw and get them pregnant, but I forgot, you not a real nigga. You one of those niggas that runs away from their responsibility."

She was pissing him off with all that extra shit she was talking. Mekco never wanted to be the type of nigga that walked away from their child and just didn't give a fuck, but at the same time, he didn't want a baby with Toya. He was cool with Nicole being pregnant with his seed. She was who he really wanted to be with.

Toya had talked all that shit, but she ended up crying.

"Mekco, look, I really don't want us beefed out like this. I mean, everything was just all good between us. If anything, this baby is our blessing and should have brought us closer."

"Man, Toya, I hear what the fuck you saying, but at the same time, I got a girl. Do you understand that she will fucking kill both of our asses?" Mekco tried to explain to her.

He knew if this shit got to Nicole, she would go crazy.

"Look, Mekco, I understand you have a girl now, but when I got pregnant, *I* was your girl, or did you forget that?"

It was silent over the phone for a minute. They both were thinking about the situation at hand.

"Shit. Man, I was wrong for asking you to get rid of our baby, but just let me get my shit together on my end. I'm not no ho-ass nigga that's not gonna be in my baby life. You just caught me on a bad day."

Toya was no longer crying. She was smiling at the fact that he was talking like he finally had some sense.

"OK, Mekco, I understand. But just to let you know, I'm not trying to come between you and your girl. I just want you to help me take care of our child."

"You know what, Toya? I feel much better now that we actually talked about this shit. I'm going to hit you up tomorrow, but if you need anything, just hit me up."

"OK, cool. I will do that," Toya said before hanging up.

Once off the phone, she felt relieved that Mekco was now acting right. She still didn't give a fuck about his girl's feelings, but she was willing to act right for Mekco to be there for their child.

Mekco was cool with getting shit straight with Toya. Now, he was headed to Nicole's apartment to be honest with her. He knew it was gonna hurt her, but the way he looked at things, it was better to tell her now than let another muthafucka tell her. He only prayed that she didn't nut up and kill his black ass.

When he walked through the door, Nicole was lying on the couch, knocked out. It looked like she had popped her some popcorn but fell asleep on the movie.

He watched her sleep for a moment. She was like a little angel at peace. Too bad his news was gonna destroy her and might end his life.

He was getting cold feet as he thought about the time she tried to kill herself when he broke up with her ass. As time passed, he decided he wasn't ready to say anything to her.

Instead of waking her up to have that talk with her, he woke her up with kisses and showing love. They soon were in bed holding each other like they didn't have a care in the world. Nicole couldn't have been happier to have him by her side.

Sleep didn't come easy for Mekco; he had so much on his mind. It was crazy how fast he was to run the streets and kill a nigga when it was necessary, but it scared him to tell the woman that he loved that another bitch was carrying his baby too.

The next morning, Nicole woke up and saw that Mekco was still asleep, so she hurried and jumped out of bed. She went into the kitchen to make sure the bottle of Hennessy was out of sight. Nicole knew he was gonna have a fit if he found out she was still drinking.

She did try to stop once before, but drinking had become a part of her everyday living, and she was having a hard time quitting cold turkey. Last night, when he was ignoring her, then making her wait all night for him to come over, she had started drinking. She ended up taking a shower to freshen up. Afterward, she popped the popcorn but ended up dozing off on the couch.

"What you doing in this kitchen? I don't smell any food or hear no pots rattling in this muthafucka," Mekco said, sneaking up behind her.

"Boy, I don't feel like cooking. Why don't you go get us something to eat?"

"Damn, Nicole, your ass don't ever feel like doing shit. Go get dressed so we can go."

Nicole hurried and jumped into the shower so she could get dressed.

Mekco opened the cabinet and moved the two boxes of cereal in front of the liquor bottle. He shook his head before pulling it out, then pouring it down the drain.

"Sneaky alcoholic bitch."

He was pissed that she had been lying to him about not drinking. It looked like they both had secrets in their closet. They both had been on some bullshit, but he felt like her shit was worse 'cause she was playing with the safety of his baby's life.

Mekco went to the living room and sat on the couch. He tried to calm himself down, but he couldn't shake the hate that he was feeling toward her.

"I'm ready, baby. Let's go," Nicole said, appearing in the living room.

Mekco jumped up, not trying to hold back his feelings. "Bitch, you must really want me to beat your fucking ass. What the fuck I tell you about that drinking shit?"

Nicole was caught off guard and honestly thought she was getting away with sneaking a drink. "Mekco, I don't know what you're talking about."

Before Nicole knew what hit her, Mekco had her folded up in the corner.

"Stupid ass gonna look me in my fucking face and straight-up lie to me, like I ain't see you hide the bottle this morning."

Nicole stayed on the floor crying. She held her face down, scared that he was gonna hit her in her face again.

"Mekco, I'm sorry," she mumbled.

"Yeah, I know you're sorry, but I'm sorry for ever fucking back with your ass. I'm out."

Mekco grabbed his phone from the coffee table and walked toward the door.

Nicole finally got off the floor and yelled out, "Wait, Mekco, what about the baby?"

Mekco laughed before turning her way. "Man, do whatever the fuck you gonna."

He walked out the door, and Nicole allowed her body to slide down the floor as she cried her eyes out.

Once again, she felt lost. How was she supposed to live without Mekco in her life?

Chapter 4

"OK, Ms. Collins, we'll see you in two weeks for your follow-up," Tanisha said, sitting at the front desk at the doctor's office.

"Thanks, girl, I'll see you then," Erica said before she walked away.

She went to the front door to wait for Pierre to pull up. While she was waiting for her appointment slip, he had gone to get the car.

Seeing that a woman was coming toward the door, being friendly, Erica opened the door for her.

"Thank you," the young lady said before looking up, but once she did, she saw a familiar face.

"Hey, Erica, right?" Toya said with a devilish smile on her face.

She didn't even have to be messy about shit 'cause she knew Erica was gonna run her mouth.

At first, she didn't care about Nicole finding out about her baby, but for the last week and a half, Mekno had been MIA. After a million calls and texts, he still acted like she didn't matter to him. The way she looked at it, bumping into Erica was a blessing.

"Yeah, Toya, right?"

"Yes, girl. I haven't seen you in a minute. How is the baby?" Toya asked, playing it extra friendly.

"They're doing just fine. Yeah, that's right. It's twins," Erica said, excited to share the news with someone else.

"Wow, girl, I know you and your fiancé are happy."

"Yes, he wanted a boy, and I wanted a girl, and we were blessed enough to get both at the same time."

Erica was playing friendly but really wanted to know what Toya was doing at the office. It was enough of the pleasant little chitchat.

"So, Toya, what are you doing here?" Erica finally asked.

Toya smiled. It was showtime.

"Girl, I just found out I'm knocked up too. I'm not sure when I'm due, but I got pregnant around the time of the picnic. I believe you know my baby daddy."

Erica looked at her like she just told her it was the end of the world. She opened her mouth to say something, but before her words could come out, Toya started to talk. "I'm sorry, I gotta go. I don't wanna be late for my appointment." And just like that, she walked off, leaving Erica stuck with her mouth wide open.

Erica got herself together, then went out to the car, but when she got in, she slammed the door.

"Damn, what the fuck wrong with you?" Pierre asked.

"I wanna slap the shit out of somebody."

"Who pissed you off, baby? They got you cussing and shit. Who I gotta fuck up?"

"Mekco."

Pierre looked at her like she had lost her mind before asking, "Damn, baby, what the hell he do to you?"

If she had said any other name, he would have pulled up on whoever and rocked their ass, but hearing her say Mekco's name made him question her and her ill feelings toward him.

"Niggas just not shit. I swear they not."

"Erica, watch your mouth, ma. You don't even sound right cussing and shit. Calm down before you upset my babies."

For the next fifteen minutes, Erica rode in silence. She did try to text Nicole, but she didn't respond. Then it hit her that she hadn't really talked to her best friend in a minute.

Between Erica being in school during the week and just living her life, she stayed busy. Whenever she did call Nicole, she was either busy herself or just didn't answer. She was gonna make it her business to pull up on her girl soon, especially after bumping into Toya. They had some shit to talk about.

"I'm hungry, Mr. Miller," Erica said, breaking their silence.

"Man, what the fuck is your problem? Oh, you mad at my nigga for whatever reason, so you gonna have an attitude with me?"

"I don't have an attitude," she said clearly with an attitude.

"Whatever, E, you only call me Mr. Miller when you're pissed off."

She didn't even bother to respond. The last thing she wanted was to fall out with him because Mekco was a dog.

"So, are you gonna tell me what the fuck is going on?" he asked.

"It's nothing, baby. I'm just hungry."

"I'm about to call my mom and see if she cooked. I mean, would you rather eat over there or go out 'cause I know you don't feel like cooking?"

"Yeah, call her. I love her cooking. I don't know why she can cook well and you can't."

"'Cause my granny made sure I ate good every day. I didn't even have to lift a finger to make a bowl of cereal or a sandwich. Then, when she died, I ran the streets, so whenever I got hungry, McDonald's and Coney Island became my personal cooks. Sometimes, when my mom was around, she would cook too. She learned all her skills from my granny."

Erica sat back in her seat as they drove over to his mom's place. She didn't wanna say too much cause she knew that whenever he spoke about his past, especially his grandma, he got into his feelings. If Pierre didn't know anything else about his mom, he knew that she had her ass in the house cooking and watching some bullshit on TV.

Kim opened her door with a smile. She loved seeing her son every other day. Sometimes, she would cry when he left as she thought about how she walked away from him as a child.

Even after she found out about his dad, Big P, dying and then a few years later his granny passing, she still didn't reach out to him, and it killed her inside.

Back then, the drugs took over her life. It didn't even allow her to sober up for either one of their funerals.

Now that the past was in the past, she enjoyed every moment with her son. It was a bonus that he had Erica in his life. Kim absolutely loved Erica. Not only was she beautiful, but she was smart. She knew her son was with the right one.

Kim also felt that Erica kept her son leveled. He might have done some dirt because he wasn't entirely out in the streets, and she had Erica to thank for that.

The way he looked at Erica even when she wasn't looking, she knew that look was only pure love.

"Hello," Nicole said, answering her phone after the fourth ring.

"Aye, boo, I'm outside. Buzz me in."

Nicole hung up the phone, then walked into the living room to buzz Erica in.

Lately, she had been to herself and just avoided everybody.

Erica walked into the apartment and sat beside her best friend. The look in Nicole's eyes told Erica that she had been crying and was upset about something. Her look made the happiness leave Erica's face.

She was now sad and didn't even know what was wrong.

Since she knew about Mekco, she somewhat assumed that was the reason why Nicole was mad.

"Hey, boo, I miss you," Erica said, trying to get a smile out of her friend.

"Hey," Nicole said dryly.

"So, we are not about to do this. Tell me what's wrong so we can fix it and make you feel better."

Nicole forced out a smile. That was the reason why she loved Erica; she always had her back.

Nicole looked her friend's way and began to cry. "Girl, everything is fucked up. Mekco left me, and I haven't heard from him in like two weeks. I can't stop drinking, and I don't want this baby anymore."

Nicole spoke so fast that Erica wasn't sure if she had heard her correctly. "Wait, what?" Erica asked, confused.

Nicole repeated herself, but this time, she slowed it down for Erica.

"Oh my God, Nicole. I think we need to stop talking now and just pray. You're going through a lot right now, and I'm unsure if I can give you the right advice."

"OK, Pastor Collins," Nicole jokingly said.

Erica smacked her lips. "Whatever, girl."

"So, do you not want this baby because Mekco broke up with you, or is there another reason?" Erica asked.

"I thought being pregnant would make him want to commit and be serious. I wanted him to really love me and not just love having sex with me. This baby was supposed to help our relationship, but he grew distant from me instead."

"So, what's the plan, Nicole? You know I got your back no matter what."

"I'm not sure, Erica. I still love Mekco, but he's a little boy with a grown man dick. He just is not ready to be a father right now, and I'm not ready to be a mom."

"Nicole, you know I love you more than just a friend. You have been like a sister to me, and I hate that I had come over here to tell you this, but I wouldn't be a real friend if I didn't say anything about this."

Nicole wiped her eyes, then asked, "What is it, boo?"

Erica wiped her tears as she looked at her friend, who was trying so hard to stop herself from crying. To be honest, it really wasn't a reason for her to stop 'cause the news that Erica came to deliver was gonna hurt her even more.

"Erica, what is it?"

"The other day, when I was at the doctor's office, I bumped into that girl Toya that Mekco had at that picnic. She was really happy to see me, just to let me know that she was also pregnant by Mekco."

Nicole dropped her head in her hands while crying her eyes out. Erica slid over to be closer to her friend. She hugged her, trying to make her feel a little better.

"It's OK, boo. You can do better than him."

Nicole spent the next ten minutes crying before she busted out laughing. Erica sat back, looking confused.

Nicole had done the crazy move that them women do in the movies right before they killed whoever was closest to them.

"Girl, I swear that nigga ain't shit. I guess that's why he's been switching up on me and shit. He just was out here doing his dirt. He had been treating me like I was wrong for being pregnant when really, the problem was, he had got another bitch pregnant. Do you know we just started fucking without condoms after all the years we've been together? That mean he was fucking that bitch raw from day one. I hate him so much, Erica."

Erica was speechless. She wasn't sure what to say to Nicole. She knew her friend was hurt, but she was trying to be strong at that moment.

"You know what, Erica? I'm not even about to waste any more tears over him. He said he was done with me, and I'm gonna let him just do him. I'm done playing the role of Mekco's little bitch. I can no longer be that weak bitch he turned me into."

"If you need anything, just let me know. No matter what, boo, I got your back 100 percent," Erica said with a smile on her face.

Nicole smiled back. "I love you, Erica, but don't worry about this shit. I'm gonna get through this shit and bounce right back."

"I know, but I want you to know that I'm here for you, and to be honest, I don't want you to do anything stupid."

"I give you my word that stupid shit is out of my system. I don't wanna hurt myself right now. I just wanna better myself and get that nigga completely out of my system. I have to do what's best for me now, but I do need your help with something."

"Anything, boo. What's up?" Erica said, ready for whatever.

"I'm not gonna keep this baby, and I'm gonna move out of this place. I don't wanna stay here 'cause he pays the rent and bills here. I don't want anything to do with him at all. I'm gonna need your help, but I don't want you to say anything to P. The last thing I want is for him to tell Mekco my plans."

"OK, boo, I got you, but where are you gonna go?"

It didn't take Nicole long to reply, so Erica knew she had already considered this.

"Probably my mom's house, or shit, I saved up enough
bread to get another apartment, and getting my old job
back is nothing. Girl, I can move on without him."

"I understand what you are saying, and you have nothing to worry about. I'm not gonna say anything."

"Thanks, boo."

"No problem, Nicole. You're my girl."

The girls ordered some pizza and spent the remainder
of the day packing up some of Nicole's stuff.

Erica was proud of how strong Nicole was being. She
knew she probably would lose her mind if the shoe were
on the other foot. She was happy that she and Pierre
weren't going through this mess, but she didn't say it out
loud. The last thing she wanted was for Nicole to think
she was trying to rub anything in her face. She knew how
Nicole could flip out and be full of jealousy.

For a whole week, Erica made it her business to go over
to Nicole's house every day after school to help pack and
move little stuff in their cars. Nicole had let Erica know
that Mekco was still avoiding her, and she was okay with
that. It actually helped her remain focused on her and
sticking to her plan.

Erica had no problem with not telling Pierre anything
about Nicole and Mekco's problem. During the day, she
was at school, and most days after school, she would go
straight to Nicole's apartment. Since Pierre was never
home, he liked the idea of her being with a friend instead
of being at home alone.

The two girls would pack up some of Nicole's things,
then chill all night.

There had been some serious stuff going on in the
streets and with the Brick Boyz. Pierre had been out in
the streets doing what he would call handling his busi-

ness. Some nights, he wouldn't even come home until the following day.

Erica knew better than to ask about his day.

Some nights, he would show up late, and after a shower, he would climb into the bed and just hold her. His scent would wake her up, but she wouldn't say anything. She would feel him kiss on her repeatedly and whisper in her ear how much he loved her. Sometimes, he would tell her he was sorry for being out all night. Erica acted like she was still asleep, but she thought it was cute how he loved her.

Erica stood in front of the mirror with only a black bra and matching panties on. She rubbed her growing stomach with a smile on her face. She had never pictured herself pregnant, especially with twins.

"You still look as beautiful as the first time I saw you," Pierre said, sneaking into the room.

Erica jumped before turning around. She never heard him come in the door.

"Boy, don't be scaring me like that. But anyway, thank you."

"It's early as hell. Where you about to go?" Pierre asked while kicking off his shoes.

"Church, baby. Today, we are cooking lunch for the neighborhood. You know, around this time of year, we start doing this every other Saturday."

"Damn, that's a nice thing to do, for real, baby. I was hoping we could chill today, but I see how important this is to you."

Erica grinned a little harder. "Since you don't have to run the streets with your buddies, I thought maybe you could go with me."

"And what the hell am I gonna do at your daddy's church?" Pierre asked.

"Serve food, silly butt. Maybe if he saw us together and saw you helping out, he would talk to me," Erica sweetly said, trying to convince Pierre to go with her.

Pastor Collins still acted like she was a stranger, and Erica was tired of him and his childish ways. She had given him enough time to get over whatever it was that was bothering him.

He had his head wrapped around the idea that she had chosen being in love over being his daughter. It was a foolish thought, but it was a thought that came between the father and daughter relationship.

"Man, I don't know about all that. I'm not trying to see your daddy, and I'm pretty sure he ain't trying to see my ass. You trying to make him hate me more?"

Erica tried not to laugh at Pierre, but she couldn't help it. "He doesn't hate you, baby. He just needs to get used to you being with and loving his daughter."

Pierre started to undress so he could jump in the shower. As he lifted his shirt to take it off, Erica's smile quickly turned into a frown.

"Oh my God, Pierre, is that blood on your shirt? Are you hurt?"

Pierre snatched the shirt off, then examined himself. "Nah, I'm cool. This must be that other nigga's blood."

Erica smacked her lips, then rolled her eyes.

"What now, baby? Damn, you the one who asked."

Erica didn't say anything. She walked toward the closet and started looking for something to wear. She ignored Pierre even after he started walking toward her.

The thing was, she knew what he was about since day one, and since then, he made sure to be honest with her. Erica's problem was that she thought that once she told him about the babies, he would at least try to calm down. If not for her, for the babies.

Pierre stood behind Erica and wrapped his arms around her waist. As he placed sweet kisses on her neck, she smiled. It felt like her body was melting right there in the bedroom.

She tried to act like she wasn't enjoying it, but he knew every spot on her body that loved the extra attention. Allowing his hands to touch all over her, Erica couldn't help but moan out just how much she loved him.

"Come jump in the shower with me," he ordered.

Erica followed right behind him. She didn't give a damn if she had just gotten out of the shower. She knew exactly what he was craving because she wanted it too.

Erica sat back in the passenger seat as Pierre drove to the church. The power of good pregnant pussy had him driving to church, ready to serve the whole neighborhood.

"Man, E, I swear you better be lucky I love your ass because you know this church shit really not how I wanna spend my Saturday."

"Pierre, the way I see it is you need to chill out. Where do you think we will get married? You have to enter a church to marry me, you know that, right?"

"I know that, girl, and when the time comes for us to handle that, I'll be ready," he explained.

"OK, Mr. Miller, I sure do hope so," Erica said dryly.

"So what the fuck you thought? I was just gonna keep us engaged forever?"

Erica giggled. "I sure hope not."

The rest of the ride was quiet. Pierre was thinking about what she had said. He knew he had to marry her in a church, but that wasn't the problem. He just wasn't in the mood to deal with her pops. He couldn't understand how someone could call their self a pastor and be all into the Lord but at the same time, be so fucking evil.

When it boiled down to it, he knew he was gonna have to deal with him, especially if Erica was still trying to deal with him.

Once they got out of the car, Erica held Pierre's hand. They stood outside of the church for a minute before going in.

"Come on, baby. I promise everything is going to be all right."

Erica led Pierre into the church, then down to the basement. Everyone turned their attention toward the couple. It kind of made Pierre uncomfortable, but he continued walking with a smile on his face, showing off his platinum slugs.

Pastor Collins shook his head but quickly got his act together. He couldn't allow his daughter and her gang-banging, little baby daddy to cause him to act a fool in front of everyone. He walked over toward the couple.

Erica was shocked when he reached out to hug her.

As they hugged, he whispered in her ear, "I don't know what the hell you think y'all doing, but please don't embarrass me any more than you already have."

Before Erica could respond, her father released her.

With a huge smile on his face and a voice loud enough for everyone in the basement to hear, he said, "I'm so glad you made it, my precious daughter."

Then he turned his attention toward Pierre. "Hey, there, my son-in-law. I'm glad you came to help out. We could really use your help today."

Pierre didn't get a chance to respond either because after the pastor put on that fake show, he walked off.

Erica laughed to herself; her father was a trip.

Sister Mary made her way over to the couple.

"Hey, Erica and her friend. We have already started warming the food. The doors open in about half an hour. Can you guys start spreading the tablecloths on all of the tables?"

"Sure, Sister Mary, and this is actually my fiancé, Pierre."

"Fiancé? Wow, congratulations, dear. Nice meeting you, Mr. Pierre."

For the first time, Pierre spoke up. "Nice meeting you too, ma'am."

Sister Mary walked over to the rest of the nosy group that she hung around. She needed to report back to the ones who didn't hear the pastor calling him his son-in-law.

Erica went into the storage room and grabbed some tablecloths. "Here, baby, let's get these tables set up before these folks get here."

Erica and Pierre finished in no time, and soon after, Sister Mary came back their way, asking them to do something else.

"Pierre, if you don't mind, can you bring out this cooler? Sister Helen filled it up with ice and water bottles in the back room like a fool, and we need it out here."

"Yes, ma'am, no problem. Just show me the way."

Erica watched them walk off. She smiled at how nice Pierre was acting. She also knew that his being nice to Sister Mary was gonna get around the church, and everyone else was gonna love him too. Maybe next, her father would see how much of a good guy he really was.

The rest of the afternoon went by without any problems. Erica noticed how her dad stayed away from her and Pierre.

The women in the church were showing Pierre so much love that Erica could tell that the older women were crushing on him.

"Girl, how did you get him in the same room as your dad?" Nicole's mother asked.

Before answering, Erica let out a laugh. "I have my ways, but he looks like he's having a good time."

"Yeah, he over there smiling, getting them old ladies' panties wet," Theresa said, laughing right along with Erica.

"Oh my God, you so silly. I meant to ask you this earlier, but where is Nicole?"

"You know, them guys were moving the rest of her stuff out today. I'm surprised she sticking to her plan. I just hope she can make it on her own 'cause you know Mekco had her so spoiled that she wasn't working or anything."

"Oh yeah, that totally slipped my mind. But she's gonna be all right. She just gotta stay focused and become the woman she was before getting involved with him," Erica said.

That Saturday, they served many families from the neighborhood. Pierre had to admit that he actually had a good time. Once the families were gone and they cleaned up, the other members just about begged him to visit the church the next day for Sunday service.

"So, Pierre, I hope we can see you tomorrow for service at 10:00 a.m.," Sister Mae said, rubbing his hand.

"Mae, get outta that young man's face. I'm pretty sure Erica will bring him to service," a jealous Deacon Thomas said while pulling his wife toward him.

Erica and Pierre laughed. "E, these old ladies want me," he whispered in her ear.

"Yeah, I see. You better stop smiling all in they face before I punch you," she said, laughing.

Pierre hugged Erica before placing a kiss on her lips. "You the only one I want."

Pastor Collins cleared his throat before interrupting the couple. "Remember, you're in a church, not in the trap."

And just like that, he walked away.

Nicole lay across her bed, rubbing her stomach. It was still flat, but it had become a habit of hers. She would cry while explaining to her unborn child why she wouldn't be able to keep it, all while rubbing her stomach.

"I'm so sorry, baby. I'm just not ready right now. Maybe when I get my shit together, I'll try again."

Nicole cried as she thought about how her appointment to terminate her pregnancy was that Monday.

Erica had class, so she talked her mom into going with her.

Nicole tried to tell everyone she was fine, and she played it off whenever Erica or her mom were around, but really, she was sad. It killed her that Mekco didn't even call her after he had beat her ass a few weeks ago. She wanted to be done with him, but at the same time, she wanted him to at least act like he still wanted her.

That Sunday, instead of going to church, she stayed home and unpacked her belongings. While unpacking her bedroom stuff, she was interrupted by her phone ringing. As she looked at the screen, she saw Mekco's name flashing. She forgot about how she was supposed to be feeling and found herself cheesing.

"Man, get your shit together, bitch," she told herself. She watched the phone ring until he finally hung up.

Mekco didn't give up easily; he continued to call her back-to-back.

Nicole eventually got tired of him calling and just turned off her ringer. She continued to unpack, feeling proud of herself.

"Man, this stupid bitch gonna make me really hurt her simpleminded ass," Mekco said out of anger.

He had decided to make up with Nicole. He figured after all this time, she was probably over their fight and ready for daddy to come home.

It pissed him off when he popped up at her apartment, and the whole place was empty. She had finally gotten tired of his shit and moved on.

He went downstairs to the manager's office to ask a few questions.

"Hey, Kevin, what's up, man?" he asked, acting friendly to a man he barely spoke to when Nicole lived there.

"What's up, my man? How can I help you?"

"I see Nicole has moved. You wouldn't have a forwarding address for her mail, would you?"

Kevin looked down at his desk. "Umm, let me see. I know she left one."

Mekco patiently waited while the fat white man searched the top drawer of his desk.

"OK, here we go. This is the address that she left behind," Kevin said as he wrote it down on a sticky pad.

Mekco took the paper from him and then walked out of the office. He didn't even bother to say thank you.

Once inside his ride, he looked over what Kevin had written down. As he recited the address, he slowly realized that the address belonged to her mom.

"I guess that bitch not as smart as she think," Mekco mumbled before driving off.

Mekco sat outside of Theresa's house. He had forgotten that it was Sunday, and that meant that they were at church. He quickly got bored, so he pulled out his phone and dialed Pierre's number.

"Damn, where the fuck this nigga at?" he asked out loud to no one.

He then put the phone down but quickly picked it up, hearing it ring. He thought it was P calling, but instead, it was Toya. His being bored was the only reason he answered, plus he hadn't talked to her in a few weeks either.

"What's up?"

"Oh, so you finally can answer the phone. I know you been seeing me call you."

"Please don't start that shit. All that mouth gonna make me regret answering your call and then hang up on your ass."

"I'm sorry, daddy. I just miss you so much. Do you think you can come by a little later? I need you, baby," Toya said.

Seeing Nicole's mother's car pull into her driveway, he hurried to get off the phone with Toya. "Look, I'm gonna hit you back up later. Let me handle some business right quick."

"OK, baby."

Mekco hopped out of his car, then jogged three houses down to her house. "Hey, ma, you know where Nicole is?" he said with a warm smile.

Theresa rolled her eyes. "Boy, don't 'ma' me. My daughter told me everything, and she don't want to be bothered with your sorry ass. Now, get the fuck away from my house before I have some real goons get at your ass."

Mekco raised his hands, letting her know he didn't want any problems from her. He slowly walked back to his car, pissed off. He put in his mind that whenever he saw Nicole, he was gonna beat her ass again, then make slow love to her. He was gonna get his girl back by any means necessary.

Mekco got into his car and sat there for a minute. Things weren't going his way, and he wasn't used to that. He was the leader of the Brick Boyz, and his bitch was tripping on him.

He pulled out his phone and then called P's phone. Once again, he didn't get an answer. He wondered where that nigga could be.

Mekco then dialed Toya's number. "Aye, I'll be there in a minute. Hook me up with something to eat. I'm starving."

Toya smiled, knowing she planned to make Mekco all hers. She was gonna make sure she and their child were gonna be straight for life. She wasn't about to play all that disappearing shit.

"What you got the taste for, daddy?" she asked, using what she thought was her sexy voice.

Mekco smiled. He was feeling the attention that Toya was giving him. She had really made his day a little better. "Besides you, it doesn't even fucking matter. Just have something ready."

He didn't even wait for a response before hanging up.

Before pulling off, he looked at Nicole's mother's house for the last time.

"Baby, I'm still so shocked and happy that you joined me in church today," Erica said as Pierre drove them home.

"To be honest, it wasn't that bad. I really enjoyed myself today," he admitted.

With a huge smile, she couldn't help but ask, "So, do that mean you will be joining me for service again?"

"Yeah, I don't see why not."

Erica waited until they stopped for a red light before leaning over and kissing him. "I swear I love you so much."

"You better with that big-ass rock on your finger and you walking around carrying my kids."

After laughing, Erica asked, "Why can't you be like other boyfriends and just say you love me too?

'Cause I'm not like them niggas. I'm me. But for real, E, you already know I love your ass. To be honest, I might have loved you from the beginning of us meeting."

Erica sat back in the seat as she blushed over his words.

Once they got home, Erica undressed and took a nap. Those babies had her so tired all the time. Sometimes, it surprised her that she could even stay up in her classes.

Pierre went into the living room and pulled out his phone. He saw he had a few missed calls from Mekco and his mom. He called his mom back first.

"What's up, Ma?"

"Hey, where the hell you been? I called you earlier, and you didn't answer," Kim said.

"Ma, chill out. I was at church with Erica. We just walked in the door."

"Church? I see Erica finally got you going to church with her. That's good. I'm proud of you."

"Thanks, Ma. I told her that I would go back with her too."

Kim was happy that her son was going to church with Erica. That was one of the reasons that she loved Erica for her son. She tried her best to keep him leveled, and she could tell that Erica really loved him.

"I was calling because I needed a ride to the market to get this dinner together."

"Damn, Ma, what you cooking? We gonna stop by and eat with you."

"Come take me to the store, and you two are more than welcome to come to dinner. You know I don't mind feeding y'all, especially my grandbabies," Kim admitted.

Kim told Pierre exactly what he wanted to hear. "All right, Ma. As soon as Erica wakes up, we'll be on our way. Love you, Ma."

"I love you too, and tell Erica I love her too."

After that, the two got off the phone, and Kim went back into her living room to finish watching her movie.

Pierre called Mekco back. He wanted to hear what mess he had gotten himself into now. Lately, his boy had been on some bullshit, getting both of his chicks pregnant, then basically telling both to kiss his ass at the same time. He didn't know what the fuck was wrong with him.

"What's up, bro? What the fuck you been up to?" P asked.

"Aye, my nigga. When was the last time Erica seen Nicole?"

Wondering what the hell was going on, P asked, "Shid, she was just over there the other day. Why you ask that?"

"Man, I went to Nicole's apartment today, and the stupid bitch done moved on me and shit. Then I go over to her mom house, and she talked shit, telling me to stay away from her daughter. I don't know what the fuck really going on."

P was confused. Erica had been going over to Nicole's apartment a lot lately, and she never mentioned that her girl was moving. "Aye, bro, she haven't said anything to me about Nicole moving, but when she wake up, I'll ask her."

"OK, bro, good looking. Just hit me back later on today."

P had been concerned about his boy. It's like he had just been spaced out for the last couple of months. He couldn't help but ask, "Mekco, you, OK? I mean, lately, you haven't been yourself. Are you good?"

"Honestly, I wanna say I'm OK, but this whole baby thing is bugging me. I don't know where the fuck Nicole ass is at, and truth be told, I love that girl, and I really need her just to hold me right now. I'm not a soft pussy-ass nigga, but I miss my girl. And when I see her, I'm gonna try to make things right with her. I gotta do right by my kids, man."

"I feel you, bro. I'll hit you up later after I talk to E. I'm glad your wild ass finally getting your mind right."

"Yeah, I can admit I was on some bullshit, but I swear I'm about to get my shit in order."

The best friends got off the phone. Pierre was proud of his boy. For a minute, he thought he was gonna have to knock some sense into him.

P thought about what Mekco had said about Nicole moving. He wondered if Erica knew what the fuck was going on. He got up and then made his way toward the bedroom.

"Aye, E, wake up right quick. I need to holler at you," he said as he shook her arm.

"OK, I'm up. What is it, baby?" she mumbled, still half-asleep.

"Aye, when was the last time you spoke to Nicole?"

"Yesterday, baby, why?" Erica asked as she sat up in bed.

"That nigga talking about he went to her crib to try to get shit right with her, and her sneaky ass then up and moved on him. That nigga sounded like he wanted to cry. Did you know about her moving?"

"Huh?"

"E, don't play with me. If your ass can 'huh,' then you can hear."

Erica giggled. "Baby, I don't have anything to do with that stuff. But anyway, me and the babies hungry," she said, rubbing her belly.

"So, just fuck what I'm talking about? You think you're slick trying to throw the babies in it."

"Baby, you woke us up, and now we hungry."

"Get your naked ass dressed. My mommy said she wants me to go take her to the market, and she will cook dinner."

"Good, let me get up then," she jokingly said.

Pierre stood there and watched her get dressed. It was hard not to place her on the bed and make love to her again.

"Baby, I just thought about something. Why don't you just let your mom get my car since you have been driving me around anyway? And you said you would get me something bigger for me and the babies anyway."

"You know what? That's a good idea, but are you sure about giving away your baby?"

"Yeah, plus once the babies get here, I was gonna have to get something bigger."

Chapter 5

Brian parked right outside Pierre's apartment. He had been hiding out after his brother disappeared. But he wasn't a dummy. He knew that could only mean that the Brick Boyz had got him.

Lately, Brian's little crew had been out trying to make a name for themselves, and for that very reason, a few members had lost their lives.

Brandon and Brian had failed to mention how the Brick Boyz got down and how they were heartless when it came to this street shit. He wanted to see Pierre and Mekco suffer, and he saw that hitting their pockets wasn't enough, so he made sure that the first thing on his agenda was to get rid of the bitches that they loved.

He had been by Nicole's apartment, but he never saw her car, so he figured she was somewhere with Mekco's punk ass.

Brian kind of felt bad for Erica because she just walked into this shit, not having a clue about just how much her nigga was hated.

"Bingo," he said as he watched the couple enter separate cars.

He noticed the budge in Erica's stomach. The jacket that she wore told everyone about her business. "That's just too bad, Pierre. You probably would have been a good daddy, fuck nigga. I get to kill you, that bitch, and that ho-ass baby. Man, I wish my brother was here to see me finally taking this nigga out."

As Brian followed the couple's cars, he held a whole conversation with himself. His being off his meds had his mind gone. If his brother were here, he would have made sure that he stayed on them, and they probably could have been on top right now.

The couple drove over to Kim's house, talking over their phones about baby names. Since they found out what she was carrying, they debated what they should name their babies.

Pierre wanted his son to be a junior and his daughter's name to be Princess or Paris. Erica wasn't sure what she wanted to name them yet.

"Look, can we just agree to let their names start with a P like my name? You can give them their middle name, and, of course, they will have our last name."

The sound of him saying "our last name" made the butterflies in her stomach dance around.

"Baby, you not gonna let me sleep on it?" she asked while laughing.

"I'm gonna need an answer soon so I can go get y'all names tatted on me."

"Oh, so, you gonna get my name tattooed on you so I'll know it's real?"

"Shid, if that big-ass rock on your finger didn't tell you, I don't know what the fuck will. But for real, E, you can take your time. You know I'm an ink junky and just ready to hit my nigga up for some new work."

"You know what, baby? I just thought about it. You have given me everything I asked for and whatever I don't ask for. I'm gonna let you name them, and that's final."

Pierre pulled into his mother's apartment complex. Once he killed the engine, he got out and opened Erica's car door. He gently pulled her out of the car and gave her a long, passionate kiss. It never failed. She continued to make him a happy man.

In between their kisses, Erica moaned, "I love you, baby."

"And I love you more."

Brian sat in his car acting like the sight of them kissing was making him vomit. "Man, fuck y'all and all that mushy shit. Bitch boy, you a dead man walking. You and that pregnant ho."

Pierre and Erica finally released each other long enough to make it upstairs to Kim's apartment.

"Damn, Ma, it smell good as hell. What you got cooking?"

"I kept it simple tonight, but I cooked some greens, mac and cheese, and fried chicken. I need to go to the market to get some eggs for my corn bread. Erica, you gonna love my corn bread, baby. That shit will have you thick like you from down South somewhere," Kim said while laughing with everyone else.

Erica gave Pierre a look, letting him know to tell her about the car.

"OK, Ma, so we decided to let you have Erica's car. She is about to have them babies in a few months and is not driving herself around anymore. She would like for you to have it."

Kim covered her mouth before yelling, "Are you fucking kidding me? Y'all better stop playing with me."

"Ms. Kim, we are so serious right now. Plus, we know you wouldn't want to be stuck in the house all the time," Erica said sweetly.

Once Kim got them keys in her hands, she fought back her tears. "Pierre, you just don't know how much I love you. I really appreciate everything. And that goes for you too, Erica. I love your ass too."

Both Pierre and Erica told Kim that they loved her as well.

She took no time at all grabbing her purse from her bedroom. Before walking out the door, she stepped back into the kitchen and hugged them both, saying, "Y'all watch that last batch of chicken for me."

Brian sat in his car listening to his homeboy Tommy tell him how the previous night, the Brick Boyz had raided one of their spots, killing a couple of his already-small crew. His blood boiled hearing that the Brick Boyz was still murking his little team. Brian thought that if he brought in some niggas from another state, they would be able to sneak around and kill their enemies, but the Brick Boyz was already on it.

Brian was so wrapped up in his phone conversation that he didn't even see who jumped into Erica's car, but once he saw it ride past him, he started his engine. With a smile on his face, he followed behind the vehicle.

"This nigga killed my fucking brother. I can't show this nigga no fucking mercy. Everyone he love must die, starting with his bitch."

Kim drove without a worry in the world. She had finally got her life on track, and her son allowed her to get back in his life. All she was waiting for was Erica to have her grandbabies in a few months. After all that she had been through, she could finally see that her life was better now.

"Damn, I was supposed to make that light," Kim said as she stopped at the red light. She only had a few more blocks before hitting the market.

"It's now or never, nigga. Let's do this shit. Make Brandon proud," Brian mumbled right before he pulled up to Erica's car.

Before the light had a chance to turn green, Brian pressed the button to roll down his passenger-side window, and without a second thought, he emptied his whole clip into the driver's-side door of Erica's car.

He then made a wide U-turn and drove off in the opposite direction from where he was initially going.

Seeing what had just happened, the other drivers around jumped out of their cars to check on Kim and call an ambulance. There had been so many calls to the same location that the police and ambulance arrived within six minutes.

"Dang, where the hell is she at? I'm ready to mess this food up."

"Baby, calm your greedy ass down," Pierre said, rubbing on Erica's belly. He smiled, knowing that she was the love of his life and was carrying his babies.

He honestly thought that after being an inmate for six years, he was gonna get out and just continue to be a street nigga. He never pictured that he would get straight, find love, become engaged, and become a father in just a few months.

After waiting for another twenty minutes, Pierre jumped up from the couch, "Man, fuck this. We about to eat. She can save the corn bread for the next time."

Erica smiled as she followed him into the kitchen. She felt her twins moving around, so she knew they were ready to eat too.

Pierre pulled out his phone as they ate, then dialed his mama's number again. He had called her three times already and still hadn't heard from her.

"Baby, I'm getting worried. Your mom should have been back from the store by now. Then, on top of that, she's not answering her phone."

Pierre didn't say much. He was worried himself. He tried to act like everything was OK because he didn't want to scare Erica. For some reason, he knew she would lose her mind if he showed how he really was feeling.

After dinner, Erica cleaned up their mess, then joined Pierre in the living room.

"I just called her again, E, and she still not picking up."

Before Erica could respond, Pierre's phone started to ring. He smiled as he saw his mama's name across his screen.

"Hey, Ma, where you at? We done ate and everything."

"Hello, my name is Christine, and—"

Before the stranger could finish her statement, Pierre cut her off. "What you doing with my mama phone?" he asked.

"Oh my God, she's your mother?" Christine asked with a shaky voice. She tried her hardest to hold in her tears.

"Man, Christine, why do you have my mama phone? And what the hell is going on?"

Erica didn't say anything, but she had a strange feeling in her heart. She silently prayed for Kim and Pierre as she paced the floor.

Christine hurried and blurted out the story. "I was walking down the street when a car pulled up to the lady in the red car, and he just started shooting into her car. Once he drove off, I ran over to make sure she was OK. I held her hand until the ambulance came to take her to the hospital. I rode with them, and that's how I ended up with her phone."

Pierre jumped up from the couch. "What you just say? My mama was shot? What hospital is she in?"

Pierre asked every question, but the one he really wanted to know, and that was if she was still alive.

Erica was right on Pierre's heels as he put on his shoes and grabbed his jacket. Whatever happened, she was gonna make sure she was there and had his back.

"Thank you. I'm on my way."

"Baby, what's going on?" Erica questioned, hoping he would fill her in on everything.

Pierre looked at her with tears in his eyes. "Somebody shot her; somebody tried to kill my mama. We gotta go to the hospital."

Erica hugged Pierre. She felt the wetness from him crying on the side of her neck. She prayed everything would work in their favor. Kim meant more to him than she could ever believe.

"Come on, baby, let's go. Everything's gonna be OK," Erica whispered in his ear before they released each other.

Pierre was quiet the whole ride to the hospital. Erica drove in silence. She could tell that his mind was racing, and he just needed to chill until he found out what was happening with his mom. It messed with both of their minds as they both wondered who could have wanted to kill her.

A ride that usually takes fifteen minutes had only taken Erica a good eight. She was breaking the law that night, trying to rush to the hospital.

"I'm looking for Kimberly Miller. I was told that she was brought in," Erica said to the old white lady at the front desk.

The lady worked her magic on the computer and told the couple where they could go. As they got to the area where Kim was being treated, Erica talked to another lady sitting at a desk in the waiting room. She told them to have a seat and wait for a doctor to come out and speak to them.

Erica turned around to go sit down, but Pierre didn't. He stood there for a minute. Erica saw the hesitation and wondered what he was up to.

"For the patient Kimberly Miller, can you please tell me if she is OK? Is my mom still alive?"

"Sir, I can't answer any questions for you right now. Like I said before, the doctor will come out and talk to you."

Erica could tell that Pierre was pissed and was ready to go off on the lady, so she grabbed his hand and pulled him toward the seats.

"Come on, baby, let's just have a seat, please."

Pierre allowed Erica to walk him over to the seats. Erica looked around and saw a young lady sitting in the corner, crying. She wondered if that was the lady on the phone with Pierre. She took Pierre's phone out of his hand to dial his mom's number.

The phone rang twice before the young lady answered it. "Hello."

Erica hung up and then walked over to where the woman was sitting. "Hi, I'm Erica. You talked to my husband about my mother-in-law."

"Hi, I'm so sorry about what happened to her. It was so crazy. She was sitting at the red light when this guy just started shooting into her window."

Christine repeated the story to her and started crying again. Erica found herself crying as well. Over the short period of time that she had known Kim, she had learned to love her.

"When you guys arrived here, was . . . She still alive? Me and her son are very worried."

"Yes, she was holding on. I rode with her and held her hand. She is a fighter."

"Thank you for being there for my mom," Pierre said, standing behind the girls.

Christine nodded, showing that she accepted his kind words. Pierre sat next to Erica, then turned his attention toward Christine. "I have a few questions for you."

"I don't know what else I can tell you. I told you and your wife all that I saw already."

"Just tell me who you saw shoot into her car."

Erica looked at Pierre and could see the fire in his eyes. As much as she hated when P came out, she understood precisely why Pierre was leaving. He had just got his mom back in his life, and now, somebody was trying to take her out.

"I'm sorry. I really can't describe the shooter other than saying it was a Black guy, and he looked somewhat young. Maybe around 24 or 25."

"What kind of ride did he have?"

"It was a black Tahoe."

"Christine, did the police talk to you already?"

"No, not yet. Why?" she asked.

"Do you think you can get ghost before they start poking around? I really don't care for the muthafuckas, and I don't need them in my fucking face."

"Umm, I understand. And I have no problem disappearing. I'm not a big fan of them anyway."

"Thank you."

"Kimberly Miller's family."

Pierre, Erica, and Christine hurried to see what the doctor had to say.

"Mrs. Miller was rushed in after being shot three times. As a result, she has lost a lot of blood, but she is alive."

Before the doctor could finish talking, Pierre smiled, then asked, "Can I see her?"

"Sir, she just got out of surgery and is being transported to her recovery room. Just give us a few minutes."

With that being said, the doctor walked away.

Erica gave Pierre a long hug. She cried on his chest after receiving the good news.

"I'm so happy that she is OK, and I'm about to get ready to get out of here," Christine said as she grabbed her jacket from the chair.

"Wait a minute. I really wanna thank you for being by Mama's side. I mean, you didn't know her, and you were there."

Pierre dug in his pocket and pulled out a few hundred-dollar bills. "It's not much, but it's all I have on me."

Christine cried as she shook her head. Even though she could use the money, she couldn't see herself taking the money for being a good human being. "You don't have to pay me for doing what was right."

"You are a good person, from what I can tell. Just take the money. It will make me feel better," Pierre said. Then Pierre took out his phone and called Mecko.

"What's good, bro?"

"Yo, I'm up here at the hospital with mom."

"Say what? Is everything straight?"

"Nah."

"Say less. I'm on my way."

Christine looked at Erica as if she was making sure it was OK. Erica smiled at her, followed by a hug. She then whispered in her ear, "It's OK, Christine. We really appreciate you."

Then Christine took the money and put it deep into her purse. "Thank you both so much."

"No, thank you," Erica said as Christine walked away.

Erica and Pierre took their seats and waited for the doctor to return. Pierre was ready to see his mom. Even though the doctors said she was OK, he needed to hear her say it herself or see for himself.

As he sat back, he thought about Christine's description of the car. He couldn't put his mind on who the fuck he was gonna kill next, but somebody was gonna get it.

"Damn, bro, I got here as quick as I could," Mekco said as he walked into the waiting room.

Pierre stood up to give Mekco a dap. Erica looked up but didn't speak. She was Team Nicole forever.

"Man, how Kim doing?" Mekco asked.

"Doctors just came out and said she was hit three times, but she good."

The doctor had said a few minutes, but that turned to another hour. By this time, the other members of the Brick Boyz and Nicole had shown up. Pierre and his friends talked among themselves while Nicole and Erica sat on the opposite side, talking. Erica noticed how Nicole tried not to look Mekco's way, and he was doing the same.

Just the sight of seeing Mekco made Nicole's feelings fuck with her. Deep down inside, she still loved him, but she knew he wasn't shit. She was still young and could find a better nigga one day.

The doctor had come out to get Pierre. His mother was very weak and didn't need a room full of people, so they would only let her son in.

Now, knowing that she was good, everyone else started leaving, everyone except Nicole and Mekco, that is. She stayed behind to be with Erica, and he stayed behind, waiting for the perfect opportunity to check Nicole about the bullshit that she had been on lately.

Mekco grew tired of waiting and decided to handle his business.

"So, you really gonna sit your stupid ass over there like shit all good, and you don't deserve for me to slap the shit out of you?" Mekco said very aggressively.

"Get out of my face, sneaky bastard."

Mekco looked at her, confused by her statement. He knew there wasn't a way in the world she knew about what he had been up to.

"Yeah, that's right. I know about your bitch and bastard child. Now, get out of my fucking face."

Mekco instantly got pissed, and before anyone knew it, he was lifting Nicole out of her seat by her neck. That had become his favorite move on her lately.

Erica jumped up, "Come on, Mekco, let her go. This is not the time or place for that."

Nicole started to cough as she tried to remove his hand.

"Erica, sit your ass down. This ain't got shit to do with you," Mekco yelled.

"What the fuck you say to her, nigga?" Pierre asked as he walked back over toward them.

Mekco released a crying Nicole. "My bad, bro, but this is between me and my girl."

"I'm *not* your girl, remember?" Nicole yelled.

Before Mekco could respond, Pierre pulled him out to the hallway. Erica held Nicole to make sure she was all right.

"Bro, you can't be up in here acting like a damn fool. The police already lurking around and shit," Pierre tried to explain to his friend.

"Man, that girl been on some bullshit. She knows I love her ass, and she acting like she really done with a nigga."

Pierre had so much on his mind at that moment, and dealing with Mekco and his relationship problems was not one of them. Yeah, his mom was OK, but he knew she had a long way to go until she was completely herself again.

Mekco felt bad and couldn't help but shake his head. "My bad, bro. You almost lost your mom, and I'm out here crying like a pussy over a bitch. Let's go find the nigga that did this and bury him."

With a devilish smile, Pierre responded, "Yeah, now, I like your way of thinking. But them niggas goin' have to wait until tomorrow. I can't leave her alone."

"Understood."

Pierre returned to the waiting room to find the girls in deep conversation. Once they noticed him coming back their way, they quickly stopped talking. He wondered what the big secret was but was gonna wait to ask Erica about that.

"E, I want you to go ahead and head home. I'm gonna stay here with my mom. I know she would like to see a familiar face when she finally wakes up."

"OK, baby, just call me if you need me. I'm gonna ride with Nicole, so here are your keys," Erica said, followed by a hug and kiss.

Nicole stood up from her chair. "P, I'm glad your mom is OK. I'm still keeping her in my prayers."

"Thanks, Nicole."

Erica kissed Pierre one last time before she and Nicole left the hospital. Pierre returned to his mama's room. He couldn't picture being anywhere else that night but with her.

"Girl, you really hooked the new place up," Erica said, looking around Nicole's new apartment.

Although she had her mail forwarded to her mom's house, she didn't want to stay there, knowing that Mekco would have stopped by to look for her.

"Thanks, boo. I'm happy you decided to stay over with me. I swear I be so bored in this bitch by myself."

"Well, since you needed me to drive you home from the clinic, it only made sense that we stay together. Nicole, are you sure you really wanna do this? I mean, you see the way he was acting at the hospital. Maybe he misses you and is sorry for how he's been acting."

"Man, fuck him, straight-up. I'm nobody's fool any more. I had more than enough time to get over his sorry ass, and I feel much better knowing that I'm finally free from the bullshit. Tomorrow, I'm gonna go handle my business, and next week, I'll return to work. I don't need him for shit."

"OK, boo, as long as you got your mind made up, I can't do nothing but support you and have your back."

"Erica, did you see how that nigga choked me up? He is fucking crazy. How he think he gonna get another bitch pregnant and still try to string me along like a dummy?"

Erica didn't say anything. She was caught up in a text that Pierre had just sent her.

"I'm about to cut your ass off too."

Both started to laugh. "My bad, Nicole, this boy is so freaking silly, I swear."

"Well, I'm about to take a shower, then go to bed. You can sleep in there with me or stay on the couch. It's your choice, boo."

Erica lay on the couch as she talked to Pierre. She was gonna get in bed with Nicole after she got off the phone, but she didn't want to disturb Nicole's rest, especially since she was having that procedure done in the morning.

Mekco pulled up to Toya's crib. He was pissed at Nicole and that bullshit-ass role she called herself playing at the hospital.

He was willing to bet any amount of money that if he would have thrown some bills at her that she would have been all on his dick. Toya's pussy was about to get a real workout. He needed to release a lot of built-up stress.

"Open the fucking door," he demanded.

Toya hung up the phone and then rushed to open the door for her baby daddy. Once she had the paperwork from the doctors stating that she was pregnant, she couldn't wait to show everyone. She would no longer be known as "Toya from the hood," but "Toya, Mekco's baby mama."

"Hey, daddy, you ready for me to heat up your plate so you can eat?"

Mekco walked straight to the bedroom, then started to undress. Toya was right on his heels.

"So, I take that as a no." She climbed into bed, ready to receive what she had been missing for the past few weeks.

Mekco lay back on the pillows and chilled as Toya made his dick disappear in her mouth. She was a nasty bitch, but he loved every moment of it. She was the type of bitch that would leave a nigga ass cheeks wet from her super soaker-ass mouth.

As good as she made him feel, his mind stayed on Nicole. How could she not want him after all that they had been through? He had promised P that he wasn't gonna follow Nicole home that night.

On his way to Toya's house, P had let Mekco know that he had some info on the nigga who shot his mama and needed him to ride with him later on. P could handle his own business, but it always made him feel better when his bro was by his side. The last thing P needed was for Mekco to get locked up for slapping up on a bitch.

"Man, come ride this dick," Mekco demanded, and just like that, Toya had become a professional jockey.

After letting her feel like she was in total control of the situation, Mekco flipped her ass over and beat her pussy senseless. She was no longer doing that cute little moan that he loved. She was now begging for mercy. Too bad he wasn't trying to hear all that shit.

After their little session ended, Toya cuddled up with Mekco like they were a couple.

She was happy to have him in her bed finally, but it didn't even matter to him. If it wasn't her tonight, then there wouldn't have been a problem finding another bitch who was waiting her turn to fuck a Brick Boy.

"I'm so happy that you came over. I mean, it's been a minute."

"I told you I been handling some business and didn't need no distraction."

Besides good head and sex, Toya was known for running her mouth and not knowing when to shut up. So, like always, she allowed her mouth to dig her into a hole.

"I ran into that girl that P had proposed to at the picnic. She really has got bigger since the picnic."

"Really? Did you tell her you was pregnant?"

"Yeah, we were at the fucking doctor's office. I think she is smarter than a fifth-grader."

"Whatever, bitch. You probably couldn't wait to run your big-ass mouth."

Toya sat up in the bed. "Mekco, you really need to watch how you talk to me. I mean, I *am* carrying your baby. I told you from day one that me and this baby will not be a secret, and you got me fucked up if that's what you were thinking."

"Bitch, I told you from day one, I have a fucking girl, and you not about to fuck that shit up. I also told your ass that you should get an abortion. Why would you want a baby by a nigga who don't want you or a fucking baby by you?"

Toya stormed out of the room, crying. She had known how he really felt, but to hear the shit over again really hurt her feelings. She sat on the toilet, crying her eyes out.

Mekco now knew why Nicole was on that independent shit. Erica had run her mouth to her, and now she didn't even want him around her.

Mekco had to find a way to get his girl back, and the first step was to stop dealing with Toya. He wasn't sure how that was gonna be possible since she was having his baby, but he was gonna figure it out.

Mekco was putting on his clothes when Toya appeared back in the room. "So, you just gonna leave me like that?"

"Look, Toya, it's been fun, but I told you from jump, the moment you start catching feelings and start fucking up my life, I was gonna be done with your ass."

"So, I'm good enough to fuck and tag along with you when you wanted to make that bitch jealous, but I'm not good enough to carry your child and be with you?" she asked.

"Damn, now, you get it. Plus, my girl is about to have my baby too. I'm not a ho-ass nigga. I'll help take care of this baby, but I'm not about to be with you like that. Do we got an understanding?"

Toya's face dropped at the news. She really couldn't be mad at what he was saying 'cause he kept it real with her since day one. She knew she would never replace Nicole, and her getting pregnant by him didn't change shit.

She wiped her eyes and tried to pull herself together. The last thing she wanted was to be weak for a fuck nigga because it was oblivious that he didn't give a fuck about nobody but himself.

"Just get the fuck out, you heartless piece of shit," Toya yelled.

Mekco dug in his pocket and then tossed some money at her. "This all your trick ass wanted anyway. Call me when the baby is born so I can help out. Until then, stay the fuck away from me and Nicole."

Mekco walked out the door, making sure he slammed it.

Toya didn't give a fuck. Truth be told, she was only 60 percent sure he was the father, and she needed every last dollar he let hit her floor.

Before pulling off, Mekco pulled out his phone and then texted Nicole's phone.

Mekco: Baby, I swear I'm sorry for everything. Please, baby, I need you in my life. I'm not whole without you. I love you and just want us to be a family.

Nicole read the text and contemplated on whether she should text him back. He was saying all the right things, but it was too late to act like he cared. She had her mind made up to get an abortion in the morning, and that was final.

Nicole's phone went off, letting her know she had a new message.

Mekco: Nicole, I know you see my text. Can you please text me back? Baby, I'll do whatever to make things up to you. What do you want? A new car, a new house? Damn, what is it? Fuck it, let's go to Vegas tonight and get married. Is that what you want, a fucking ring?

Nicole cried. Why did he have to be the way that he was?

He knew she would have loved all that, but he had to get it through his head that she wasn't about to play any games with him.

Nicole reread each message repeatedly and ended up crying herself to sleep.

She tried to be strong, but his texts had reopened her feelings for him that she thought she had buried.

Brian sat in the motel room, watching the news. He got the shock of his life seeing that an older woman was shot down in traffic yesterday and not Erica. He hit himself as he realized that he had fucked up again.

"Damn, bro, don't be mad at me. I swear I thought his bitch was driving that car. I was only trying to make you proud."

Brian sat back, trying to put together a plan B. It was harder than he thought because he didn't have anyone to steer him in the right direction, and he had been off his meds for too long to get his brain to work the way he needed it.

Brian began to cry loudly, "Oh, brother, I need you."

***

Erica knocked on Nicole's bedroom door. "Hey, boo, are you ready to go?"

"Hell yeah. Well, I guess so."

Erica paused for a second. "Are you sure you want to do this, Nicole? You are not sounding too sure about this plan. It's not too late to change your mind. Just remember, no matter what, I got your back 100 percent."

It took Nicole a minute before she could say anything. It was a hard decision for her to make. She had loved Mekco and couldn't wait to carry his baby, but the fact that they could break up for a hot minute and he foolishly got someone pregnant hurt her to the core.

He had always been so careful with using protection with her but rushing to dick down the next chick was the killing part. She had been his fool for too long, and now, it was her turn to turn her back on him and move the fuck on.

"I'm ready, Erica. Just promise not to leave my side."

"I promise I'll always have your back, boo."

The best friends gave each other a tight hug before leaving the house. They might not have agreed on everything that each other did, but they had a tight bond.

They arrived at the clinic around 8:45 a.m.; her appointment was at 9:00 a.m.

Erica had got caught up in a phone conversation with Pierre about his mom. The doctors had said that her vitals weren't as strong as they would like, but she was a fighter. Pierre wanted Erica to say a prayer for her.

Erica had no problem praying over the phone, and once she finished and said amen, she heard Pierre repeat after her.

Someone had called for Nicole to go to the back. She hurried and jumped up. Erica hugged her before she disappeared to the back.

"Where the fuck you at, E? It don't sound like you at school?"

"Huh?" she said, acting deaf.

"I told you if you can 'huh,' you can hear. Now, where are you?" he asked again.

She didn't want to tell him because he would tell Mekco, and that would cause a big problem. So she told him the truth but not the *whole* truth.

"Baby, we are at the doctor's office. She had an appointment today."

"Oh, OK. Since you are with your homegirl, why don't you tell her that my bro is sorry, and he wanna be in her and the baby's life."

Erica smacked her lips, "Yeah, OK, baby. Anyway, kiss your mom for me and tell her that I love her."

"Yeah, OK, baby," he said, mocking her.

"All shit, baby, let me call you back and get these doctors in this room. Something not right," Pierre yelled into the phone.

Erica could hear Kim's machine going off right before Pierre hung up. She wasn't sure what to think. All she knew was her tears began to roll down her face.

Nicole lay on the exam table in her hospital gown as she waited for the doctor. Her phone had gone off again. She knew it couldn't be anybody else but Mekco's crazy ass. She sat up and grabbed her phone to read his message.

Mekco: Baby, let me take you to breakfast. I got something special for you.

Nicole shook her head. Mekco was back on his bullshit again. Just then, two more messages came in.

The first message was a picture of an engagement ring.

The second message was him begging for her love again.

Mekco: I love you, baby. Marry me. I promise I'm a changed man.

Nicole lay in the bed crying. She was so sure she was doing the right thing, but now, she wasn't. Reading his texts made her think that maybe Mekco might have changed his ways and really wanted her.

She wiped her face as the doctor and assistant entered the room.

"Are you OK, ma'am, or do you need a minute?" the doctor asked.

Nicole didn't say anything. She just looked crazy, like a deer caught in the headlights.

Being concerned about Kim's health, Erica tried to call Pierre's phone. After trying the second time, she still didn't receive an answer. She figured Nicole was gonna be in the back for a while, so she went to the front desk.

"Excuse me, I came in with a friend, but I need to leave right quick. Can I leave a message with you to give to her?"

"Sure, just write it down on this sticky pad, and I'll give it to her."

Erica wrote a note stating that something had gone wrong at the hospital and that she would be right back. After giving the receptionist the pad, she turned to leave.

Good thing she drove and still had Nicole's keys.

Erica rushed to the hospital to check on Pierre and Kim. She prayed the whole way there. She made it to the floor Kim was on. She saw Pierre standing by the waiting room door. She ran to him and hugged him. That's all it took for him to break down.

Erica held him as he cried. "She gone, baby, my mama gone, E."

Nicole walked out of the room with her head down. She was ashamed of what she had done, but at the end of the day, she knew what she wanted. As she walked into the waiting room, the receptionist stopped her.

"Hey, your friend left you this note," she said, handing her the paper.

Nicole read the note, then tossed it in the trash. "So much for always being there for me." She pulled out her phone and sent out a text message. After only waiting ten minutes, her ride pulled up.

"Hey, baby, I missed your ass like crazy," Mekco said before kissing Nicole's lips.

Mekco drove off with the biggest smile on his face. He had his girl back, and they were on their way to Vegas just like she had agreed to. Love was in the air, and wedding bells were about to be ringing.

Maybe they were each other's true soul mates, after all.

Chapter 6

"Oh my God. I'm so sorry, baby," Erica whispered into Pierre's ear as she held him in her arms.

He was at a loss for words and couldn't do much but hold her and let his tears fall.

It had been years since he cried, and it hurt him down to his soul. He had just got her back into his life, and just like that, some heartless-ass bastard had taken her away from him.

Only this time, it was for good.

Erica also cried her eyes out. She had just gotten to really know Kim and instantly fell in love with her bright personality. She was an easy woman to get along with.

Erica couldn't believe that she was gone. It was crazy how all she talked about was holding her grandbabies; now, she would never be able to do that.

"Let's get the fuck from out of here, baby," Pierre mumbled.

"Baby, I swear I don't want to leave your side right now, but I dropped Nicole off and need to pick her up. I'm sorry."

Erica felt terrible, but she knew once she dropped Nicole back off at home, she would be able to be by Pierre's side and help him deal with his mom's death.

Pierre gave Erica a small peck on her lips. "It's OK, baby. Just meet me at the crib."

Erica watched as Pierre walked away from her. She secretly felt like shit.

He had just lost his mother, and she was leaving his side. She lost her mom at a young age and knew how hard it was for the woman who brought you into the world to no longer be there for you. She also knew he was pissed by the way he walked away from her. She told herself that he was going through something and not to stress him out any more than he already was.

As Erica drove back to the clinic, she dialed Nicole's number.

She wanted to let her know that she was returning, but she didn't get an answer.

Erica ended up calling her a good three more times, but she never received an answer.

"Man, Nicole, please pick up the phone. I'm on my way to get you now. I'm sorry for leaving, but Pierre's mom just died," she cried out over Nicole's voicemail.

When Erica arrived at the clinic, she walked in, expecting to see Nicole waiting. Instead, when she walked into the clinic, she found it half-empty, and Nicole was nowhere to be found. Erica approached the front desk to talk to the lady she had spoken to earlier.

"Hi, I came in not too long ago with my friend. Her name is Nicole. Is she still in the back or something?"

"Umm, she came out a little after you left. I'm sorry, but she's gone now."

"Really? Did you see who she left with?"

"All I could see was a guy with a head full of dreads. I hope that can help you out a little."

"Yes, it did. Thank you," Erica said right before she stormed out of the clinic. She wasn't sure what bullcrap Nicole was on, but the fact that she was back with Mekco made her question what was really going on.

Erica was pissed. Not only did she leave Pierre's side when he needed her the most, but Nicole was acting stupid and not answering her phone.

Before driving off, she went on Facebook to see if she had updated her status. Anyone who knew Nicole knew how she stayed on social media.

She threw her phone down on the passenger seat of Nicole's car after realizing Nicole had deleted her page.

Erica drove to Nicole's apartment, only to realize she was still driving Nicole's car and had her house keys. She didn't have a clue where her girl was, but at that moment, she knew she needed to get back to Pierre. He needed someone to have his back.

Walking into their place, Erica was shocked to find Pierre sitting on the couch with a fifth of Hennessey, a Red Bull, and, of course, he had his weed and blunts all over the coffee table.

Erica remembered a conversation that they had awhile back. He had promised to slow down on all that, and if he did decide to have a little fun, he wouldn't do it in the house.

Erica knew he was hurting, so instead of reminding him about what he said, she put her feelings aside and prepared herself to do whatever it took to put his mind at ease, even if it was just for the moment.

Erica took a seat next to Pierre and held his hand. "Baby, I'm about to cook. You need to eat something."

Pierre continued to smoke and sip on his drink like she wasn't even there.

"Did you hear me, baby? Are you hungry?"

Picrre coldly responded, "Nah, I'm good. Go play with your little friend."

His attitude and response hit her hard. Not once had he ever talked to her in such a nasty way.

She tried not to trip only because she knew he was hurt while she went out on a dummy mission looking for Nicole.

"Baby, I'm so sorry for not being able to come straight home. There's just some stuff going on, and I got caught up in the middle of it," she said, trying to get back on his good side.

Pierre still didn't say anything to her. He was pissed off, and it wasn't just the fact that she left him to be with Nicole. He was pissed about everything.

He loved having his mom back, and now she was gone. He was hurt and felt that if nobody else understood him, Erica should have.

Erica leaned over and kissed his cheek, trying to show some love, and he still sat there like she wasn't shit to him.

He was hurting her feelings, and she wasn't used to him acting like that toward her.

Erica felt like she was really with the infamous P and not Pierre, who she had fallen in love with.

"I'm sorry, baby," she said again with tears in her eyes.

"Yeah, I see that now," he replied, blowing the smoke out from his blunt. He didn't even care if it hit her in the face.

At that very moment, Erica felt like the enemy, and how he looked at her scared her. For the first time, he looked at her without that loving stare. He showed signs of hating her. It was like he was disgusted even being near her.

A teary-eyed Erica got up from the couch and then went into the bedroom to cry. She cried until she had fallen asleep.

Pierre sat in the living room faded. For a minute, the weed and liquor numbed his heart from the hurt and pain. But after a while, everything hit him all over again.

He knew he had pissed off Erica, but truthfully, at the moment, he didn't give a fuck. How the fuck, in his time of need, did she decide that it was a good idea to go hang with her girl? She had even skipped school to be up under that bitch.

He tried to play it cool when it came to Nicole only because of his bro, but he saw her for what she really was. That bitch had kept Erica around, watching her every move, smiling in her face, while all along being insanely jealous of her. That bitch was a regular paper chaser, just like any other bitch that Mekco fucked with. That nigga had a type, and it had always been hoes that chased after niggas with money. He liked hoes that acted needy, so he could always feel like he was doing something.

Thinking about his bro, Pierre pulled out his phone to dial Mekco's number. He had a bad choice in females, but he also knew that he was one person who Mekco could count on to be in his corner.

It surprised him that he wasn't even answering his phone, and after the third time calling him, Mekco's phone had gone straight to voicemail.

"Aye, bro, I'm not sure where you are right now but hit me up when you can. I'm just fucked up right now and got some shit I need to get off my chest."

One thing about him was that he hated leaving voice messages, but he felt it was necessary in this case.

Pierre hung up, hoping his friend would call him right back.

Sitting back on the couch, he lit his blunt back up and necked more of his drink. He allowed his choice of drugs to do their job and clear his mind a little more.

After it was all gone, Pierre made his way to his bedroom. He stopped in the doorway and stared at Erica. She was still asleep, looking so beautiful as always. Her pretty brown skin glowed even more now that she carried those babies. He loved the fuck out of Erica, but now he questioned if she had his back a hundred percent.

Today, he never needed her more, and she left him hanging for a bighead bitch who was only out for self.

He didn't want to hurt her any more than he had already done, so he decided just to pack up some of his clothes and get the fuck on. He needed his space, and she just needed to focus on herself and school.

Erica had finally woken up after hearing Pierre move around. She sat up in bed and watched the love of her life pack up some of his belongings. She knew what it looked like, and her heart dropped.

She knew it was wrong that she had left him, but he was taking it a little too far, trying to leave her.

"Pierre, where are you going?" she asked.

"Look, I'm really not in the mood to be bothered with you right now. I know you probably don't have nowhere to go, so I'm just gonna let you stay here, and I'll get the fuck on."

"What?" she asked.

She heard exactly what he had said, but she had to ask what to make sure that was what he actually wanted to say.

Before Pierre could respond, she continued to talk.

"What did I do that was so wrong that you would want to leave? I said I was sorry earlier. What more do you want from me?"

"We good, E. I just don't want to bother you with my personal issues. That's it."

"Baby, please don't do me like that. It's just that I got caught up in some of Nicole's mess, and I apologized a million times. I'm here now, baby. Please, forgive me," Erica cried out.

Instead of responding, Pierre turned his attention back toward packing his clothes. He wasn't trying to hear what she was saying at all.

Erica grabbed Pierre's arm to try to stop him from leaving.

"Man, get your fucking hands off me!" Pierre yelled as he pushed her against the wall.

Erica was scared as she stared at the man standing before her. She could barely recognize the man who was looking back at her. It wasn't Pierre, the man she fell in love with. It was P, the wild, crazy, and dangerous man niggas on the streets feared.

Pierre could feel his blood boiling as he stood there watching Erica. He was at the point that he didn't even want to talk to her anymore. He grabbed his bag and walked out of the room. Erica sat on the bed and cried.

She wasn't sure where he was going or when he was coming back, but with the way he had just handled her, she didn't care.

Pierre jumped into his ride and drove off. He just needed some space, and being around Erica was only gonna make his ill feelings for her grow.

After crying her eyes out, Erica got herself together and pulled out her phone. She needed her best friend to answer her phone. Whatever she and Pierre were going through had her in her feelings, and she needed to vent to someone. She knew the role that she had played and could now understand why he was hurt, but she wasn't ready to deal with him not wanting her anymore.

She called Nicole's phone three times before she finally left her a voicemail. "Nicole, where are you? I've been calling you all day. Please, call me back."

Erica then walked into the kitchen to warm up a slice of pizza from the other day. As she ate, she thought about Pierre and how he had flipped out on her. This was the second time that he had done that. The first time was when she told him about her being pregnant and how there was a chance he wasn't the father.

Seeing him turn into P was scary. He became cold-hearted, and if she didn't know any better, she would say that his eyes were pure black.

She began to cry again. He had done so much to prove his love to her. She wasn't about to let him just walk out of her life like that. She was determined to get her baby back. Even though she was scared, she weighed her options and decided to call him anyway. The worst that could happen is he could either not answer or hang up.

Pierre saw Erica's name flashing across his screen and contemplated if he wanted to answer her call. After the fourth ring, he picked up. He was pissed off at her, but his heart hadn't turned completely cold. She was still in there somewhere.

"What's up?"

Erica could tell that he still had an attitude but continued to talk. She tried so hard not to cry, but between the babies messing with her hormones and the way he answered the phone, she couldn't control her tears.

"Pierre, can you please come home? I'm not used to you being mad at me; I just want us to make up. Can we do that?"

"Look, Erica, I just need some time to myself, and truthfully, I don't know when I'm coming back home. There's money and shit there, so you should be straight if you need anything," he explained to her.

"Pierre, what is it that you don't get? I don't care about no freaking money. All I want is you," Erica yelled into the phone while still crying.

Pierre knew he had to let her go for his own personal reasons. All that drinking and smoking had brought up some shit in his mind, and he knew that if he stayed, he was only gonna bring her pain . . . or even worse. She had his heart, and he couldn't live with himself if anything happened to her or the babies. The only thing he could do was push her far away from him and the lifestyle that he lived.

"Look, I said all that I had to say. Why can't you just deal with the fact that I don't wanna be bothered with you?"

"So, now you don't want to be bothered with me? So, what about the babies? You don't wanna be bothered with them either?" she asked, just trying to see where his mind was.

Pierre shook his head. He hated it when she put the babies in everything. But he was somewhat glad she had brought them up. He now knew what to use to hurt her. The next few words were gonna hurt her, but at the same time, they were gonna kill him.

"What about them, E? If I'm not mistaken, you said they might not be mines anyway, right?"

"What? I can't believe you said that to me, but I'm glad I know how you *really* feel about this whole situation. It's fucked up because *you're* the one who begged me to keep them, and now you bitching up. It's all good. You no longer have to worry about us, you fucking asshole!" With that being said, Erica hung up the phone and went to the closet.

She cried as she packed her clothes. She wasn't sure where she was going, but she knew she wasn't about to deal with Pierre while he acted that way. She was gonna make sure that whenever he did come back, she wasn't gonna be anywhere in sight.

His words replayed over and over in her mind as she packed, and each time, she cried harder. She couldn't see herself ever forgiving him after this.

After getting her things in the trunk of Nicole's car, she drove to her father's house. She didn't want to return home, but she didn't have anyone else to run to.

She prayed that her father didn't have too much fun laughing and saying he told her so. After all, he was the one who warned her that she wasn't shit to Pierre but a fool.

Pastor Collins opened the door for his daughter with a smile. She thought he was about to be on that petty stuff, but he was actually happy to see her.

"Hello, my beautiful daughter," he said, allowing her to walk into the house.

"Hey, Dad. How are you?"

"I'm fine, but what's wrong with you? It's all on your face that something is bothering you."

Pastor Collins wasn't a fool and knew his baby girl too well. He wanted things to be how they were before when she actually liked him, would come to him for advice, and talked about her problems. So, instead of running his mouth, he gave her a chance to come clean.

"I'm OK, Daddy. These babies just got me so tired," Erica said, hoping that he would leave the situation alone.

Just thinking about what really was bothering her made her wanna cry, so she knew she couldn't talk about it, especially to him. With the hate he carried for Pierre, this would only cause more problems.

He could sense that whatever it was, she wasn't ready to talk about it, so he just left it alone. "Why don't you go ahead and lie down in your room? I just put dinner on, so 'bout time you wake up, it should be ready."

"Thanks, Daddy."

Erica got up from the couch and went to her old bedroom. Not even ten minutes later, she was knocked out.

Pierre lay across his mother's couch, deep in his thoughts. He had moved her into this nice apartment just for someone to take her away. It was crazy how the world worked at times.

After all the dirt that he had done over the years, and all the families he done hurt by killing their loved ones, he never imagined hurting the way that he was.

Before Erica had made it home earlier that day, he thought about everything that had happened, and that's when he realized that his mom wasn't supposed to die that day. Muthafuckas around the way knew that was Erica's car and that the hit was supposed to be for Erica. That shit hurt him to the core that someone would want to hurt her just to hurt him. She was innocent all the way around.

The way he looked at things, if he pushed her away from him and made sure she hated him, he wouldn't have to worry about nobody else trying to hurt her.

At the beginning of their relationship, he talked to her about shit like this, and as much as he tried to stay away from her, he couldn't. It was now too late. He had already fallen for her and made a family.

He sat back, thinking about those cold words he had spoken to her, and it hurt him knowing that she was probably somewhere crying her eyes out. He made a promise to make it up to her whenever he killed the muthafucka who was responsible for killing his mom. He just prayed that she would forgive him and take him back after he explained everything to her.

Pierre held his phone in his hand, staring at a picture of Erica. She stole his heart from day one and still had it, but he was gonna have to learn to live without her until shit cooled down.

Chapter 7

"Oh my God, baby, I can't believe we are actually about to do this. I swear I've prayed for this day to come for so long," Nicole said as she stared out the airplane window.

Mekco had promised Nicole that if she forgave him and took him back, he would take her to Vegas and marry her. It had been torture living without her. He was at the point that whatever she wanted, he was gonna make sure that she got it. He had already promised her a new car and a nice big house for them to raise their child in. He was willing to do whatever it took to make her happy again.

"I told you, baby, I got you from now on. I will never leave your side again." He then kissed Nicole to seal the deal.

Nicole was in love but still didn't want to be made a fool of. She let him promise her everything under the sun, but at the same time, she was still worried about the other bitch with his baby. Mekco had fucked up so much that he made her have trust issues.

"You talking a good game, but what about that big-headed bitch Toya? When we get back home, you still gonna fuck around with that bitch?"

"Nah, baby, I already told her that I wasn't gonna fuck with her anymore and not to contact me until the baby is born. After that, we gonna get a test done. Baby, it's all about us right now," Mekco explained.

"I still can't believe you got that bitch pregnant."

"Nicole, let's not get into that shit right now 'cause when it all boils down to it, I'm marrying your stupid ass. Plus, did you forget where the fuck I just picked you up from? You were about to really say fuck me and all that we had been through and kill my damn baby. You gonna pay for that shit."

Nicole didn't respond. She knew she was wrong for that. She loved Mekco and wanted the rest of their trip to be perfect, so instead of going back and forth with him, she kissed his cheek, then lay her head on his chest.

During their flight, Nicole thought about how she made a promise to herself not to fuck with Erica anymore. She loved her and knew it was gonna be hard, but she realized Erica wasn't a good friend. Erica had left her at that clinic to go be up under Pierre's ass after she promised to be by her side.

The sad part was that she had no idea what was happening back in Detroit. She hadn't answered any of Erica's calls and deleted her voice messages without even listening to them. She wasn't about to let her ruin her day with her bullshit.

Mekco rented a car, and then they drove straight to the hotel. He was tired and just wanted to chill for the rest of the night.

"Mekco, when are we gonna get married? I'm ready," Nicole whined.

"Damn, baby, you ain't tired from the flight? We can take care of that shit first thing in the morning. For now, let's take a shower, order room service, and then fuck until we pass out."

With a huge smile on her face, Nicole started to strip before she even could make it to the bathroom. "I like that plan, baby."

Nicole got the water at the right temperature before jumping in. Mekco was right behind her with a hard dick in his hand. The smile on his face, plus the hard dick greeting her, told Nicole that she had been missed.

The couple took their time washing each other's bodies. Nicole went first and took her time making sure her soon-to-be husband was clean. When it came down to Mekco cleaning her body, he did a rush job. He was never into that entire romantic shit. He just wanted to fuck.

Erica had talked to her bestie on many occasions about how romantic Pierre could be and how he took his time getting to know every inch of her body. Nicole was trying to bring that side out of Mekco, but he wasn't having it.

Before all the soap was rinsed off Nicole's body, Mekco had already picked her up and had her back on the shower wall. Nicole wrapped her soapy legs around Mekco's body as he slowly entered her.

"Damn, baby," Nicole moaned out as Mekco worked his way in and out of her. Mekco was working with that get right and had Nicole sprung and wilding out in that bathroom.

Nicole continued to moan out while Mekco made sure to hit deep into her pussy. The deeper he went, the louder she got.

"OK, Mekco, put me down, baby," she whispered in his ear.

He hesitated at first, but after a couple more strokes, he slowly released her. She stood there catching her breath before she dropped to her knees. She knew he was always a big fan of hitting the back of her throat.

Nicole held her mouth wide open as she allowed him to push every last inch into her, making sure to hit her tonsils. Mekco grabbed the back of her head and fucked her mouth faster. Really, she had started thinking about him with Toya and how she probably had done the same thing. It had turned her off.

"Whatever. Look, I didn't bring your ass all the way out here just so you could be on that bullshit, Nicole."

"I said I'm not feeling that shit right now, Mekco."

Mekco shook his head. He couldn't believe how stupid she was acting. "All right, bend your ass over then."

Nicole bent over in the shower and waited for Mekco to enter her from behind.

Mekco didn't like how she acted and planned on making her pay. He slowly entered her pussy from behind, then, without giving her a chance to get used to his size, he began to fuck her hard. Her body was jerking so hard that she almost fell forward on her face.

Even that didn't make him ease up. Instead, he continued to fuck her while slipping his thump up her ass.

"Damn, Mekco, calm the fuck down, nigga," she yelled.

"Man, this my pussy. I can fuck it however I want it. Remember that shit." He continued to pound into her with full force.

With ever stroke, she moaned out loudly.

Nicole was relieved when he finally pulled his dick and thumb out of her. But that was short-lived once she felt him enter her ass with his brick-hard dick.

She yelled out in pain, but that didn't stop him at all.

"Nicole, shut the fuck up. Don't act like you ain't never did this shit with me before. Now, take this dick," he ordered.

Nicole knew the only way to please him was to do as he said. Since he had begged her to get back with him and promised her a new house and car, she allowed him to do whatever he wanted to her body.

That was gonna be her husband the following day, so she knew she was gonna have to get back to pleasing him, even if it hurt her in the process.

"Shit, I'm about to come, baby. Where you want it?" he asked, slowly stroking her ass.

Nicole jumped right into the program of being the best wife she could be. She even forced herself to block out of her mind the image of him and Toya fucking. "Wherever you want it, baby."

Mekco laughed on the inside. He had her right where he wanted her. She was gonna pay for thinking she could just leave him.

"Get your ass back on your knees. I don't even know why you got the fuck up in the first place."

Nicole did as she was told. As soon as she opened her mouth, he shot his semen down her throat. The look on her face had let him know that she didn't like the taste and was about to spit it out.

"Swallow that shit and stop playing with me, girl," he ordered.

Without taking a second to protest, she swallowed. After making sure it was all gone, Mekco stepped out of the shower and entered the bedroom. Nicole got out of the shower and quickly brushed her teeth, making sure to rinse her mouth out with mouthwash. She hated when he made her swallow his cum. She thought she would have gotten used to the awful taste by now.

Mekco lay across the bed with the hotel phone in his hand. "What do you wanna eat?" he asked.

Nicole pulled out a T-shirt from her luggage and put it on. "Baby, we are in a city that is full of fun. Why are you trying to keep me locked in here? I wanna go out."

"Man, I told you when we got here, we were chilling today, and then tomorrow, we can do whatever you wanna do."

"OK, baby. I want to get married first. Then we can go shopping as husband and wife. After that, I wanna go home so we can start looking for a house big enough for our family."

Mekco looked up, feeling confused. He had totally forgotten that he had promised her a new house. All that begging and making promises that he had done was biting him in the ass now. He didn't want to move out of his crib, so it looked like he was just gonna have two places to rest his head at. There was no way he was letting that crib go. That place was his baby.

"OK, baby, it's your world. Whatever you want, I got you, girl."

That night, the couple made love again before finally dozing off. Mekco went to sleep first, but Nicole was too anxious to become Mrs. Richmond in the morning.

She almost fucked around and called Erica to share the good news, but then she thought about how her so-called best friend had turned her back on her. For the life of her, she couldn't understand how she just got up and left her because she wanted to be up under Pierre's ass.

Nicole had put in her mind that she was gonna just walk away from that friendship. She had always had Erica's back in her eyes, and in return, she got fucked over. For now, it was only gonna be her and her husband.

The following day, Nicole jumped out of bed with a huge smile on her face. Today was the day that she would become Mekco's wife, and nothing in the world was gonna fuck up her day.

Looking through her belongings, she pulled out a short lavender dress she planned on getting married in.

They had already decided they didn't have to go all out since they flew to Vegas to rush and get married.

After showering, Nicole entered the room to find Mekco picking out his clothes.

"Are you ready for this?" he asked with a smile.

"You know I've been ready for this day. You were the one who was on that bullshit."

"Yeah, but I'm ready now. Let me jump in this shower so we can do this."

Mekco placed a kiss on Nicole's lips before walking out of the room and entering the bathroom.

Later, Mekco drove to the Little Neon Chapel in downtown Las Vegas. He had already arranged for everything for them. Elvis was gonna marry them off that morning.

"Bae, how do you feel knowing that you are about to be my wife and your best friend not here to see it and share this special moment with you?"

Without a second thought about what was going on, Nicole hunched her shoulders. "Man, fuck Erica. I'm not fucking with that girl anymore. She wasn't loyal to me. All she cared about was herself and Pierre's ass."

"Damn, ma, what's the beef about now? Y'all were good."

"She is just not my friend anymore, and I don't feel like I should have to compete for her attention because she has a li'l boyfriend now. Besides, we are about to get married and start our family. I don't need her."

Mekco knew how Nicole could be at times, and he also knew she could be jealous-hearted sometimes, so he didn't respond to her answer to keep the peace between them. There was no telling what really was going on between them.

"I see she was calling me, but I turned my phone off. I don't need her fucking with our wedding."

"OK, baby," was all he could say to continue to keep the peace between them.

Mekco wasn't trying to get her started. He was ready to marry her crazy ass, then head home so he could find her a house.

Mekco and Nicole sat in the chapel and witnessed three other couples say their I dos before it was finally their turn.

Nicole was so excited and couldn't help smiling as each bride cried from marrying the love of their lives.

Finally, they stood before the reverend dressed as Elvis, ready to take their relationship to the next level.

"Mekco Richmond, do you take this woman whose hand you now hold to be your wife? And do you solemnly promise before God to love, cherish, honor, and protect her until death do you part?"

Without a second thought in his head, Mekco quickly said, "I do."

Elvis turned his attention toward Nicole. "Do you, Nicole Jackson, take this man who now holds your hand to be your true and wedded husband? And do you solemnly promise before God to cherish, honor, and protect him until death do you part?"

Without any hesitation, Nicole repeatedly yelled out, "I do, I do, and I do."

Mekco chuckled at how excited she was to become Mrs. Richmond.

"I now pronounce you man and wife. You may kiss your beautiful bride," the Elvis impersonator said, acting like he was playing on a guitar.

Everyone who witnessed their wedding cheered them on as they locked lips.

As they drove away from the chapel, Nicole couldn't help herself having a huge smile on her face. She was the happiest woman in the world at that moment.

Becoming his wife and not just being a bitch he fucked with was gonna give her the attention and street credit that she wanted. She couldn't wait to go back home to show off her ring. Nicole knew Toya and Erica were gonna be jealous, and she really didn't give a fuck.

"Baby, where we off to now?" Nicole asked as she took a minute to stop looking at her reflection in the mirror. She swore being a married woman now changed her appearance.

With a li'l smirk, Mekco responded, "Nicole, I got a couple of racks to blow through. We are about to spend the rest of this day shopping and gambling. The casino has a blackjack table with my name on it. Let's go fuck up some shit."

"OK, I'm down, but you know I'm not fucking with those tables. I'm gonna have my ass on those slot machines."

"Yeah, OK, scary ass."

"That's *Mrs.* Scary Ass Richmond, nigga."

They both laughed as he continued to drive.

The newlyweds spent hours driving around spending money. Nicole made sure to get everything that she knew bitches in Detroit weren't gonna have. She was gonna go back to the hood shitting on bitches, all while rocking that huge rock Mekco had placed on her finger.

"All these damn bags . . . We finna go back to the room and drop them off. After that, we can go blow this bread at the casino," Mekco announced as they made their way to the hotel.

After three hours of gambling and drinking, Mekco found Nicole at the slots just like she said she would be. Mekco was drunk and ready to go back to the room. Hennessey always made his dick wanna play in some pussy.

"Damn, baby, before we go back, can we at least get something to eat? I am with child and hungry, remember?"

Mekco took her by the hand and walked her over to the nearby restaurant. "I do need something to soak up this liquor."

They took a seat at a table located in the back.

Soon after, a young lady walked over to their table, passing out menus. "Hello, my name is Mercedes. Can I start you guys off with a drink?"

"Can I have a sweet iced tea with extra ice?" Nicole asked.

"Yes, ma'am," she replied before looking toward Mekco's side of the table. "And what can I get for you, sir?"

Nicole sat back in her seat as she watched Mekco stare at the waitress. She tried not to start anything but felt like he was testing her. He could be a disrespectful-ass muthafucka at times.

"Damn, Mekco, answer her so she can get the fuck away from our table."

Mercedes rolled her eyes but didn't say a word. She knew her job was already on the line from always being late. And she wasn't about to get fired over this big-mouthed bitch at this table.

"Damn, Nicole, calm the fuck down. I was just thinking about what I wanna drink. I swear you tripping for no reason. Didn't I just marry your crazy ass?"

Mercedes tried to get on Nicole's good side just to make sure she didn't cause any problems for her.

"Congratulations on the wedding. You guys are so beautiful together."

Now, Nicole was all smiles. "Thank you so much. And you can just get his drunk ass some water, please."

"OK, well, I'll be back with your drinks, and that should give you guys enough time to decide what you want to eat."

Mercedes walked away with a little extra swish in her hips only because she knew Mekco was still watching. She didn't want any real problems, but looking at the size of Nicole's ring, she knew he was paid, and a decent tip would have been wonderful. Her pockets were empty and could use a little come-up.

"So you wanna fuck her, Mekco?"

Mekco laughed. "Man, you be trippin', I swear. You my wife now, and you need to stop acting so jealous of these other bitches."

"You right, baby, and I'm gonna stop being like that. But you were just staring at her like I wasn't sitting right here in your face. How was I supposed to handle that situation?"

Mekco had a little devilish smirk on his face. He knew exactly what he wanted since he sat down.

"Bae, you're supposed to act like a caring wife. If you think I'm checking out another bitch, instead of checking me or acting all ratchet, why don't you ask the bitch if she would be down to join us for some fun or something?"

Nicole's face turned cold. "Are you fucking *serious?* You such an asshole, Mekco. What the fuck did you marry me for if you still wanted to be out here fucking other bitches? Why the fuck are you playing these games with me?"

"Look, when we first got together, you knew how I was about pussy. But you also knew that you were the only bitch that I'll ever love for real, so what's the big deal? Now, be my wife and hook that shit up when she gets back with our drinks."

Nicole sat there with tears in her eyes. She was trying so hard not to cry behind his bullshit, but at the same time, he was only being him. How stupid could she be thinking a ring would stop him? In reality, its only purpose was to keep her tied down to him. She knew he had a problem with commitment, and them saying their I dos wasn't gonna change him.

"Nicole, you know I love the fuck outta your ass and always will. Go ahead and fix your face. Here she comes."

It was hard, but Nicole fixed her face like he said, putting a fake smile on it.

"Attagirl. You're so beautiful when you smile. Now, be friendly to this bitch so we can leave Vegas with a wild story that only you and me would know about. You know the old saying, 'What happens in Vegas stays in Vegas.'"

Nicole was back smiling at the fact that she had the chance to make her husband happy.

She could tell by the way he talked about them fucking Mercedes that he was gonna be a happy camper, so she got ready to do her wifey duties.

When it came to Mekco, she was blinded by his love and was willing to do whatever he wanted her to do. Now that she carried the title of being his wife, she was gonna have to step up her game, starting with making sure he left Vegas with a smile on his face.

Mercedes walked over to the table with a tray carrying the couple's drinks. "Here you guys go," she said, placing their drinks in front of them.

Mekco grabbed his water, then drank half of it. "Thank you, Mercedes."

He gazed into her eyes while Nicole kept a smile on her face. She was trying to show him that she could handle anything, even when she wasn't feeling what was happening. Nicole had never been with the same sex, even though Mekco had talked to her about it before. Now, he was basically forcing her to do it. But at the end of the day, she was his wife now, and if that was what he wanted, she was gonna make it happen.

"So, did you figure out what you wanted to eat yet?"

Mekco stared at her camel toe in her tight uniform pants and knew exactly what he had a taste for. He just wanted to see if Nicole was about that life.

Nicole knew he loved pussy, and he was gonna get it with or without her. The decision was all hers.

Mekco knew he was gonna have to give her that jump start. He grabbed Mercedes's hand and gently massaged it. He moved his fingers in a circular motion. Mercedes blushed as she listened to him talk.

"Good question, Mercedes, but I was hoping you could tell me and my wife what's the best thing to eat in this bitch. We need something wet, sweet, and juicy that we could take turns sucking on."

Mercedes was hip to the game and knew what he was talking about. She couldn't help herself but to play right along with him. "If you guys are looking for something to match that description, I'm sorry but you won't find it on these raggedy-ass menus, but I might be able to help you with that."

Mekco gave Nicole a look, telling her to go ahead and pull the bitch all the way in. Nicole pushed her true feelings aside to ensure her husband was happy. "So, if what we're looking for is not on the menu, can you tell us what's the ticket to get what we really want?"

Mekco smiled at his wife. She was a pro and had just started the job. He was proud of how she took over and handled the situation.

Now that they were talking about money, Mercedes was in. "It's gonna cost a few bands for something like what you described. Ain't shit cheap out here, if you know what I mean."

"Yeah, I figured that. So what time do you get off?"

Mercedes looked down at her watch. "In another two hours, but we are getting busy, so time is gonna fly quickly."

Nicole took Mercedes's pen out of her top pocket and made sure to place a soft touch on her D-cup-size breast. Mekco watched with a smile as Nicole wrote down their hotel and phone number.

"Just call us when you get off, and we'll order the Uber."

Mercedes looked down at the paper before folding it, then placing it into her pocket. She smiled while walking away from the table.

After Nicole and Mekco finished their meal, they left the bill money and a tip before leaving.

"I'm so proud of you, baby. You really down for a nigga," Mekco said, wearing a smile on his face.

Nicole also smiled. If she was making him happy by being a ride-or-die wife, she was willing to do whatever.

The newlyweds returned to their room, ready to play with Mercedes. Mekco was excited that his wife was down, but Nicole was secretly nervous. She was somewhat mad that she was pregnant because a good cold drink would have made her night. She really needed to ease her mind but played it off so well that Mekco didn't suspect it was a problem.

After a long, hot shower, the couple jumped into the Jacuzzi to relax. Mekco made his way over toward her side and stood in front of her. For a moment, he took his time admiring how beautiful she was.

"Baby, you're so fucking beautiful, and I am so glad that you're my wife and carrying my baby."

Nicole allowed him to place a kiss on her forehead before she spoke. "Yeah, baby, that's nice and all, but you haven't forgotten that you have another bitch pregnant too."

Mekco floated away from Nicole. "Man, don't start that shit. We were just having a good time. Both of y'all my baby mamas and just gonna have to deal with that shit. Fuck that she my baby mama, and you're my fucking wife, so you'll always have one up on her."

Nicole cheesed so hard after hearing that. Hearing him say that she was above Toya was like music to her ears. She then went over to Mekco's side and stood before him. While kissing him, she used her right hand to massage his already-hard dick.

"Mekco, you do know I love you, and I'll do anything for you, right?" she asked between kisses.

"Yeah, baby, I know. That's why you were the chosen one. And I love you too."

Right before Mekco was about to stuff his dick into her, Nicole's phone rang. She looked at Mekco, then asked him if she should answer it.

"Go ahead. That might be that bitch, Mercedes."

Nicole carried her wet self over to the nightstand to answer the phone. "Hello."

"OK, give me the address, and we're gonna send the Uber to pick you up," she said into the phone.

Mekco chilled in the water, listening to his wife hook up their fun for the night. He knew Nicole was the right woman to marry because she was down for him, but that gold-digging bitch Toya was only around for the money.

When they got back to Detroit, he was gonna make sure he put her in her place. He felt like he was a little too soft on her the last time he spoke with her.

Nicole walked back over to Mekco, then continued to jack off his dick. He leaned his head back and puffed on his blunt. He was enjoying the work that she was putting in but was low-key ready to fuck.

"Damn, Nicole, slow down a little before I come."

"OK, baby, my bad. Mercedes is on her way, and you'll be able to release yourself in a minute."

Mekco grabbed Nicole's face and tongued her down. "I love you, girl."

"I love you too, daddy."

"Man, when this bitch gets up here, I don't want you to bitch up. We about to fuck the shit out of this bitch, then send her ass home. We're leaving first thing in the morning happy," he said, laughing.

"Ok, baby. You know this gonna be my first time, so I'm a little nervous, but I promise I won't mess this up for you."

"Man, hit this blunt and take some shots before that bitch get here."

Nicole gave him a crazy look. "Boy, stop playing. You know I'm carrying your child, or did you forget already?"

Laughing, Mekco took the shot he tried to give her. "My bad, baby. You so small I almost forgot, but I'm glad you on that shit 'cause I'm fucked up right now."

In reality, Nicole had just been drinking the day before she was supposed to get her abortion, but only because she thought she wasn't keeping the baby. Now that they were married, she was gonna try to put her problems behind her so their baby could be healthy.

Mekco kissed Nicole to ease her mind. "Look, you ain't got shit to worry about. You know how I lick and suck on that pussy and how good that shit feels?"

Just thinking about the images he had put into her mind made her smile. She couldn't deny that he was the man when it came to pleasing her body. She had only been with two other guys before him, but he was the only one who could make her squirt back-to-back with no problem. And that was why she had no problem screaming out daddy to the top of her lungs every time he was deep in her pussy.

"Yeah, baby," she moaned out as he sucked on her neck and fingered her tight pussy under the water.

"What I want you to do is let that bitch do you the same way, and don't be scared to eat on her pussy, either. Just mimic what I do to you, and everything will be OK."

Mekco had her so far gone that she heard what he had said but was still in her own world as she felt his fingers enter and exit her. Nicole was just about to come when her phone started to ring.

"Go answer it. That's that bitch, Mercedes," Mekco ordered.

"I hope you don't call her bitches when she get in here," Nicole jokingly said as she walked over toward the bed to answer her phone.

Mekco didn't respond. He was just that confident that no matter what he called the bitch, she was gonna stay and let him fuck the shit out of her. He felt that way because of how easy it was to put in the order for her pussy. She was thirsty for the dick.

"All right, baby, that was Mercedes. She said she was about to get on the elevator and come on up to us," Nicole said with a slight smile. She was ready to do whatever to please her husband.

Mekco stepped out of the Jacuzzi, then wrapped his towel around his waist. Nicole sat on the bed, still ass naked. Her mind was doing a little countdown for when Mercedes knocked on the door.

A few seconds later, a light knock on the door alerted them that their playmate for the event was there. Nicole walked over to the door to let her in.

Mercedes walked in wearing a short tan trench coat. It was 96 degrees in Vegas, but she wasn't worried about the heat. Underneath her coat, she wore only a cherry red thong. Mercedes came to play no games with them.

She undid her coat, allowing it to hit the floor. Mekco grinned, seeing her sexy thick ass standing there with only a thong on. He knew right then that he had picked the right bitch for them.

"Damn, girl, you came ready to do the damn thing," Mekco said, squeezing Mercedes's right ass cheek.

Mekco then signaled for Nicole to come over to where they were standing. Nicole stood up from the bed and nervously walked over to the two. To make her feel a little comfortable, Mekco kissed her before speaking to Mercedes.

"Look, this my wife first time fucking with a chick, so show her a little extra attention," Mekco ordered.

Mercedes turned toward Nicole. For a moment, she looked at Nicole's naked body. She smiled, liking what she saw. She grabbed Nicole by the hand and slowly started kissing on her, all while cupping her breasts.

Mekco stood there watching Nicole get tongued down by Mercedes. He couldn't lie, that shit was sexy as fuck and had turned him on. He then let his towel hit the floor as he jacked off his dick. Nicole didn't hesitate to move when Mercedes walked her over to the bed.

"Lie down, sexy," she whispered.

Nicole was used to following instructions, so she had no problem listening to her new friend. Lying flat on her back, Nicole enjoyed feeling Mercedes's mouth covering her pussy.

Mekco was enjoying the sight of his wife getting head from another bitch and the fact that Mercedes was face-down, ass up. Waiting for him to enter her from the back had his dick jumping in his hand.

Mekco watched the two women go at it for a few seconds before he began to suck and lick on Mercedes's clit from the back. She was so wet that he couldn't help but suck up all her juices.

At any other time, Nicole probably would have been jealous hearing another female moan out her man's name, but she was in her own world. Mercedes kept her satisfied with her mouth. She licked from her clit to her asshole, making sure not to miss a beat.

Never in her life did Nicole ever think she would receive head from another woman and enjoy it the way she did. She thought she was gonna lose her damn mind when her legs started to shake, and Mercedes didn't ease up.

Instead, Mercedes sucked on her clit a little harder, which caused Nicole to release down her throat.

"Oh my Gawd," Nicole barely managed to yell out.

Soon after, Mercedes was moaning out from all the tongue fucking she was receiving from Mekco. Instead of letting her catch her breath, Mekco quickly stuffed his dick inside of her.

He made sure to feel her waterfall splash all over his dick. He moved in and out of her tight hole while Nicole was now in the doggie-style position getting her ass licked and fingered.

It was finally time to change positions, and Mekco was ready to get some attention from these two bitches.

After dropping his first load off in Mercedes, he took a seat on the edge of the bed, and just like magic, both girls dropped to their knees. They both slurped on each side of his hard dick. Mekco felt like he was in heaven. If he had known how easy it was to talk Nicole into doing this shit, he probably would have talked her into doing it years ago.

Mekco ended up lying back on the bed and letting the ladies take over. They took turns sucking and licking on his dick and balls. Mercedes kept deep-throating his shit like she was his fucking woman, and Nicole wasn't scared anymore and was up for the challenge. She played the li'l game that Mercedes was playing, and when she was handed the dick back, she stuffed her mouth with every inch, all while playing with her husband's balls. She was the wife and wasn't about to let no bitch outdo her.

For the rest of the evening, the three fucked, sucked, and chilled. Nicole now looked at things differently. She now loved how a woman could make her feel and was willing to let another one join her in the bedroom.

Mekco always left her feeling good after busting back-to-back, but that night, both Mekco and Mercedes attacked her body, and she loved it.

The next morning, Mekco woke up to Nicole and Mercedes, who were going back at it again without him.

That shit looked sexy as fuck, but he knew he had created a fucking monster. He watched as Nicole ate Mercedes's pussy. Since she already had her ass tooted in the air, she was the one who would be punished with his morning wood. Without a good morning or anything, he rammed his hard dick in her wet pussy without any mercy.

Mercedes left the hotel with a smile on her face. She really didn't want to leave, but she had to go to work, and they had a flight to catch.

Even though she was walking away with ten Gs in her pocket, she still knew she had to take her ass to work. That money was gonna be a down payment on a house. She had already grown tired of living with her mama. Hooking up with them was really a blessing for her.

That afternoon, they boarded their plane to return home. They both were homesick and ready to pick up their life in Detroit.

After being up all night and morning fucking, Mekco and Nicole were drained. As soon as their bodies hit their seats, they were knocked out.

Before they had left the hotel, Nicole had damn near begged him if they could stay for another day just to get some much-needed sleep.

Mekco wished they could stay, but he had some business to take care of, and there was money to be made.

He was already pissed that Nicole had forgotten to grab his phone out of his car before they jumped into the Uber and made their way to the airport. He prayed that P and the fellas were handling business.

Chapter 8

Erica woke up ready for whatever the day had to bring. She didn't have class, but her doctor's appointment was 10:00 a.m. She was ready to see how her babies were doing.

It had been three days since she had talked to Pierre, and she felt like the babies could sense that they weren't around him. They moved around but weren't that active. They must have missed him talking to them and all that good stuff.

Pastor Collins had been pushing Erica to discuss what was bothering her and why she was back home. At first, he was cool and didn't bother her, but it soon started to kill him, not knowing what was going on.

Even though Erica was pissed at Pierre, she just couldn't find it in her to talk about his actions. He had crushed her by his cruel words, and every time she thought about what he said to her, she cried her eyes out.

Climbing out of bed, she showered, then got dressed. Like every other morning, her dad was already gone for the day.

She was happy he had stuff to do because she hated having him sitting up in her face, thinking he could read her mind.

It was still a little early, but she had to stop by McDonald's to get her favorite. She loved their sausage griddles and hash browns.

After getting her food, Erica jumped into Nicole's car and made her way to her appointment. It was crazy how Nicole had totally been ignoring her, and she had her house and car keys. She wasn't sure what her problem was, but she wasn't about to kiss Nicole's ass.

Erica hated how she had Nicole's back and messed up her happy home being a real friend.

Erica sat in the parking lot of her doctor's office, eating her breakfast. She thought it was cute how her babies moved around when she ate. She knew they were gonna be some greedy babies.

Erica pulled out her phone to try to call Nicole again. Although she said she wasn't gonna kiss her butt, Erica at least wanted to return her stuff. If Nicole didn't want to be her friend, then that was gonna be OK with her.

Nicole rolled her eyes as she saw Erica's name flash across her screen. "Man, this bitch just doesn't get it."

"Man, answer that shit and stop tripping on your girl," Mekco ordered.

With an attitude, Nicole answered, "Hello."

"Hey, Nicole, I don't know what the problem is, but I've been trying to reach you. I have your car and house keys. I thought maybe you would want your stuff back."

"Look, I really don't fuck with you anymore. That's the problem that you seem not to understand. But just take my car to my house and put the keys in my mailbox," Nicole said with an attitude.

"Girl, what's your problem now?" Erica asked.

"I just don't like you. You fake, and I really don't have time for all that shit. I have a husband now and a baby on the way, and that's all I need to worry about."

Before Erica could respond, Nicole hung up. She got her point across and let it be known that she kept the baby and was married.

Erica was in her feelings but put her phone away in her purse. She signed in, then took a seat. She tried to calm her nerves, but her legs kept shaking for some reason. Half of her wanted to cry, but the other half kept telling her to be strong. The last thing she needed was to break down crying and upset her babies.

Erica tried her hardest to act like she didn't care, but at the end of the day, her feelings were hurt. She had lost her best friend and the person who promised to love her forever all at once, and she didn't have a clue why everyone was suddenly against her.

Something else bothered her. For the life of her, she couldn't understand why her appointment was at 10:00 a.m., and it was now going on 10:45 a.m. She now felt like Pierre whenever he came to an appointment with her.

"Erica Collins."

Hearing her name being called, she placed the magazine back on the table and walked to the back. She lay down on the examining table, then lifted her shirt up, exposing her round belly.

"I see you ready," the doctor jokingly said.

"Yeah, I'm just so ready to have these babies."

The doctor laughed. "You still have a good five months to go."

The doctor started squeezing the gel tube onto Erica's stomach, but a knock on the door interrupted him.

"I'm with a patient, Tammy," he said to the assistant, who was peeking in the door.

"I'm sorry, Doctor. I just wanted you to know that Dad is here."

Erica sat up a little and saw Pierre walk into the room. She was happy to see him but didn't smile to show her true feelings.

She could tell that he hadn't been getting any sleep. His eyes were puffy as if he had been up for days or had even been crying.

Erica wanted to hug him, but then those hateful words replayed in her mind again. That made her wonder why he was even there if these babies weren't his. At times, Pierre could be a bipolar, emotional wreck.

Pierre came right in without saying a word to anyone and took his seat.

"Glad you could make it, Dad. We were just about to check on these growing babies."

Pierre didn't say a word. He just sat there watching the monitor. Erica tried to pay attention to the babies but couldn't help herself. Her eyes stayed on Pierre. As much as she wanted to hate him, she couldn't change her feelings overnight.

"These two are doing just fine. Their heartbeats are strong, and they are growing at a fair pace," the doctor announced.

Pierre grabbed the white towel and wiped the blue gel off Erica's stomach. He was happy to see her and glad the babies were doing well. With all the bad going on in his life, he needed to hear some good news.

Pierre had tried staying at his mom's house, but after the first night of being there, he just couldn't. He ended up having a breakdown, then leaving.

That night, he drove around lost and hurt. His mind jumped from his mom's death to getting revenge on whoever was trying to hurt Erica.

As much as he wanted to push Erica away, he needed her in his life. After finally getting himself together, he went back to his place, only to find that Erica had left, too. That's when he knew that he had truly fucked up with her.

For the last couple of days, he had been thinking about his life and planning his mom's funeral. There really wasn't much to plan; they didn't have any family left, and she wanted to be cremated. He had everything set up for the following weekend.

The plan was to view her body, and then afterward, she would be cremated.

It was around 3:00 a.m. when he walked in the door, and he realized Erica had packed up her shit and left his ass. He was so pissed because he knew that she only left because of the bullshit that he had said. He really didn't mean it. He just wanted to protect her and his babies.

Erica didn't say a word to him. After fixing herself up, she returned to the front desk for her next appointment. Pierre followed her out the door and to Nicole's car.

She knew he was trying to get her attention, but she acted like she didn't even see him. Erica opened the door, and as she was getting in, Pierre pushed her over toward the passenger side. It was a light push, so she barely moved.

"Man, stop playing with me and move your ass over," he coldly hollered. He really wasn't mad at her, but he knew he carried that certain tone in his voice to make anyone listen.

Erica was in an awkward position and felt smashed, so she hurried and moved over.

"What do you want, Pierre?"

"Man, I need you, E. I know I fucked up, but truthfully, I can't live without you. You are my world, and I love you and the twins."

Erica smacked her lips and rolled her eyes. "Pierre, leave me alone with that bullcrap. I swear you are so freaking bipolar. You told me how you really felt the other day."

Pierre grabbed her face and although she put up a fight, he managed to plant a kiss on her lips.

"Stop playing with me, Pierre. You didn't want me, and you said these weren't your babies. So why are you even here? Why did you even show up at my appointment to check on somebody else's kids?"

He wasn't pissed before, but now he was. "Man, don't ever fix your mouth to say some bullshit like that. I'll fuck around and hurt your ass."

Although she didn't like his tone with her, she tried not to show any fear. She had to show him that he wasn't the only one who could talk out of the side of their neck.

"Oh, really, Mr. Miller? You say that punk-ass shit to me, then expect me to not say anything back to you? It doesn't work that way."

Pierre sat there in deep thought, rubbing his beard. She was absolutely right, and he was wrong, and she was able to get back at his ass. She had won that battle and hurt his feelings. He was a big softy when it came to her and the twins.

"Stop all that cursing and yelling, man. You upsetting my babies," he demanded as he softly rubbed her stomach.

Erica gave him a strange look. She couldn't believe how he was acting, but at the same time, she loved his touches.

"E, I'm sorry, baby. It's just that there's some shit going on, and I'm fucked up behind the shit. I swear pushing you away was the wrong way of handling shit. I know you're hungry. Let me take you to get something to eat, and I swear I'll talk to you and be real."

Erica didn't say anything at first. She wasn't sure if she wanted to play this game with him, but she had to admit that the way he held her hand and the look in his eyes made her wanna forgive him, or at least see what the reason was for him tripping on her.

Erica hated how weak she was when it came to that man, but she still had to stand her ground.

"You know what, Pierre? If you had just said you didn't want to be bothered with me, I would have been able to deal with that, but for you to take the most painful thing that happened to me and throw it back in my face was just wrong. Now, I don't wanna be bothered with you. I mean, how could I ever just forget about what you said to me?"

Pierre felt the hurt coming from her. He knew he was wrong, but it was only to protect her. But until she let him explain everything to her, Erica would never understand that.

"I just can't live without you, E, and I don't want to. Can you just give me a chance to explain, please?"

"I have something to do. Can you please get out of the car?" Erica said, even though it hurt her to say it.

Pierre sat there for a minute to decide on his next move. He wasn't about to give up that easily. She was his love and was gonna be his wife soon.

"Fuck all that shit you talking about, E. We about to go talk now."

Erica started to laugh at him. "Pierre, you are not about to bully me into talking to you. I don't have to, and I really don't want to. I need to go return this girl's car and try to get my shit together for me and my babies."

"All you need to do is listen to me and come home so we can fix this shit."

"Nah, love. I'm good. Enjoy," Erica said, being petty.

Pierre wasn't up for all that bullshit. Forgetting that he was trying to be nice, he snatched her closer to him. "Do it look like I'm playing with your ass? Stop playing with me right now, E. You just don't know what the fuck really going on. This shit not a fucking game out here."

Erica snatched her arm back from him. "Look, I'm not in the mood to deal with your bipolar self right now. If I'm up to it, I might call you when I wake up from my nap."

She didn't want to call him, but she knew he would leave her alone if she told him that.

With a grin, Pierre quickly said, "Cool, OK. Just hit me up later. There's some shit that I really need to explain to you, and you'll see why shit went south."

Pierre opened the car door to get out. Erica opened the passenger-side door, then walked around to the driver's side. She was dead wrong thinking that she was just gonna jump in the car. Pierre quickly hugged her.

"You know deep in your heart that all that bullshit that I said was just that—bullshit. E, I swear I love y'all and can't shit stop that," he whispered in her ear as he held her.

Erica didn't pull away from him. She actually felt good in his arms and had missed his scent. There was no way that she could deny that she still loved him, and maybe he had a reason to push her away.

From what she had learned from him awhile ago, when stuff got rough, he pushed her away.

After a few seconds, he released her. "I love you, E."

She didn't get a chance to respond 'cause he was tonguing her down in the parking lot before she knew it. Once they stopped kissing, Erica got back into the car.

Before Pierre walked away to get in his car, she called him back toward her.

"Pierre."

He stopped walking and came back to the car. "What's up?" he asked.

"Baby, I love you too," she said in the sweetest voice ever.

"Yeah, I know. Now go handle your business and call me later."

Both lovebirds drove off with a slight grin on their faces. Pierre knew he had to get shit back right with Erica, and he was gonna start by buying her a new car.

As soon as he got done meeting up with Cross and Mekco, he was gonna go take care of that.

Erica rode back to her dad's house, thinking about whether she was playing herself by giving Pierre a chance to explain himself. She just prayed that he wasn't about to be playing with her heart and have her all messed up in the mind.

Growing up, she told herself that she would never become that woman, and here she was, letting Pierre put her through all this mess.

Erica pulled up to her dad's house and was surprised that he was even at home. It was still early. He usually would have been still out and about handling business for the church.

"Hey, Dad, you came back home early," Erica said, hugging her dad.

Pastor Collins pulled away from Erica. "Girl, you been here for the last couple of days moping around about the same nigga. You smelling about now. I guess you're just a big-ass dummy like your simpleminded friend. Two big dummies pregnant by two drug dealers."

"Come on now, Dad, we've been doing so well these last few days. Why do you always gotta act so jealous of Pierre and talk so reckless? I swear, you are not a normal pastor," Erica said before walking off to her room. She knew it was only a matter of time before he had her running away from him again.

Erica slammed her bedroom door. The way she felt, she knew she had no other choice but to go back home to Pierre. She hated how she had become so dependent on everyone else to take care of her.

After getting herself together, she walked out of the room with her bag in her hand. There was no way she was gonna stay with her dad. She had to be a fool even to think that was gonna last.

It didn't even surprise her that he was sitting on the couch eating a turkey sandwich like he just wasn't acting an ass.

"I see you got your bag. Are you about to run back to the gangbanger?" he asked, but not once taking his eyes off the TV screen.

Erica didn't bother to respond to his pettiness. She walked out the door, making a promise to never come back.

There was only so much she could take from him. Maybe one day they could rebuild their relationship . . . or maybe not.

It was crazy how the pastor always had a way of getting under the skin of people around him, even before Pierre was in the picture. But since he was the pastor and the community loved him, nobody close to him said anything.

Erica knew she had to drop off Nicole's car and keys, but she had no idea about where she would go after. She loved Pierre but didn't want to run back to him so fast. She wasn't about to get used to him acting out and hurting her, just to leave and come straight back.

She knew that she needed to do something and fast. She was sleepy, hungry, and needed to get caught up with her schoolwork for the next day.

After thinking a little, she finally drove off. She made it to Nicole's crib, and just like Nicole requested, she locked her car and placed her keys in her mailbox. If Nicole was saying forget her, she was gonna have the same attitude toward her.

Usually, she would be somewhere wondering what she did and how she could fix it, but not this time. She was about to be a mother, and her kids were all she needed to worry about.

Erica weighed her options and ended up at one of the persons in her life who would look out for her.

Standing on the doorstep, she became nervous and wished she had at least called first. Then she knocked on the door and waited patiently, hoping someone was home.

"Girl, what the hell are you doing this way?" Cross yelled before stepping to the side to let her in with her bag.

"Baby, where are you going? I thought we were chilling today," Nicole said as she flipped through the channels, looking for something to watch.

"Bro, you on some real bullshit. I already missed out on some shit because your dumb ass threw my phone away when we were in Vegas, acting like you had lost it. My bro moms died, and shit, and I couldn't have his back because you were on some jealous-type shit. Don't you think if I wanted to get in touch with Toya, I would just pull up on her ass?"

With an attitude, Nicole yelled, "I said I was sorry, but what the fuck you want me to do about it now?"

"I gotta go meet up with Cross and P. We gotta handle some business. I'm not sure what time I'll be back. You need to find something to do with your miserable ass."

"Whatever, Mekco."

Mekco drove off thinking about how his baby was making Nicole so fucking evil. He still couldn't believe how she handled Erica over the phone and how she was acting, period. Then when he told her about P's mom dying, she just said OK and went back to looking through a fucking magazine like it wasn't shit.

Mekco pulled up to Cross's house and saw that P hadn't arrived yet. He felt bad for not being there for him.

Since he returned, they had linked up and had a few drinks. P had talked to him about how he put shit together and figured that whoever had killed his mom was really after Erica to hurt him.

When he told him how he had hurt Erica and pushed her away, Mekco said to him that was the worst thing that he could have done. He should have had her up under him at all times to protect her.

Pierre knew his boy was only speaking the truth, and he also knew that he had fucked up and needed to fix everything.

Cross let Mekco in after the doorbell went off. "What's up, young boy? Where the hell P crazy ass at?"

"Man, that nigga said he was on his way," Mekco answered.

The two then stepped into his office and took a seat.

"I'm glad your black ass is back to work. Your ass really just jumped up and left town? To make matters worse, nobody could get in touch with your ass. I guess it was a good thing ain't shit jump off."

"You know how shit be, Cross. Once the fall hits, we are on our grind and stacking all winter, and then in the summer, we go crazy," Mekco said with a grin.

Hearing the doorbell go off, Cross jumped up from his seat. "This must be that nigga P now."

Cross opened the door for P. Before he could even get in the door good, Cross was talking shit.

"What the fuck going on between you and my niece? And why the fuck she not at home with you getting some rest with them babies?" he asked as Pierre followed him to one of his guest rooms in the back.

When Cross slowly opened the door, Pierre looked across the room and saw Erica knocked out in the queen-size bed. It really pissed him off that she was there because if there was a problem, she should have just called him instead of running to Cross. Now, she had another muthafucka in their business.

Uncle or not, he didn't want people all in their shit like that.

Before Pierre could say anything, Cross turned to him and began speaking. "I don't know what's going on between y'all, and it really ain't my business, but fix that shit. She'd been through enough dealing with my brother's crazy ass, and right now, we are the only ones that have some type of sense around her."

Just like that, Cross walked away. He was never the type to be in another nigga business.

Yeah, Erica was his niece and all, but when she showed up at his house, she didn't have any bruises or marks on her, and she never told him anything terrible happened between them, so he wasn't worried. Plus, he knew Pierre wasn't cut like that. He was a beast in the streets, but with Erica, he was a big soft-ass nigga in love.

Pierre went over to the bed, then began to shake her softly. "E, baby, wake up," he said kindly.

Erica opened her eyes to find Pierre standing there. "What's wrong, Pierre? Why did you wake me up?" she questioned.

"What the fuck you doing over here, man? I know this ain't where you've been staying because I was just here the other day."

Erica rolled her eyes. Pierre was always asking a million questions when she was sleepy.

"I was at my dad's house, but you know he started cutting up, so I came here. What's the problem, Mr. Miller?"

Now, Pierre was sitting on the bed and Erica was leaning on him. As pissed as he was, her soft touch made him calm down and not even wanna trip on her. He also knew that if he let the beast out and tripped on her, she wouldn't leave with him.

"Why didn't you just call me, E? You know I would have come to get you."

"Pierre, I'm just so tired. After my appointment, I went to my dad's house, and he flipped out on me, and then Nicole got on my nerves, acting like a bitch. But I still had to take the car back to her. I'm not trying to stress myself out dealing with her crazy self, and I'm really not caring about her not wanting to be my friend anymore. Then, with you, I just really wanted time to decide what I wanted to do when it came to us. Cross was the only person that I could turn to."

That wasn't what he wanted to hear, but he had to respect the fact that he was the one who pushed her to that point. He made her hate him all for nothing. He didn't even stick to the plan of keeping her away from him. The love he felt for her made him realize that he couldn't live without her, and he was gonna make sure that he never had to.

"Let me take you home and explain everything to you, and if you still don't wanna be around me, then I'll bring you back over here."

Erica didn't say a word. She sat back, thinking about what he was saying.

Pierre had really hurt her when he reminded her that there was a chance that the babies weren't his. She loved him, but this was a tough situation for her.

Pierre stood up from the bed and took her by the hand. She didn't even try to fight him. When it all boiled down, her heart only wanted him.

"Grab your shit so we can go," he ordered.

Mekco and Cross sat in the office, talking and smoking while waiting for P to come join them.

"What's up, bro?" Mekco asked as P stepped into the room.

"What's up, nigga?"

Mekco saw Erica right behind him and quickly spoke. "What's up, E?"

"Hey, Mekco. Congratulations on the wedding," she softly said.

"Aye, Cross, I know we're supposed to be having this meeting today and shit, but I really need to get her home," Pierre warned.

"Go ahead and handle that," Cross answered.

Mekco jumped into their conversation. "Yeah, bro, I'll hit you up later and fill you in on everything."

Everyone said their goodbyes, and then Pierre and Erica left.

He couldn't wait to get everything off his chest and just be there to make her happy.

Pierre held the passenger-side door open for Erica before going over to his side. As they drove off, Erica quickly dozed again. Those babies were draining her and kept her tired all the time.

While she slept in the car, P stopped by a Taco Bell drive-thru. He knew she was gonna be hungry, and tacos were her favorite. He was trying to get shit right and knew the first way to win back her heart was food.

Nicole lay across the bed, still watching TV. She hadn't moved out of that spot since Mekco had left. She had to admit that she couldn't wait to have her baby so that she could have something to do when Mekco wasn't around.

Now that she wasn't friends with Erica anymore, she really didn't have anyone to talk to. Her mom was pissed off after she got back with Mekco and ran off to get married.

Nicole's phone went off, letting her know she had a text message. She rolled her eyes, not knowing who was interrupting her movie. She opened her messages and smiled as she read the text.

Mercedes: Hey. I swear that pussy was so good. I can't stop thinking about your sweet taste. I wish you were still in Vegas with me.

Nicole blushed at the message. To hear how her sweet pussy had a bitch begging her to catch a flight turned her on. She hurried and texted back.

Nicole: Bitch, you so fucking crazy. Lol. But I'm glad you enjoyed it. You had me so fucking wet.

Mercedes and Nicole had secretly been texting each other since Nicole and Mekco had left Vegas. The morning they had left town, Mercedes had awakened Nicole with a light shake. Nicole opened her eyes, and Mercedes placed her finger over her mouth before she could say anything. That was her way of asking her not to say anything and just go with the flow. Nicole had never been with a woman before that night, and never in life did she think that she would sleep with a female, but there was something about Mercedes that turned her on.

Mercedes: I'm about to move to my place in a few days. I'd love for you to come visit me. Why don't you catch that flight?

Nicole couldn't help herself but smile. She loved the attention that Mercedes was giving her, but she had to think about her reality. She was happily married to a man she loved and would have his child soon. There wasn't no way in hell she was gonna let a bitch come and fuck it up.

Mercedes: Nicole, your sexy ass still there?

Nicole texted Mercedes's impatient ass back.

Nicole: What the fuck you not getting? I have a husband who I love. I told you that a million times.

Mercedes wasn't giving up. She knew Nicole was full of shit and was an easy catch.

Mercedes: Stop playing with me, Nicole. If you weren't feeling me, your ass wouldn't have texted me back when I first hit you up, telling you how sweet and juicy your pussy was. And as far as that husband shit, girl, I'm not trying to hear that shit.

Nicole set her phone down on the nightstand. She wasn't sure why she even entertained Mercedes on the phone. It was all fun and games for her. But she needed someone to talk to when she got lonely.

Nicole's phone notifications for her text messages went off again. "Damn, bitch," she mumbled. She was surprised to see that Mercedes had sent her a picture of her standing in front of a mirror with nothing on.

The picture came with a caption that said, "You want another taste?"

Nicole giggled but didn't respond. Suddenly, she heard the front door open and knew Mekco was on his way upstairs. She gave the picture one last look before locking her phone, then setting it back on the nightstand.

"Hey, my beautiful wife, what you up here doing?" Mekco asked, walking into the room and handing her a long-stemmed rose.

Since they returned from Vegas, Mekco had really been trying to do right by her. He realized that when he had almost lost her, he couldn't stomach being without her. Nicole held his heart, and he never wanted her to let it go.

"Aww, Mekco, you are so sweet, and this rose is so beautiful. Thank you, baby."

"Hey, I saw your girl today. Her ass was at Cross's house when I pulled up," he said, forgetting that she wasn't fucking with Erica anymore.

"Good for her. What, you want me to give the bitch a fucking cookie?" Nicole coldly asked.

"Damn, Nicole, don't be like that. You know that girl only left you because bro moms had died. You acting bitchy when she left bro to come back to get your ass. Baby, I love you, but you wrong as fuck. How you still gonna act cold like that toward her and know the fucking truth?

Nicole smacked her lips. "Man, if you don't leave me the fuck alone about that bitch. You're starting to piss me off, and I'm gonna start treating you the same way if you don't get outta my face."

Mekco held up his hands, showing that he had thrown in the towel and surrendered. "Damn, you a mean muthafucka. I hope my baby is not about to be like your mean ass."

Nicole giggled. "Boy, shut up and get me something to eat."

"Man, I had come home early so I could take you out. You wanna go eat, and then go to the movies or something? I know your ass is tired of sitting up in this house all day."

Nicole loved how Mekco acted now. He had somehow become a totally different person. Lately, he had been trying to go out of his way to show Nicole he was the best husband in the world.

He had once told her that he was changing his ways and would do better at loving her, and that's exactly what he's been doing.

After thinking about what Mekco said, Nicole jumped up to shower. She really wasn't feeling like going to the movies because she was watching movies all day, but she was ready to eat.

As she let the hot water hit her body, she washed herself with her strawberry-scented body wash. Her body felt so good and slippery that she soon was touching on her freshly shaved pussy. To her surprise, she couldn't help but think about Mercedes.

Nicole couldn't deny that Mercedes had her hot and bothered, even though she tried her hardest not to lust after her.

Instead of going to the movies, the couple spent their time at the bowling alley.

"Damn, Nicole, you really just gonna beat my ass like that?" Mekco asked while looking at the scoreboard.

Laughing, Nicole responded. "Hell yeah, baby. I told you I didn't come to play with your ass."

Mekco gave her a funny look. "Girl, you only whipping my ass 'cause I've been drinking. Don't fool yourself, girl."

The two played another round before their time was up, and Nicole was tired. As they went toward the front, they bumped into a familiar face.

"What's up, Mekco? Long time no see," Toya said with a sneaky grin.

Mekco couldn't believe how she approached him, seeing that Nicole was right by his side. "Yeah, you do remember me saying that I wasn't fucking with you no more like that. And to call me when the baby is born."

Nicole didn't say a word because she saw how Mekco was handling her. She felt relieved that he had told her the truth about telling Toya that he wasn't fucking with her bigheaded ass.

"Whatever, baby daddy," she said to him, but at the same time, giving Nicole an ugly look.

Nicole raised her hand to show off the large rock Mekco placed on her finger. Toya rolled her eyes out of jealousy.

"Yeah, that's right, bitch. I'm wifey."

"Fuck both of y'all," Toya said before storming off.

She couldn't believe that Mekco had married that bitch. And to top it off, he was talking to her like she was a fucking nobody.

Mekco opened the passenger-side door for Nicole, then went over to his side. Once he got in, he turned his attention toward her. It was clear that she had a fuckin' attitude.

"Baby, fix your face. I know you not mad at me because she was here, are you?"

"No, baby, I'm actually glad that we ran into her. She needed to see us together, and she definitely needed to see my ring so she could know her place."

"I told you I was a changed man, baby. You are the only one I want, and I put that on anything," Mekco said while staring into her eyes.

Nicole was turned on by him and couldn't help herself. She slowly unzipped his pants, releasing his monster. Before he could say anything, his dick was disappearing into her mouth. Mekco let his chair back and then got comfortable. That was why he was glad he married her wild ass.

Their love was so strong for each other that even being in the bowling alley's parking lot couldn't stop Nicole from showing her husband how much she appreciated him.

Chapter 9

"So, are you telling me that the hit was for me, and I'm the one who is supposed to be dead? Why would someone want me and my babies dead, Pierre?" Erica cried out while sitting on the couch next to him.

They had finally made it home, and Erica was wide awake and ready to listen to him. He had broken down his theory and explained to her how whoever killed his mom thought Erica was the one driving her car that day.

Pierre hated to tell her the truth, but she needed to know it. He held her in his arms, trying to calm her down. "E, baby, don't cry. I promise everything will be OK."

As he rubbed her back, Erica tried to fight her tears. She was scared out of her mind, and soon, instead of calming down, her body began to shake.

"Man, baby, you got to calm yourself down. You know I'm not gonna let shit happen to you or my babies, and I put that on my fucking life."

Erica felt it in her heart that he was telling the truth. She knew no matter what, he was gonna protect her with everything in him. She lay in his arms, trying to calm down, and after a while, the shaking stopped, and her breathing was just about normal.

"When we first got together, I had pushed you away when shit got hot in these streets. I never wanted you to get caught up in this street shit. I can remember you were pissed and felt like I didn't love you. Hurting you only hurt me. When I put shit together and realized you were the target, I panicked and thought that if I hurt you again, that you would stay away from me. I don't know why I thought I could live without you, and I know you can't be without me."

Erica didn't say a word as she rested against him, listening to Pierre pour his heart out. She was so mad at him just days ago, but now, she understood why he said those hurtful things to her.

"E, I'll kill myself before I let a muthafucka hurt you. I apologize from the bottom of my heart for that bullshit that I said to you. I know that was wrong of me, but I know for a fact that them my babies."

Erica sat up with a grin on her face. "Baby, I forgive you. I swear I do, but I have a question for you. How do you know for a fact these are yours?"

"Because I fucking said so," he laughed.

"Pierre!"

"Nah, I'm playing with you. I know because before you even told me that you were pregnant and before all that shit happened, my grandma came to me in a dream and told me I was about to be a daddy. I wasn't sure the shit was real until you said something about it."

Erica smiled. "Are you for real right now, baby?" she asked.

"Hell yeah, baby. I never lied to you before, have I?"

Erica quickly answered, "Nope, you always been real with me, and that's what made me fall for you."

Erica stood up from the couch, then started cleaning up the mess they made from Taco Bell. She was happy that they could talk things out and get their relationship back on track.

Pierre followed Erica into the kitchen. It had been a minute since he had her, and his body craved her. As she washed the few dishes in the sink, he stood behind her with his hands wrapped around her waist. She giggled as she felt his soft kisses on her neck.

"Baby, let me finish this kitchen and put some clothes in the washer. Then I'm all yours."

Pierre didn't let her go. "Nah, baby, I'll finish up everything when I put your ass to bed."

With that being said, Erica allowed Pierre to lead her into their bedroom. That evening, the couple made sweet love, like it was their first time being together.

Pierre made a promise never to push her away again, and Erica promised never to stop loving him.

Pierre drove Erica to and from school for the next few days. He had told her he could take her to pick out a new ride, but that only made her cry. She had been holding back her feelings, and just the thought of her driving on her own scared her to death.

Erica feared for her life and nothing that Pierre had said changed that. Other than school, Erica stayed up under Pierre.

It was Saturday afternoon, the day of Pierre's mother's home-going service. And Pierre was back at his lowest. All week, he had kept himself busy, trying to keep his mind off everything, but that day, it hit him that she was really gone.

"Come on, baby. I know this hard, but you gotta push yourself to get through this today," Erica said, trying to console him. She had lost her mom at a young age, so she could relate to how Pierre was feeling.

"I don't wanna do this, baby. It's too painful. Growing up, I spent so much time hating her for leaving me, and when I got older, it was easy for me just to pretend that she was dead. When she came back into my life, I realized how much I loved her. And now, it's too late for me to show her just how much I loved her," Pierre confessed.

"Pierre, baby, don't think like that. Your mom died knowing that she was loved. Before she passed away, you showed her nothing but love, and she felt that. I'm willing to bet money on that."

Pierre smiled. That was the exact reason why he loved Erica. She always knew what to say to make him feel better.

Pierre stood up from the bed, and Erica followed. She stood in front of him, then fixed his tie for him. She had to admit that he looked so handsome standing there in his tux.

"OK, baby, you all set? Now, let's get out of here. The limo is waiting outside."

Pierre held Erica's hand as they made their way out the door. In no time, they were on their way to the church. They rode in silence but hand in hand. This was gonna be a long day for Pierre.

"Come on, Nicole, before you make us late," Mekco yelled. He was already dressed and ready to go, but she was taking forever, playing in her head.

"I'm ready, baby. Sorry for taking so long. My hair wasn't acting right. Plus, I told you from jump that I didn't want to go."

Mekco shook his head; she was irritating.

The couple walked out the door and made their way to the church. Nicole felt funny going since she didn't know P's mom and because she knew deep down inside she was on some bullshit when it came to Erica. She really wasn't ready to see her or apologize for being a bitch toward her.

Entering the church, Mekco went to the front to sit next to P and Erica. He gave both a hug, then took his seat. Nicole sat beside Mekco after speaking to P. She looked Erica's way but let her pride stop her from speaking. After everything that had been going on, Erica tried not to let anything bother her, especially Nicole's jealous, bipolar self. It was the day to say their final goodbyes to Pierre's mother, not worry about fake friendships.

After the service was over, everyone went to the repast. Pierre had rented out a little hall for everyone to get together. He didn't think too many people would show up, but the hall was packed with his mom's so-called friends. It was a good thing that there was enough food for everyone.

"Aye, bro, you know you're my nigga, and I got your back on whatever," Mekco said, giving his boy dap.

Pierre had a slight grin on his face. "Yeah, nigga, I know. Don't start getting all soft on me, bitch. I'm still P."

The best friends started laughing. Mekco couldn't lie. P was still P when it all boiled down to it.

Erica came over to the table with a plate full of food. "Here, baby, put some food on your stomach."

"Yes, ma'am," he said, laughing.

Erica gave him a peck on his lips. "Why you gotta be so dang silly? But for real, baby, it's nice to see you smiling and laughing again."

"E, where your plate at? You better go get you something to eat before it's all gone. I see some folks done went up for seconds already."

"I'm about to go get mine. I just wanted to make sure you were good first," Erica said before walking away.

Mekco saw Nicole coming out of the restroom, so he got up to meet her. "Look, you can go take a seat, and I'll fix your plate."

"Mekco, I'm really not that hungry, so don't make it too big. But anyway, where are we sitting?"

"Over there with bro," Mekco answered.

Nicole rolled her eyes, then walked off. She knew Mekco was about to be on some bullshit and try to make her talk to Erica, but she wasn't for it. Nicole sat across from P. "P, I'm so sorry for your loss. Keep your head up, bro."

"Thanks, Nicole."

Erica walked back toward the table with her plate and sat. She looked at Nicole but didn't bother to speak. If Nicole wanted to play this stupid game, then she was gonna play too. One band, one sound.

"Damn, baby, why your plate so little?" Pierre asked Erica.

"Because I wasn't that hungry, silly butt."

"That's not gonna be enough food for my babies. So you better eat now 'cause I'm not stopping nowhere for no food on our way home."

Erica couldn't help but laugh. "Baby, this is enough. You know I get full fast."

Mekco returned with Nicole's and his plate. With the girls not talking, the whole table was quiet, and it was very awkward. Once they were done eating, the fellas started talking about random shit. Erica just sat there while Nicole texted on her phone. She was trying her hardest to ignore the fact that Erica was at the same table. It was true pettiness at its finest.

They only had the hall for two hours, and time did fly. After everyone left. Erica cleaned up. Pierre tried to help her, but she refused to allow him to do anything. While she cleaned up, he was on his phone talking to Cross. Even though Cross had just left the hall fifteen minutes ago, whatever he said had Pierre's full attention.

"Baby, I'm done, and John is about to lock up this place."

Pierre nodded, letting her know that he heard what she said. "OK, Cross, I'll hit you back up later. Let me get Erica home," he said into the phone.

***

Erica and Pierre arrived home in a matter of minutes. As soon as they got in the door, Erica started to undress.

"Damn, baby, what's up with you?" he asked, thinking that she was on some freaky shit.

"Baby, that food got me so sleepy. I'm about to jump into bed and take a nap."

Pierre took a seat on the couch while Erica went to bed. His mind was racing, and he needed to stay focused on everything. Cross had called him to inform him that the streets had been talking, and a name popped up. According to the streets, Brian was responsible for his mother's murder. He was supposed to be trying to get revenge for his brother's death but was now hiding out. They also said that Brandon had died without telling his brother where the money was at, so now, he was broke and couldn't skip town. Pierre knew that meant that he should be easy to find. Pierre was ready to hit the streets, but he had a feeling that later that night, if he tried to leave, Erica was gonna try to stop him. Since she found out the truth about her being the target, she had been really clingy.

Pierre turned off the TV, then went to the back. He was thinking that maybe if he acted really nice and made her feel good, then she might let him out. It was crazy how he went from doing what he wanted to checking in and asking his girl for permission to go out. But when you're grown and in love, shit like that comes with the relationship.

Pierre climbed into bed with his future wife. He placed sweet kisses on her forehead, and just like any other time, she moved closer toward him. Pierre held Erica and whispered in her ear, "E, I love you. I will do whatever to make you feel safe again. I will kill for you and damn sure will die for you."

Pierre stayed up a little longer thinking about how he was gonna enjoy killing Brian's bitch ass. He had already made up his mind that he wanted to torture him and watch him die slowly. He wanted him to beg for mercy. Brian was gonna pay for killing his mom and for making Erica scared to be by herself.

After doing a whole lot of plotting in his mind, he was knocked out asleep with her. He just hoped that Erica didn't give him a hard time when it was time for him to go.

"Damn, Nicole, you really ain't say shit to your girl today," Mekco said as he sat down in the recliner chair in their room.

"Mekco, don't start with me. I told you I wasn't fucking with that bitch anymore. Plus, if our friendship was so important, she would have said something to me." Mekco shook his head. It was crazy how she sat there talking all that shit just to justify the bullshit that she was on. Mekco wasn't no fool, and when they all were eating, he could tell that both girls had wanted to talk to each other but didn't want to be the first one to start.

"Man, who the fuck you texting? Lately, your ass been glued to that fucking phone."

Nicole locked her phone up before she placed it down on the bed. "Man, I was texting my mom. She still pissed that I married you and wanna sit up and go back and forth about the bullshit."

Nicole was lying her ass off, but Mekco believed her because he had never had a problem with her before.

"All that's your fault anyway. You shouldn't be having muthafuckas in our fucking business, and they wouldn't have shit to say," Mekco said coldly.

"You right, but I don't wanna hear your shit either. I'm so tired of muthafuckas and their bullshit opinion of my life."

At first, Mekco didn't say anything. He knew the baby had her acting bitchy. He walked out of the room and chilled in his office to keep the peace. Nicole was evil, and he prayed his baby didn't come out acting like her mean ass.

It wasn't long before he was asleep at his desk.

Pierre woke up looking at the time that flashed on the clock on the dresser. It was 11:35 p.m., and he knew it was almost time for him to hit the streets. That bitch-ass nigga Brian had to die that night.

He slowly crept into the bedroom, trying to make sure he didn't wake his sleeping beauty. He made it to their walk-in closet, then started pulling out his all-black gear. He quietly put on his clothes and then his black Tims. After that, he opened up his safe that he kept in the back of his closet.

Not smelling or feeling Pierre near her, Erica woke up to sit up and find Pierre pulling out two guns from their closet.

"Pierre, what are you doing?" she asked, even though it was clear what he was up to.

"Damn, E, go back to sleep for me. I'll be right back, baby. I got some shit to handle."

"No, you not about to leave this house like that."

This was the exact reason why he didn't want her to wake her ass up. He knew she was about to be on his head talking shit, especially seeing his guns in his hands.

"E, please, I'm not trying to argue with your ass about this shit tonight. A muthafucka gotta die tonight, and I need you to understand that. Baby, this ho-ass nigga was after you, then fucked around and killed my mama. It's only law that I send him to his maker."

Erica sat in the bed crying. It was strange how she understood that he was pissed and hurt, but at the same time, she didn't want him out in the streets. She honestly was scared, and a lot of what-ifs popped into her mind. She worried that he wasn't gonna make it home to her.

Pierre shook his head at Erica and her tears. Her tears usually made him give in to whatever she wanted, but not this time. He was determined to put another body under his belt before sunrise.

"Pierre, please," Erica cried out.

"Erica, please stop that crying shit. I already got my mind made up, and I'm leaving. This is something that I have to do."

Erica stood up from the bed, then walked toward him, "You don't have to do nothing. You wanna do this."

"Look, E, I know you don't understand this street life, but I'm trying to make you understand that when a muthafucka hurt a person that I love, I have no choice but to kill them. When that nigga snatched your ass up, do you know how many people lost their life that night?" Pierre yelled.

Erica was now shaking her head at him. "No, and I don't wanna know."

"Look, I gotta go, but I'll see you in a minute," he said, kissing her lips.

Pierre left the bedroom and grabbed his keys from the coffee table. Erica followed him to the living room. She hated knowing what he was about to go out to do, but she knew even her tears weren't gonna stop him from walking out the door.

"Pierre, wait," Erica yelled, stopping him in his tracks.

"What's up, E?"

She wrapped her arms around him. He knew she was hurt by his actions, but he had thrown in the towel with the situation. He lifted her head and gave her a passionate kiss.

"I love you, E," Pierre admitted as their kiss ended.

"I love you too, and you better be safe and come home to us unharmed."

With a grin on his face, he responded, "You already know I am. Now, go feed my babies and get some rest."

With that being said, Pierre walked out the door, and Erica sat on the couch, crying her eyes out and praying for the man who held her heart.

P jumped in the all-black Country & Town minivan that Cross had dropped off for him earlier that day, and just like he said, the keys were in the glove box. His next stop was to go get Mekco.

It was crazy how they were in charge, but when it came to putting in work like this, they only trusted each other to have each other's back.

"Aye, bro, I'm three minutes away," P said into the phone.

Mekco kissed Nicole before grabbing his gun from the dresser drawer. Nicole smiled. "I'll see you later, baby."

"Yeah, see you in a minute."

Mekco stood outside, letting the cold air hit him. He was happy that P wasn't lying about being three minutes away because it was colder than he thought.

"Damn, bro, it's cold as hell out here," Mekco said, getting into the van.

"Hell yeah, but anyways, you ready to do this nigga dirty?"

"Hell yeah, bitch. I was born ready," Mekco answered.

The best friends rode in silence just like any other time they were out about to put in some work.

They knew they needed a clear mind, but Erica's face kept popping up in P's mind. He loved the fuck outta her, and just knowing how close someone got to taking her out hurt him.

He turned some music on to try to block out her cries. Thinking about her was gonna fuck around and get his ass killed.

It wasn't long before they pulled up to the motel that Brian had been staying at.

"So, you got a plan or what?"

"Yeah, nigga, the plan is to go put this nigga out of his fucking misery," P replied.

"Say less, bro."

"Come on, bro, let's go handle this nigga. As a matter of fact, I owe it to my mom to handle him myself. You can keep your ass in the car and watch my back from here."

"Nigga, you lost your fucking mind. You know we don't roll like that."

P jumped out of the ride, then shut the door. He wasn't trying to hear the shit Mekco was talking about. He was about to get his revenge, and that was that.

Mekco felt P's pain and knew how much he wanted that nigga Brian dead, so he got out of the car and just stayed in the background.

This was P's kill, and he had to accept the fact that he wanted this for himself.

P walked around to Brian's motel room. The sight of seeing his room number put a smile on his face.

After killing muthafuckas most of his life, you would have thought that he would be tired of that shit, but he promised himself that for the sake of not hurting Erica, this was gonna be his last kill. He knew if he wanted her to be his wife and be happy with him, he was gonna have to walk away from all this street shit.

Pierre was gonna be a Brick Boy for life. That wasn't gonna ever change, but he had a family to take care of now.

P could hear the TV volume up loud, so he knew Brian was there. Then he pulled out an old ID to unlock the room door. It was a damn shame how these old motels were too cheap to upgrade the doors.

As P slowly opened the door, a strong smell that he was so familiar with hit his nose. It didn't take a fucking rocket scientist to figure out that Brian's ho ass was already dead.

P let his curiosity get the best of him. He walked a little farther in the room, and from what he could tell, the nigga had shot himself in the head.

Before walking out, P smiled at the fact that the same gun Brian used to kill himself was the same gun he used to take his mom out with. Maybe she came back to hunt his ass.

P shut the door behind him, then jogged back to the car. Mekco jumped back into the car, right behind his boy.

"You good, nigga?" Mekco asked.

"Yeah, bro, I'm gonna always be good."

They both laughed as P drove off. He couldn't wait to drop Mekco off so he could go home and hold his baby.

"Aye, bro, when I walked in the room, that nigga Brian was already dead. That nigga had shot himself in the head."

Mekco shook his head. He could never understand why a nigga would take their own life. The way he looked at life, it was a sign of weakness.

"Damn, bro. I know you wanted to do that nigga in, but at least he gone now."

Pierre pulled up to Mekco's place. "All right, bro, thanks for riding out with me."

After opening up his door, Mekco looked P's way. "Nigga, you already know how we get down. We brothers for life."

Once Mekco was in his place, Pierre drove off. He parked the van back where he got it and then placed the keys in the right spot.

When Pierre got upstairs to his place, all the lights were off and it was pitch black. He quietly walked to his bedroom, hoping to find Erica knocked out. Usually, when she cried, she fell right to sleep.

Entering the room, he hit the light switch to put his guns up and undress. He was surprised to see that Erica wasn't in bed.

"Man, what the fuck. This muthafucka so fucking extra, I swear."

Pierre put on his shoes again, thinking he was gonna have to leave and find her crazy ass. He walked back toward the living room and flicked on the light so he could grab his coat. The temperature in Detroit had dropped too damn low for him that night.

"Damn," he yelled as he finally saw Erica on the couch. She must have fallen asleep waiting for him to come back.

Pierre went over to the couch and picked her up. Even being pregnant, she was still lightweight to him. Erica barely opened her eyes but knew that Pierre had her. His smell always filled her nostrils, and that made her smile. She knew her baby was home, and he was OK.

"I'm glad you're OK, Mr. Miller," she said as he laid her on the bed.

"Just know that I'll always come back to you, girl. You ain't never gotta worry about me."

Pierre undressed, then climbed into bed. Usually, after putting in work, he would have come home, taken a shower, and fucked the shit out of Erica. But tonight was different. He didn't do shit but waste gas. He lay in bed with her and just held her.

"Baby, I think we need to decide on a wedding date. I'm ready to do the damn thing."

With a huge smile on her face, Erica gave him a kiss. "Really, baby? I'm ready too, but I was thinking about it after I have the babies. I didn't want to be too big in my dress."

"Well, why we can't do it sooner, you know, before you get too big?" he asked.

"Are you serious, baby? Please don't play with me about this," Erica said, full of excitement.

"A nigga not playing with your beautiful ass. Life too fucking short to be bullshitting and waiting to marry the person you love. Especially when the love is real, and you only wanna be with that one person."

Erica began to cry. His words hit her hard, and she felt everything he said.

Pierre held her a little tighter in his arms. "Don't cry, baby. I'm just keeping it real with you. I love your sexy chocolate ass."

Erica used her T-shirt to wipe away her tears. One thing about Pierre that she loved was the fact that he didn't have to try too hard to make her feel good or make her smile. And that was one reason that she knew they were supposed to be together.

At first, their cuddling turned into heavy kissing, and before either knew it, they were making sweet love. The way he was putting it on her was everything. If she weren't already pregnant, he would have got her pregnant that night.

***

Mekco walked in the door with the smell of food invading his nose. He walked straight into the kitchen to find Nicole standing over the stove cooking.

He looked over to the counter and saw that she had cooked some bacon, eggs, grits, and waffles. "Damn, baby, it's almost one in the morning. Why the hell you in here cooking all this for?"

"I was hungry, and this was what I had a taste for, but I did make extra just in case you came home hungry," she said, placing the last waffle on the tray.

"Thanks, baby. I swear you make me so happy to be your husband."

Nicole smiled as she made his plate.

The newlyweds ate their food and jumped straight into the bed. It was just like Black folks to eat, then sleep. They had only been sleeping for twenty minutes before Mekco woke up. He had just remembered to get his phone and put it on the charger. He returned to the living room to grab his phone from his jacket pocket.

When he came back into the room, he felt on the side of the bed for his charger, but instead, he found something that he didn't need to see. On his side of the bed, he found one of Nicole's dildos.

"Man, what the fuck?" he yelled.

See, he and Nicole only used that bitch when they were really feeling freaky, and he never knew her to use it on her own.

"Nicole, Nicole, get your ass up!" Mekco yelled while shaking her, trying to wake her up.

"Man, what the hell you want?"

Mekco held up the dildo. "What tip you on, bitch?"

Nicole rolled her eyes, knowing she was caught. She quickly thought about what she was gonna say. "Man, you act like I can't get horny when your ass not around. Now, put my shit back in my drawer."

Mekco threw the sex toy at her, knocking her in the head. "Don't fucking play with me. Since when did you get your rocks off by your fucking self?"

Nicole couldn't help but laugh. "Boy, you tripping. You acting like you the only thing that can make me come."

Nicole got out of the bed to put her little friend away. Mekco was tripping hard, and she could tell that he was clearly jealous.

"I'm just saying, man, I'm not good enough for you no more? Do my shit suck to the point that you need to be sticking plastic fake dicks up your pussy?"

Nicole kept laughing at her husband. "Come on now, daddy. You know you all the man that I need. I just couldn't wait for you to get home."

Mekco was smiling now. Nicole had boosted his ego just that quickly. He then went over to the dresser and took it out again. "Look, I don't like that shit, Nicole."

Nicole's mouth dropped open when he tossed her toy in the garbage. "From now on, you wait until I get home, and I'm not fucking playing with your ass."

Before Nicole could get back into the bed, Mekco lifted her, setting her on the dresser. Then he snatched off her T-shirt. She knew what was next. He kissed all over her body, making sure she was satisfied. He picked up his wife and carried her over to the bed when he finished. Mekco took his time and made love to Nicole.

She wasn't sure how to feel about that night. He acted like the dildo was his competition, and he had to prove to her that his real dick was better than the plastic dick that was now in the garbage. Afterward, he fell asleep, and she was left thinking about her night before he came home.

Nicole picked her phone up after hearing that she had a message coming through her phone. She smiled when she saw that the sender was Mercedes.

Mercedes: What's up, sexy wyd?

Nicole quickly texted her back: Lying in bed bored out of my mind.

Mercedes: FaceTime me so I can see your sexy ass.

Nicole didn't hesitate to press the button to connect the call. "What's up, Mercedes?"

"Damn, girl, you looking good as hell. I was thinking about coming to see you before it gets too cold in Detroit," Mercedes said.

Nicole knew exactly how she was feeling 'cause she low-key wanted another night with her, but without Mekco. "What you trying to see?" Nicole asked, flirting.

Mercedes smiled. "Stop fucking playing with me, Nicole. You already know what I wanna see. I wanna see that juicy wet-wet."

Nicole stood up from the bed, pulling off her shirt. She wasn't wearing anything under it, so Mercedes was more than happy to see her naked body. Picking up the phone again, Nicole smiled at seeing that Mercedes was also naked.

"Damn, you're so fucking sexy, baby," Mercedes moaned as she began to play with herself.

"You sexy too, Mercedes," Nicole had to admit.

The girls played with themselves over FaceTime. They watched each other play with their own pussies while moaning each other's names.

"Nicole, you ain't got no toys?" Mercedes asked. She was gonna make it her business to turn out Nicole. She was gonna be all hers real soon. Fuck Mekco.

Nicole pulled out her pink dildo, then climbed back into bed. It had been a minute since she used it because Mekco was giving her all the dick that she needed.

Mercedes watched as the dildo entered and exited Nicole's juicy pussy. It turned her on just seeing Nicole's sexy ass moan out. She pictured it as her pleasing Nicole.

Nicole was on the verge of coming, and her moaning became louder and louder.

"Go ahead and come for daddy," Mercedes demanded.

Nicole couldn't help but yell, "I'm coming."

"That's right, Nicole. Who do that pussy belong to?"

"You. It belongs to you," Nicole moaned, not fully understanding what she was saying.

"That's right, girl. That pussy belongs to me. Don't be scared. Call me daddy," she ordered.

Nicole could feel herself about to explode all her sweet juices all over the bed, but that didn't stop her from screaming, "I'm coming, daddy."

As Nicole came to her senses again, she realized exactly what she was doing. She sat up on the bed and saw that Mercedes was still on the phone playing with herself.

"What the fuck am I doing?" she asked herself right before hanging up.

Nicole felt funny about what had just happened. She couldn't lie; she did enjoy it, but now that the deed was done, Mekco crossed her mind. How could it be possible to enjoy sex with both Mekco and Mercedes?

Later, Nicole cuddled up to her husband, and the whole night replayed in her mind. She sort of wished there was a way she could control her feelings that were growing for Mercedes. She loved the fuck out of Mekco, and she could tell how he was trying his best to be the man that she wanted him to be. She needed to get her shit together before she fucked around and lost her husband. Nicole soon passed out with some tough decisions on her mind.

Chapter 10

Toya sat on the couch, debating whether she wanted to call Mekco. It had been a good two months since she last saw him.

Even though he had pissed her off acting brand new since he was with that bitch Nicole, she still couldn't believe that he married that ho.

The thing was, by her being pregnant and staying sick all the time, she had to stop working, and because of that, she was behind on rent and bills. Toya was kind of scared, but he told her to call him if she needed anything. Not for her but for the baby, and right now, the baby needed a roof over its head.

Putting aside her pride, Toya picked up her phone, then strolled through her call log to call his cell.

"Yeah, what's up?" Mekco asked after the fourth ring.

"Look, Mekco, I'm not even about to beat around the bush with this. I'm gonna be straight-up with you. I need your help. I had to quit my job, and I don't have any money," she cried into the phone.

Mekco's words slurred as he responded to her. "Look, I got you. Just give me a minute, and I'm gonna slide through."

"OK, thanks."

Mekco hung up his phone, then slid it back into his pocket. It was Face's birthday, and the team decided to go out and get fucked up.

"Let's get another round in this bitch," Corey yelled.

He was already fucked up, but since he wasn't driving, he didn't care how fucked up he got that night. The team got a few more bottles and continued to party.

"Aye, bro, I'm about to get the fuck out of here," Mekco said to P.

"Shit, I'm right behind you. I told Erica I wasn't gonna be out all night, and you know I'm not trying to piss her off."

They laughed before letting everyone else know they were about to leave.

Mekco jumped into his ride, and P got into his. They both drove off, going their separate ways.

P shook his head because he knew if Mekco wasn't going his way, which led to his house, then he was about to go to some bitch's house. That made him wonder what the point of Mekco getting married was.

"Hey, Mekco," Toya said while opening the door for her baby daddy.

Mekco stepped in, taking off his winter coat. "So, what's this shit you were talking about?"

Toya took a seat on the couch, and he followed. He couldn't help but stare at her ass. The baby wasn't really fucking up her figure, but it was making her thick as fuck. He shook his head and told himself not to fall for her.

For the last two months, he had been good to Nicole. He took her out more and spent more time at home. He even stopped talking to other females just to prove to Nicole that she was the one. And that was the reason that she didn't bitch when he wanted to go out that night.

She trusted him completely now, or it could have been that she could do her own thing when he wasn't around.

"This baby been having me so fucking sick that my job laid me off. So, right now, I don't have any money for my rent or bills. I need your help," she pleaded.

Mekco didn't say a word, making her look over at him. She couldn't believe that he was knocked out. "Drunk bastard," she mumbled before she picked his pockets.

Mekco was known for carrying money, so she decided to help herself to it. After grabbing just a few bills, she went into her room and stashed it in her top drawer.

Then she went back into the living room and took her seat next to Mekco. She couldn't believe how this nigga was dead asleep like that.

When his phone started to vibrate, Toya made it her business to see who it was, even though she had a feeling she already knew.

Just like she thought, wifey popped up on the screen.

"This stupid bitch," she mumbled.

Toya allowed the ringing to stop. She giggled as a crazy idea popped into her mind. She slowly unfastened Mekco's pants. It was no surprise that he was already hard just from fantasizing about her ass when he was watching her.

Toya released his dick from the split of his boxers. She smiled as she watched his monster pop out and almost hit her in the nose. She couldn't help but lick on it before she put her plan in motion.

Mekco still didn't budge when she took a picture of his dick stuffed in her mouth. When she finished, she fixed his pants and took her seat.

She debated with herself on whether she should send the picture. But then she said fuck it because she was supposed to be his wife anyway.

Toya quickly put his phone on silent so he wouldn't hear when she called back. Then she sent the picture to Nicole with the caption, "He's busy right now, bitch."

After sending the message, she erased it from his phone.

"Wake up, Mekco," Toya yelled as she shook him. "Mekco, you gotta get up and go. I don't want your wife tripping on me."

Mekco was half-asleep, but hearing her mention Nicole, he jumped up. He grabbed his phone from the coffee table in front of him, then dug into his pocket.

"Here you go, Toya. My bad. I've been drinking too much," he said as he gave her half of the stack of money. He had so much money on him that he didn't even notice she had taken anything.

"Thank you. I really appreciate it."

"You know it's whatever. I told you before just because we are not together, that doesn't mean I'm not gonna be in my child's life. So if you ever need anything, just let me know," Mekco said before walking out the door.

Mekco drove home without a care in the world. He was ready to go give his wife that drunk dick that she loved.

Nicole paced the bedroom floor and cried. She wanted him to walk through the door at that very moment so she could knock the shit out of him. She felt so stupid believing that he had changed for her.

"Man, why he gotta be so stupid? How could he do this to me?" she mumbled to herself.

She cried a little more, thinking about how she was gonna handle this situation. After a while, she finally dried her eyes and decided not to say anything to him but to play this little game with him.

Nicole looked at the message one last time. She was about to play his game and beat him at it. Nicole was determined not to cry about his sorry ass anymore. If anything, she was about to have the leader of the Brick Boyz crying.

Nicole climbed back into the bed as if nothing happened. She was gonna enjoy getting the last laugh.

Mekco walked through the door, stripped out of his clothes, and then approached the bedroom. Nicole was knocked out, and he knew how to wake her up.

He cuddled up behind Nicole and started rubbing her pussy through her panties. Nicole was really awake and felt sick to her stomach, knowing that he had just fucked Toya, and now he was trying to put his dirty dick inside of her. He didn't even smell like soap, so she knew he didn't even wash after digging all in that bitch pussy.

"Come on, Mekco, this baby is hurting me right now," she lied.

"Damn, Nicole, let me get just a little bit, baby," he begged.

Nicole wanted to remind him that he just had some pussy, but she held her tongue. She just kept telling herself that she was about to get revenge, and there wasn't no need for her to bust his head open right then.

"So, Mr. Miller, if you're not gonna be busy, I'm gonna need your help."

Pierre set the remote down on the coffee table. "What's up, E? What do you need?" he asked.

"As you know, Halloween is coming up, and the church has a trunk or treat. I want you to help with some of the games and take me to go get a couple of bags of candy for the kids."

Pierre laughed. "Are you fucking serious?"

Swaddling his lap, Erica kissed him on the lips.

"Yeah, baby. Plus, it's not just me. Other members of the church wanna see you too."

"Man, I already been to church with you every Sunday for the last two months. Do I really have to do this?"

"Yes, or I'm gonna be mad at you," Erica said, pouting.

Pierre couldn't believe how spoiled his soon-to-be wife was. Since she has been in his life, he found himself doing things he never thought he would ever do.

"I'm telling you this now, I'm not scared of your spoiled ass, and I'm not scared to tell you no. You lucky I actually like going to church and being around those folks. Just tell me when we need to go get the stuff."

Erica laughed before kissing Pierre again. "Thanks, baby. I swear you are my Superman."

At first, Pastor Collins tried his hardest to ignore Pierre stepping foot inside his church, but after a couple of weeks of seeing his face, he became proud. He had to give Pierre the credit that he deserved. Not only was he impressed, but the rest of the church members were falling for his charm.

Pastor Collins was happy with the positive feedback he received about Pierre. It turns out that he was very helpful and kind to everyone.

He even thought about giving him a second chance. Maybe he was too fast to judge him when he didn't ever try to get to know him.

Erica and Pierre spent the next three days discussing what games they could play with the kids and exactly how much candy they were gonna buy. Erica wasn't a big candy eater, but Pierre was, so she turned down everything that he said. When it was all said and done, they still ended up with a trunk and backseat full of candy.

It was no surprise to the pastor when Erica showed up at the church with Pierre by her side. The pastor watched as Pierre helped her take a seat at one of the tables in the basement before he left the building.

Walking outside to see where his future son-in-law was heading, the pastor was pleased to see him pull out a few big bags from Walmart with treats for the kids. With a smile, he walked over toward Pierre's car.

"Hey, do you need some help?" he asked.

Pierre turned around to find his father-in-law. It surprised him that he didn't try to attack him in the back of the head or some crazy shit like that.

Instead of being an asshole, Pierre popped the trunk. "Yeah, I could use some help. That will save me the trip of coming back out here in this cold."

Once again, the pastor was impressed. The trunk was filled with cases of water, juices, and pops.

"You know, I'm feeling like I owe you an apology. You have shown me that you are not the person I thought you were. So far, you have been an OK guy for my daughter."

Pierre hesitated to respond at first, not because he didn't appreciate those words but because he was shocked that the pastor could actually say nice words to him. He was surprised but responded to keep the peace between them.

"Thank you, sir. I really appreciate it. To be honest, you raised a wonderful young lady. Erica came into my life and changed my way of living."

It took Pierre and his new friend, the pastor, three trips to bring everything into the church basement.

"OK, everyone, I would like to thank you all for showing up and helping get this basement prepared for the children. Trunk or treat will be a success. We still have a few hours to get everything together."

Since it was so cold outside, they decided to make the children goody bags full of snacks. Erica and Theresa worked with Sister Diana to make sure each child had a nice-size bag.

Pastor Collins called Pierre into his office. Seeing that they had just bonded, Pierre didn't have a problem stepping inside the big man's office.

"What's up?" Pierre let flow out of his mouth before he could remember who he was actually talking to.

"My bad. How can I help you, sir?"

"I wanted to get in your business and ask you a few questions. Is that all right with you?"` Pastor Collins asked, hoping the young man wasn't gonna trip on him.

Pierre looked at him as if he had lost his damn mind. They had just bonded, and he was already about to be on that bullshit, Pierre thought.

Erica always told him how bipolar her dad could be.

"Sir, with all due respect, I believe my business is just that . . . *my* business. If it's not concerning your daughter, then we really don't have anything to discuss."

Pastor Collins sat up in his chair. "Well, it does have a lot to do with my daughter. I was just wondering when you were planning on marrying her. I hate for a guy to drag on an engagement for a long time, just stringing a woman along."

Pierre shook his head, but he wasn't about to let this man fuck up his night. "Look, to be honest, I'm not stringing her along. I love her, and we just started talking about dates for our wedding."

"Pierre, I really don't want any problems with you. I was just asking because I wanted to do the honor of walking my baby down the aisle and pay for the wedding," Pastor admitted.

Pierre smiled. "I'm glad you are coming around, Pastor. I was trying to make a closer date, but your daughter kept pushing it back. I know that she would love for you to walk her down the aisle, which was why she didn't agree on a date for the wedding. She was giving us enough time to get our relationship together."

Pastor Collins smiled. "I'm glad we could talk about this. And I just want you to know I'm here to support you guys."

Pierre stood up and reached out to give the pastor a handshake, but the pastor pulled him in, giving him a tight hug. Pierre knew that was a sign that he had finally won over the pastor.

After releasing him, he said, "We family now. We don't do that handshake stuff. We hug over here and show love."

Pierre laughed a little before they walked out of the office.

While stuffing the candy bags with goodies, Erica made it her business to keep looking at her dad's office door. She wasn't sure what was happening, but she was scared that they were gonna start arguing and fighting each other.

Seeing them walk out smiling, like they were actually getting along, was a surprise. The weight of the world had lifted off her shoulders as she witnessed for the first time them hitting it off.

Pierre walked over to where she was sitting. "What's up, baby? What you need me to do?"

"I put the order in for the pizzas, and we're almost done, so you can just chill for a minute."

Pierre and Erica made it back home by 10:00 p.m. They were both tired but happy because the kids had a good time.

Pierre found himself enjoying the little activities at the church, from doing events with the kids to feeding the community. He knew that if his mom were alive, she would have been proud of him.

On a couple of Sundays, he even beat Erica waking up for church. Pierre really was changing for her, and he couldn't find a reason to complain about it. It was crazy how love could change your whole life around.

Chapter 11

"Good morning, my loving wife. Why the hell you up so early?" Mekco asked.

Nicole was still pissed, but something in her wouldn't let her cry over him anymore. "I was up thinking about going to see my mom today. You know, I haven't seen her since before we went to Vegas, and that's been a minute."

"Yeah, OK. You go ahead and do you. I'm about to take my ass back to sleep. I got a fucking headache outta this world."

Nicole looked at Mekco and didn't like what she was seeing. Lately, she couldn't stand to look at him without thinking about that night when he came home and had just got done fucking Toya's rat ass.

She was slowly starting to hate him. Even though it had been a good two weeks ago, she still couldn't shake what he had done. All that talking about how he changed was for the birds. But it was all good. She had a plan of her own.

Mekco rolled back over without even noticing that his wife was about to be his worst enemy.

Nicole had once tried to kill herself over him, and now, she wanted to kill him. She hurried to get dressed because she couldn't wait for her day to begin.

She arrived at her mom's house and wasn't surprised she wasn't even there. Nicole felt foolish about not bothering to call before driving over there. She pulled out her phone to give her a call.

"Hey, Ma, where you at?" she asked.

"Girl, what do you want? I thought you don't mess with me since you're somebody's wife now," Theresa said, trying to be funny.

Awhile back, Nicole had become sick and tired of Mekco's shit and him putting his hands on her. She ran to her mom and ran her mouth 'bout his ways. Since then, Theresa stopped dealing with Mekco and was pissed off that her daughter was stupid enough to not only run back to him but to actually marry his no-good ass.

Nicole had built that fence between her mom and her husband, but now, she wanted her mom to forget everything she had told her. Theresa wasn't having that shit and wasn't about to kiss their ass.

"Ma, I'm at your house. Where are you?"

"I'm out with Eric. What can I help you with today?"

Nicole smacked her lips. "Ma, why you gotta be like that? I'm still your daughter, or have you forgot that?"

"Nicole, what do you want? You been acting real funny toward me since you ran off to get married, so please don't think I'm about to kiss your butt."

Nicole wasn't too quick to respond because her mom was right. She had been very disrespectful toward her lately. When she got back from Vegas, they had got into an argument, and she had told her mom that she wasn't fucking with her anymore. She also told her mom that she didn't need her in her life, that all she needed was Mekco and their baby.

Now that Mekco had hurt her, she wanted her mom to hold her and tell her that everything was gonna be OK. Nicole held the phone, crying. She knew that she had fucked up her relationship with her mom, and there was a chance that it was too late to get it back right.

"Ma, I'm sorry. I just need someone to talk to right now. Can I come back to see you later?" Nicole asked.

Theresa could hear the pain in her voice, but she, for once, was tired of her daughter's bipolar ways.

"Look, Nicole, when I get home, I'll call you."

Nicole hung up the phone. She was mad, but at the end of the day, she couldn't blame anyone but herself.

Feeling overwhelmed and emotional, Nicole only had one place to escape. Being back with Mekco and chilling at his house, she had forgotten all about her place. It was a good thing that she had taken some of Mekco's money out of his safe and paid her rent up for a few months.

After getting comfortable on the couch in front of the TV, Nicole tried to clear her mind with a nap, but that didn't work with her phone going off.

"Hey, what's up, Mercedes?"

"Hey, sexy, why you sounding so sad? What's going on with you?" Mercedes questioned.

Nicole sat up as she felt her tears build up. She hated herself for even crying over Mekco again, but she was hurt. She cried into the phone, "I'm just so tired of all this bullshit. I'm tired of crying over his no-good ass."

Mercedes rolled her eyes. She couldn't help but get pissed as she heard Nicole cry over that dog she got for a husband.

"Damn, girl, what did he do now?" she asked, trying to be supportive of her friend.

Nicole was so caught up in her feelings that she couldn't stop crying. She loved him so much that she hated him. "He's back messing with this bitch named Toya. He had promised me that he wasn't dealing with her anymore, and I found out he was still fucking her," Nicole cried out.

Mercedes shook her head; she hated that Nicole was crying over her dog of a husband. She hated how he played her but took this situation to build up her relationship with Nicole.

"I'm so sorry you hurting like that, Nicole. Come on, baby, just calm down, and we can talk like we been doing."

After a few minutes, Nicole finally stopped crying. She was able to calm herself down. She liked that Mercedes was there whenever she got in her feelings.

"*Woo*," Nicole said, wiping away the tears that were left around her eyes.

Both girls let out a little laugh. Then they sat on the phone discussing their feelings about Mekco and their being with each other.

"Nicole, I tell you this all the time, you are too beautiful to be sitting up crying over a no-good nigga. Baby girl, you can do much better," Mercedes said.

Nicole listened to the advice that Mercedes was giving her. She had to admit that what she was saying was true, and maybe it was time for her to look for love somewhere else. At the end of the conversation, Nicole concluded that Mekco was not about to be her final answer to love.

After getting off the phone with Mercedes, Nicole lay down again on the couch, thinking about what Mercedes said. Before they got off the phone, Mercedes told Nicole that if she wanted her to, she would come to Detroit just to be on her support team.

Mercedes actually had Nicole thinking about just letting her come. She could always stay at Nicole's house. That way, she wouldn't worry about paying for a hotel room.

The thought ran through her head, and before she dozed off, she decided that she was gonna call her back later and tell her to come be with her in Detroit.

It was a good thing that she kept her place.

***

Erica walked around the grocery store, trying to make sure she had everything that she needed for Thanksgiving. Once again, her father's church was feeding the neighborhood, and she and Pierre were out shopping for the event.

Pierre met up with Erica in the fruits and vegetables section of the store. His basket was full of hams and turkeys.

"Dang, baby, that's a lot of meat."

"Well, your dad asked me if I could get a little extra just in case we get more families to feed this year. I'm just following orders," Pierre said with a smile.

"Baby, I appreciate you helping out, but you do know that other people are gonna bring food too, right? You really don't have to try to do everything on your own," Erica explained.

Pierre felt what she was saying, but truthfully, he had a lot of money that he didn't know how to spend, so he had no problem helping the next person out.

"Baby, ain't nothing wrong with having extra," he replied.

After leaving the market, the couple went home. Pierre brought all the groceries into the house. It was a good thing that he had a deep freezer for everything.

As they got comfortable on the couch, Erica began thinking about some stuff to help Pierre out.

"Baby, I was just thinking about something you told me awhile ago."

"What's that?"

"Do you remember telling me that you needed something to do to keep you busy and out of trouble?" Erica asked her future husband.

Pierre sat there playing in her hair, thinking about what she was saying. It took him a second 'cause he always talked to her about everything.

Mekco was his boy, but Erica had become his best friend. He confided in her about everything under the sun, and not once did she give him any bad advice.

He figured out from the beginning that Erica was really his true soul mate.

"Yeah, baby, I remember. Why, what's up, my love?" Pierre asked, curious to see where she was going with her questions.

"I was just thinking about how you act when dealing with the church. I think you should open up your own center for the kids. It could be a place where they could go after school to have fun or do their homework. You could provide meals and snacks. Then during the summer, you could open up every day and just make sure they have fun."

Pierre listened to his future wife run her mouth. She went on and on about this center. He couldn't lie; she had everything thought out.

He couldn't help but smile at her. She was so fucking brilliant, and he was actually considering doing this center thing. Erica had made things sound good.

"Damn, baby, I love that idea. I wish you had mentioned something earlier in the year before it got too cold outside. I hate that I'm gonna have to find the perfect building with the right-size yard when it's cold outside. We need to make sure they can play baseball indoors and outdoors. Plus, a football field is a must."

Erica placed a kiss on Pierre's lips. She was happy that he liked her idea, but it didn't surprise her, not one bit. She knew kids were his soft spot, and her idea was right up his alley to help the children.

Nicole finally woke up from her nap to see that Mekco had called her five times, and Mercedes had texted her twice. She wasn't in the mood to deal with anyone at that moment.

Mekco had her all the way fucked up, walking around like everything was OK, and he had really changed since they had got married.

He would come home early to spend time with her some days. The way Nicole looked at it now was that he was trying to get her all buttered up so she wouldn't think he was back to his old ways.

Nicole felt stupid and betrayed by his actions but promised she was done crying over him.

Now with Mercedes, it was a whole different story. She was talking a good game, and Nicole was wide open.

Over a short period of time, Nicole and Mercedes talked or texted on the phone every day. Nicole discovered that Mercedes was everything that she needed in her life at that moment.

When it boiled down to it, the only problem Nicole saw was that Mercedes was a female. For once in her life, Nicole actually cared about what the next person thought about her.

Nicole lay there rubbing her stomach. She hadn't eaten all day, and it had started to growl loudly. She climbed out of bed to get dressed. She didn't feel like going to get anything, but she hadn't been there in over a month and knew everything in the kitchen was old. Besides, Taco Bell was calling her name, and she was craving some tacos and cheese fries.

As Nicole jumped into the car, her phone rang. She looked down and saw that it was Mercedes.

"What's up?" Nicole asked.

"Hey, baby, I was just checking on you. I know you were feeling down and shit," Mercedes explained.

Nicole smiled. "I'm OK for now. I took a much-needed nap, and now, I'm about to go get me something to eat.

My stomach is rumbling, and I need to feed this damn baby."

"All right. Call me once you return to the house if you feel like it."

Before Mercedes could hang up the phone, Nicole called out for her to wait a minute. "Hold on, Mercedes. I was thinking about what we were talking about earlier. I would love for you to come to Detroit. I could really use a friend right now."

Mercedes was now grinning from ear to ear. Since the first time Mercedes saw Nicole, she wanted her for herself.

Mekco, being a dog, hitting on her, and then suggesting a threesome, was just what she wanted to get close to Nicole. After all that time of talking and texting, she finally got Nicole to remove that wall she had built around her heart.

"Damn, baby, are you for real? You really want me to come be with you?" Mercedes questioned.

She was excited to hear that Nicole was finally seeing things her way. She was pregnant and needed someone to be beside her since Mekco wasn't doing her right.

Nicole began to drive away from her place. "Yeah, I'm serious, but I'll talk to you about everything later."

The two got off the phone feeling happy about what was to come of their relationship.

"Damn, I'm so confused right now. I want that perfect family with a husband and kids, but I want to be loved and happy at the same time. Right now, Mekco's not playing his part, and Mercedes is talking right. Man, why she can't be a man?"

Nicole went on and on talking to herself and trying to clearly understand what exactly she was doing with her life.

It was crazy how, after all this time, she finally had what she thought was the perfect family; you know, the giant house, multiple cars in the driveway, million-dollar rings on their fingers, and now a baby on the way. But now she had to deal with her husband, who decided to fuck up her happy dream by fucking with bigheaded sluts like Toya. It was bad enough that the bitch was pregnant, and she was willing to deal with that, but for him to still be creeping, she just couldn't do it. She felt like that night that they had run into Toya at the bowling alley was a big setup to keep her thinking it was all about them and their marriage.

Nicole felt played, and now that she was done crying, she was ready to play his game.

"Damn, E, I swear it gots to be something else you wanna eat besides this shit. You know you're not a fucking Mexican, right?" Pierre teased as they pulled up to Taco Bell.

Erica loved tacos, but now, with these babies, she eats them even more. During the very beginning of her pregnancy, her emotions were all over the place, and she used to cry about his jokes, but now, all she did was laugh at his jokes.

"Whatever, Pierre. You know this all your babies crave."

Pierre laughed as he opened her door and helped her out of the car. "That's only because they already been brainwashed by your ass."

The couple walked into the fast-food restaurant, holding hands and laughing. As they stood in line, Pierre looked over the menu. He had eaten so many tacos fucking with Erica's ass, he was trying to see if they had anything new that he hadn't tried yet.

They weren't in line long before they placed their order and took a seat. As Erica ate her food, Pierre watched Nicole walk through the door.

At first, she didn't see them, but after getting in line, she saw Pierre and Erica sitting down and eating. She looked at him but didn't bother to speak.

Pierre didn't give a fuck about her not speaking. He just knew she was a no-good, sneaky bitch, and he had to watch her ass.

Mekco was his bro, but Pierre wouldn't hesitate to put her ass to sleep if she ever wanted to test his girl.

Erica noticed that Pierre was no longer eating, and his attention was on something behind her. She slowly turned her head to see what or who had his attention.

Turning around in her seat, she wasn't surprised to see Nicole standing in line. Tacos had always been their favorite thing. Seeing Nicole had brought back memories of when they were friends. It was jacked up how jealousy could mess up a friendship that started when they were two years old. That made Erica question if they were ever really friends. Maybe Nicole was faking it all those years, she thought to herself.

Erica giggled to herself as she thought about how foolish she was being. There wasn't no way whatever they shared was fake.

"What you over there giggling about?" Pierre asked.

Erica turned back around in her seat. "Nothing, baby, nothing at all."

Nicole got her food, then walked to an empty table near her ex-best friend's table. She was gonna leave but thought she'll be a bitch and stay. She thought she was gonna make Erica get in her feelings.

Pierre noticed how Erica's body language had changed, and he didn't like how she could let a bitch like Nicole bother her.

"Aye, you need to chill out because we not about to leave just because she in this muthafucka. Fuck her if she wanna be a bitch toward you," Pierre said, trying to make his future wife feel better.

"I'm good, baby. I'm not even paying the dumb ho any attention."

Pierre couldn't hold his laugh in. "E, you be around me too much, ma. You don't even sound right cussing. You better stop that shit before your pops start tripping on me again."

Erica laughed. "Whatever. My dad loves you now. He finally sees you how I see you."

"Hell nah, E. I wouldn't say all that. I don't want him seeing me how you see me 'cause I know every time you look at me, you thinking about how good I look, and I don't need your dad thinking like that."

Erica was really cracking up now. "Boy, I swear you are crazy."

Nicole was pissed at herself. She thought she was doing something by staying inside the restaurant, but all she did was witness true love. She knew what Erica and P had was true love, and she was walking around with a rock on her finger just so a nigga could keep her on lock. The sad part about it was that she knew what she was getting herself into before she said I do.

The sight of seeing them together made her sick to her stomach, and she no longer had an appetite. Nicole jumped up from the table and threw her tray away before storming out the door.

Chapter 12

A couple of weeks had passed, and it was finally Thanksgiving. Theresa had invited everyone to her house for dinner.

Well, it was gonna be an early dinner because she wanted to go to the church to help the other volunteers.

Theresa had put her pride aside and invited Nicole and her son-in-law. However, she wasn't sure if they were coming.

Eric, Erica, and Pierre had arrived on time, ready to eat.

"I guess we waited long enough for my daughter and her husband to arrive. Let's say our grace, then dig in," Theresa suggested as everyone gathered around the table.

"Everything looks so good. I can't wait to eat," Erica said, looking at the food.

Theresa smiled. "Thank you, baby, and make sure you eat enough for you and those twins."

Everyone held hands as the pastor led them in prayers. Once he was done, everyone said Amen, then took a seat.

They all made their plate and started to eat. Just like Erica imagined, everything on the table was tasty.

While they were in deep conversation, nobody noticed that Nicole and Mekco had finally walked in.

"Look at this bullshit here. Y'all eating and shit. Just fuck me, right?" Nicole said loudly, interrupting the conversation at the table.

Theresa stood up, very upset. "Girl, watch your mouth when you walk into my house. When I invited you to dinner, I told you what time we were gonna start. Everybody not living on *your* time, little girl."

Nicole felt stupid and embarrassed. She wasn't expecting her mother to stand up to her.

Theresa took her seat again. "Now, you guys can have a seat and eat."

Nicole stood there for a minute, thinking about what she was gonna say next. She was pissed off that her mom had embarrassed her in front of the company. For some strange reason, she thought she was gonna walk into the house and be a bitch without anyone saying shit.

She smacked her lips before responding. "Nah, we good on that. I see you already got my replacement," she said, looking over at Erica and Pierre.

Nicole was being petty because she already knew why her mom didn't mess with Mekco anymore.

Pierre stood up from the table, ready to go off on Nicole. He didn't give two fucks if her nigga was right there.

Before he could say anything, Erica placed her hand on his, which made him look down at her. "Baby, finish eating so we can go to church."

Pierre took his seat again but couldn't help but stare a hole through Nicole.

Mekco stood there, not saying a word. It was evident that he was drunk and high. He finally spoke up. "Baby, stop tripping. Let's sit down and eat. We ain't come over to mess up the holiday."

"Fuck that, Mekco. I'm ready to go. Come on!" Nicole yelled.

Mekco pushed his chair back in. "Thanks for the invite. Sorry we can't stay."

No one said anything else. Instead, they all continued to eat.

Theresa was still a little upset and excused herself from the table. It was only a short second before Eric followed behind her.

While they were in the back room talking, Pierre kissed Erica. "Aye, baby, are you OK?"

"Yeah, baby, I'm good. I told you before that Nicole's little bitchy ways don't bother me anymore. I mean, we have been friends since forever, and it was fun while it lasted. Anyway, I don't need her, baby. You are my best friend."

Pierre smiled, hearing her say that. "You been my best friend since day one, baby, and I'm serious as fuck, E."

Pierre placed a gentle kiss on Erica's full lips. It wasn't long before they were sucking on each other's tongue.

"Not at the table, you two. Save that for the wedding," Pastor Eric said as he walked back into the dining room.

"Sorry about that, Dad. Is Theresa OK?" Erica asked, trying to change the subject.

"Yeah, she'll be OK. She really just needs to learn how not to let that disrespectful daughter of hers get under her skin."

Just then, Theresa walked back into the room. You could tell that she had been crying from the puffy red eyes she was now wearing.

Erica felt bad for her because she was a sweet woman and didn't deserve to be dogged out. She said, "Since we all are done, I'll start putting up the food and cleaning the dishes."

"No, baby, you go ahead and relax. You don't need to be doing all that while you are carrying those twins," Theresa said as she started collecting dishes from the table.

Erica stood up anyway. "I'm OK. I need to work off some of that food anyway."

Pierre then stood up. "Since you cooked all this good food, we'll clean up."

Theresa took her seat next to the pastor. She wasn't about to make anyone beg to clean up. She wasn't a fool.

Pierre and Erica tackled the kitchen the way they did at home, and it didn't take them long to finish. Then everyone grabbed their coats and headed to the church.

Mekco and Nicole returned to his crib on Coney Island. "It's a damn shame you don't know how to fucking act, and we gotta eat this bullshit for the holiday."

"Whatever, nigga. I'm not about to kiss nobody ass for a fucking plate. Fuck them, and if you wanna go against me, fuck your community-dick-having-ass too."

Mekco looked at Nicole like she had lost her fucking mind. He had been good to her since they married, but it seemed like she wanted to constantly argue and fight with him.

"Come on, Nicole, it's the fucking holiday. Sit your ass down somewhere. I don't understand why the fuck you always tripping and acting an ass," Mekco yelled.

Nicole took a seat on the same couch as him. She tried to calm herself down because she was still mad at him from that picture that Toya had sent her, but she couldn't let that slip out, or her plan was gonna fail.

She picked up the remote and cut on the TV to prevent herself from saying anything else. As she ate her food, she laughed at what she was watching and didn't pay Mekco any more attention.

Mekco sat there watching her. He could really see now that she was bat-shit crazy. He actually thought that maybe he should have let her ass get that abortion and left her ass the fuck alone.

Here he was giving her everything that she asked for, and she was doing the fucking most.

Mekco had left every one of his hoes alone to prove to her that he could be faithful and only love her. He couldn't believe how he begged her to be with him and to give him another chance so that she could start acting like a fucking psycho.

As he thought about it, she was always crazy, but since she was giving up that good pussy, he overlooked it.

Mekco hated how she was acting now. Nicole had even quit attending church once she and her mom argued about them running off to get married. Then her falling out with Erica was just crazy.

Erica did what any human would have done in that situation.

Mekco wasn't sure if it was the baby that had her tripping or if it was the fact that she couldn't smoke or drink anymore.

Mekco had one last trick up his sleeve to get her to act right.

"Baby, I see you stressed like a muthafucka. Get up and take that shit off. You ain't let me beat that shit up in a minute. You know I got what your nutty ass need," he ordered.

"Nah, nigga, I'm good on that."

Mekco stood up, then pulled her up by her shirt. "Don't fucking play with me, girl. Get your ass in the room."

Nicole hated how she always gave in to Mekco's dick. She did try to turn him down like she said she would, but it was hard, especially when he got hard.

She loved when he called out demands and let it be known that he was in charge. She stood there trying to act like she wasn't turned on, but he knew better.

Mekco knew precisely what he was doing when he stared her in the eyes, biting on his bottom lip, all while undressing.

Nicole slowly started to undress.

She was so turned on that about the time she was only left with her panties on, they were already soaking wet. Mekco had that type of effect on hoes.

Nicole slowly started walking backward toward the room, and Mekco followed. She was mesmerized by the pole that was eager to enter her.

Mekco was ready for her juices to overflow on his dick. He couldn't even wait for them to enter the room. Right before they got to the bedroom door, he ended up picking her up in the hallway and slammed his dick into her wetness.

"Oh my Gawd, Mekco," Nicole moaned out as he entered, then exited her pussy.

Mekco picked up his pace with every stroke that he gave her. Nicole was in heaven and couldn't control the shaking that her legs were doing, wrapped around his waist.

It had been awhile since they had fucked, so it ended early. Nicole didn't complain about it because even though it was short, Mekco still packed a lot of power.

Still holding Nicole up on the wall, Mekco carried her to the bedroom, then tossed her onto the bed. Nicole peeked at his dick to see what was up, and Mekco caught her.

"Hell yeah, he ready for round two," he said, laughing as he got right back hard.

After going at it for a total of three rounds, Mekco was finally knocked out.

Nicole usually would have been asleep too, but she had a lot on her mind. She felt weak for giving Mekco some pussy. Her mind replayed the conversation she had with Mercedes the day she returned to her place.

Once Nicole was done pouring out her heart and crying a fucking river, Mercedes sat on the phone listening and giving her some advice on how to keep her cool. By the end of their conversation, they had everything all set. Nicole was gonna stop giving up her pussy to Mekco and save it for when Mercedes came to Detroit to visit her.

Nicole had withheld sex for so long that her already-shitty attitude was at a hundred now.

Before dozing off, she decided to keep it to herself that she had given it up. Mercedes didn't need to know everything. Nicole just hoped that she wasn't on no bullshit when she came to Detroit.

Erica and Pierre enjoyed themselves, helping out at the church. It was a joy to see everyone happy and full.

After finally getting home, the couple couldn't wait to hit the sheets. They were tired and full, but at the end of the day, it was all worth it. Being blessed and being able to bless the next person was a good feeling.

Erica was enjoying her shower when she felt Pierre's body pressed behind hers. "Damn, baby, why the fuck you got this water so damn hot? Fuck you trying to do, boil my babies?"

"Oh my Gawd, boy, you so stupid, and it's not even that hot," Erica said, laughing at him.

Pierre stepped back a little to give Erica enough room to add colder water.

"Are you happy now, baby?"

"Hell yeah. You be trying to kill a nigga in this fucking bathroom."

Erica giggled. "Ain't nobody tell you to get in here with me in the first place. You always sneaking in the shower with me just to complain."

Rubbing all over Erica's soapy body, Pierre grabbed a handful of his fiancée's ass. "Girl, you tripping the fuck out right now. All this good shit belongs to me, and it's my job to make sure that you clean it the right way."

Erica was really laughing now.

Since the first day she met Pierre at the club, she loved how he made her smile and laugh. There was never a dull moment when she was around him, which was all the time.

"I swear you're so silly, boy," Erica said as she turned to face him.

Pierre took that moment to steal a kiss from her. Erica was now more turned on than before. She wrapped her arms around Pierre's neck. It was her turn to get kisses from the man she loved unconditionally.

It wasn't long before Pierre had her back on the wall while he slowly entered her. He took his time moving in and out of her wetness.

Erica tried her hardest to control her composure, but his stroke game was out of this world. She wrapped her arms around his neck and buried her face into his shoulder. Pierre tried not to go too fast while making love to her, but her soft moans in his ear had him going crazy, and it wasn't long before he picked up his pace.

"Fuck," he mumbled as he released his seed into her wetness.

Erica was tired before, but after their little session in the shower, she was utterly worn out. She was so tired that she didn't even want to lift her head from his shoulder.

"Come on, E. I know you're tired, but let me clean you off so you can get some rest," Pierre said as he let her down.

He then began to wash her body using her Caress body wash and her pink loofah.

Once the soap was rinsed off their bodies and they dried off, they made their way into the bedroom. It was chilly that night, so Erica put on some nightclothes before jumping into bed with Pierre.

"Baby, you know that I love the fuck out of you, right?"

"Yes, Pierre, this is something I know," Erica said with a little laugh.

"I'm serious, E. That shit that li'l bitch tried to pull really pissed me the fuck off. I swear I would have knocked her fucking head off for jumping stupid."

"Pierre."

"E, I'm for real, man. I don't like that bitch. Truthfully, I never did. I was just tolerating her because I loved you," Pierre admitted.

Erica wasn't sure how she should feel or what to say behind what he just said. She never knew that he didn't like Nicole before they had fallen out.

"I know you're probably speechless, but I saw she was jealous of you. Everything y'all did together, she made it some competition. Like whenever y'all went out, she always tried to outdo you by making sure her dress was tighter or shorter. Then that bitch would pile all that fucking makeup on her face. The sad thing about it was that you always won in my eyes. You didn't even need makeup or anything extra. You got that good brown skin that always glows. You're the most beautiful woman in the world to me, and I put that on my mama."

Erica sat there with tears in her eyes. She never paid any attention to Nicole's ways, but now that he was saying all that, she finally saw it. Besides that whole Nicole stuff, hearing him tell her how much he loved her and how beautiful she was made her very emotional.

"You don't have to cry, E. I ain't say shit you shouldn't already know."

Even though she was teary-eyed, Erica smiled. Pierre was exactly what she needed in her life. Some people didn't believe in real love or love at first sight, but what they shared was something special.

Not many people could say that their first love would be their only love and be confident enough actually to believe it.

Erica cuddled up on Pierre's chest and fell fast asleep. Pierre placed a kiss on her forehead before he turned on the TV.

Pierre always stayed up to watch the news when she was asleep, and it was quiet. He couldn't believe how all these kids were being killed or out in the streets doing the killing. That's when he thought about the shit that Erica brought up. Maybe it was time for him to buy a building and open up that center for these kids.

Pierre was ready to move up his plans. These kids needed some guidance. He wanted better for them, even though it wasn't the path he chose for himself. However, this was his way of redeeming himself.

Chapter 13

Mercedes: I'm in Detroit now. Text me the address, baby.

Nicole read the text message that Mercedes had just sent her. She smiled as she grabbed her coat and prepared to walk out the door. She had her overnight bag already packed and in her trunk.

Mekco had already left, claiming that he had to meet Cross for some business, but she knew that was a lie because she had already gone through his phone the night before and saw that Toya had called and told him that she was in the hospital, threatening a miscarriage. They had just got finished fucking, so he wasn't man enough to leave right then. So, this morning, he jumped up and left.

Before driving off, Nicole texted Mercedes her address. After that, she drove off with a smile on her face.

All this time, she had been thinking she was happy being with a man, but now, she was thinking that maybe a chick could love her and make her even happier. She even thought about the fact that if she was gonna be in a serious relationship with a female, she was gonna have to give up what she loved the most, and that was dick, especially Mekco's thick, long dick.

When Mercedes arrived at the address, she didn't see Nicole waiting for her, so she stayed in the car. She could tell that she wasn't gonna like being in Detroit.

She was born and raised in Las Vegas, Nevada, so this cold weather was killing her. Cold in Vegas was around 80 degrees.

Mercedes pulled out her phone and dialed Nicole's number. After the third ring, Nicole finally picked up the phone.

"Hey, baby, I'm turning the corner now," Nicole said before even saying hello.

"I see you, baby. Come on, I'm freezing out here," Mercedes said before hanging up the phone.

Nicole and Mercedes walked into Nicole's crib. Mercedes had helped her grab the few bags of groceries she had in the backseat.

"Damn, girl, it's cold as fuck in here too. Don't tell me you don't have no heat," Mercedes said jokingly.

"Don't try to ho me like that. I really don't be here like that, so the heat wasn't on."

After putting up the groceries, Nicole went back into the living room, where Mercedes was lying on the couch butt naked, playing with her freshly shaved pussy.

Nicole knew what time it was and slowly started to undress in the doorway. This was the day she had been waiting for.

She was tired of all the phone sex with Mercedes and was ready for some tongue action.

Nicole walked over to the couch. With Mercedes guiding her, Nicole took a seat right on her face. Mercedes had no problem taking control.

Mercedes knew this lifestyle was new to Nicole, so it was easy to mold her into the female she needed her to be.

"Damn, Mercedes, that shit feels so fucking good," Nicole moaned out.

Mercedes was enjoying tasting Nicole, but like any horny ho, she was ready to get her juice box ate. So, Mercedes made Nicole get up and change positions after a while.

Nicole had the googly eyes, and Mercedes could tell her mind was gone. Mercedes could tell that Nicole was naïve and a sucka for love. All a muthafucka had to do was eat her pussy and show her some attention, and she was wide open.

After making what Nicole wanted to believe was love, the two women cuddled on the couch as if they were a couple and had been with each other since forever and a day.

Just as she did when Mekco made her come, Nicole went straight to sleep. Mercedes got up, grabbing her phone and bag from the love seat. She quickly went into the bathroom to shower and make that important phone call that she was supposed to make when she first touched down in Detroit.

Worried that Nicole would hear her on the phone, Mercedes turned on the shower to tune out her conversation.

"Hey, baby, I'm finally here," she said as she sat on the toilet.

The man on the phone didn't care to have the small chitchat, so he jumped straight into business mode.

"How long do you think it's gonna take to get that bread and return home?"

"Damn, nigga, give me a fucking day or so, and it should be all done. Have some faith in your girl," Mercedes said, trying to convince her boyfriend Rodney that she was on her job.

"Bitch, don't play with me. I know your ass, and I know you probably in Detroit sucking the piss out of that stupid bitch. Stop trying to make that bitch fall in love with you, for real, and bring that money home to daddy."

Mercedes had to catch herself from laughing too loud. "Baby, I gotta make her fall for me to get that dough for us. Let me handle this shit in Detroit, and you make sure all your little stupid bitches know that I'll be home in a few days so not to get too comfortable trying to play my role while I'm gone."

Without waiting for a response, she hung up on him.

Mercedes pulled out her Dove body wash and the loofah she had in her bag before jumping in the shower. As she rubbed the soapy loofah all over her body, she thought about the morning she came home from the room fucking with Nicole and Mekco.

She thought she was just making a few bucks, but when she told her boyfriend, Rodney, where she had been, instead of being mad at her like a normal person, he had put together a plan to get them even more money. Plus, he wanted to get revenge on that ho-ass nigga Mekco.

Mercedes knew she had to pull Nicole's dumb ass all the way in order for her plan to work. She wasn't worried about it because Nicole had already proved to her that she was gullible as fuck already.

Nicole didn't even know Mercedes's last name or anything about her other than she ate pussy well. Foolishly, Nicole was ready to leave her husband for her.

Right before Mercedes was about to hop out of the shower, Nicole jumped in.

Mercedes smiled like she was happy to see her, but in her head, she was thinking, *Damn, this bitch is clingy. I see why Mekco be getting the fuck on.*

"Dang, baby, why didn't you wake me up so I could join you?" Nicole asked while holding on to her from the back.

Lying straight through her teeth, Mercedes quickly answered, "You're so sexy when you sleep. I didn't wanna wake you."

Nicole smiled harder while placing small kisses on Mercedes's back.

Mercedes rolled her eyes as she allowed the warm water to hit her chest.

***

Mekco sat in the chair beside Toya's hospital bed. He was pissed. He tried to keep his cool with his face buried in his hands.

The nurse had just walked out of the room. Since he had been there, the nurse had been in three times, checking on Toya and the baby's heartbeat.

"Toya, I've been here all morning with you. When you gonna tell me what the fuck you was doing last night that got you laid up in this fucking hospital and these muthafuckas running in here every five minutes checking on my baby?"

Toya rolled her eyes at Mekco. She was tired of his mouth and wished she had never texted his ass. But she knew if he found out she was in the hospital and lost the baby, he was gonna fuck her up.

"Mekco, all that ain't important right now. Let's just worry about the baby."

He sat up in his seat for the first time since he got there. "I'm trying to be nice, but don't act like I won't fuck your ass up in here."

Toya knew it was time to speak out because Mekco never made a threat and didn't keep it. He was a man of his word. After taking a moment to get her story together, Toya tried to sit up a little in her bed.

"Man, keep your ass still before you knock that monitor off your belly."

"Look, Mekco, you not about to be in here talking to me like I'm your wife. You got me all the way fucked up."

Mekco couldn't help but to laugh at her silly ass. "Bitch, don't fucking play with me. You ain't gotta be my fucking wife for me to knock the shit outta your stupid ass. Now, get to talking," he ordered.

"OK, damn!" she yelled.

Mekco stared her straight in the eyes waiting to hear what the fuck she was about to say. He just hoped she didn't lie to him, or that was gonna be her ass.

"Look, it was my girl Tameka's birthday, and we went out. And before you ask, I wasn't smoking or drinking. You can ask the doctors when they come in," she hurried to say, trying not to piss him off.

"Fuck all that shit, what the fuck happened?"

Toya continued to tell her story. "Well, we were at our table talking, and Tameka's cousin Brianna asked me why I wasn't drinking. So I told her I was pregnant. Then Tameka started running her mouth, talking about me being pregnant by you."

Mekco felt it in his stomach that when his name was mentioned, that's when shit got wild. "Oh really?"

"Yeah, but anyway, the bitch Brianna started talking shit talking about how last year she used to fuck you and got pregnant, but you made her get an abortion."

Mekco couldn't even say shit. He knew who Brianna was. That crazy bitch had tried to fight him when he told her that she had to get an abortion. She scratched his face up before he pulled out his gun and stuck it in her mouth. He could understand why she would be mad to hear another bitch was carrying his seed.

"By me being pregnant, I knew I wasn't supposed to be fighting, and I swear I tried to just walk away from that bitch, but she kept walking up in my face talking big-time shit. The next thing I know, the bitch tried to sneak me, so I beat the bitch's ass."

"Man, that bitch out of control. I'm gonna go pay her ass a visit later today," Mekco said.

For the first time since he was there with her, he touched Toya's stomach. It wasn't that big, but he prayed that it was a little boy.

He prayed that both of his babies were boys because he knew he fucked over too many females in his life. He knew if a nigga fucked over his girls, he would have to bury a muthafucka.

"So, this whole thing is your fault that I'm in here because, while the bitch was on the ground getting her face stomped in, she made sure to kick me in my stomach," Toya pointed out to get the attention off her.

"Yeah, you're right, and I'm sorry about that. I'm gonna handle that bitch. You won't have to worry about that shit happening again," he assured her.

"I beat her ass already. That's good enough. Plus, we don't need that bitch trying to lock you up for anything. I need you to be out so you can help with this baby. There's already too many children without their fathers."

"Damn, girl, you right. I wasn't even thinking like that. My mind was on fucking her up."

Toya shook her head. "You have kids on the way. You better start using your brain."

Mekco didn't respond, but he knew she was right. He sat back in his chair, thinking about what Toya had just explained. She was absolutely right. He needed to live like he was about to bring some kids into this cruel world and not like he was out for himself.

Toya stared at Mekco while he stared at the ground. She couldn't lie. She still had feelings for him, even after all the shit he had put her through.

Now, she didn't feel bad for sending Nicole that picture. She really was hoping and praying that Nicole would have got mad and left his ass, so she could slide right in and replace that bitch.

Toya knew how Mekco had a bad temper and was quick to express his feelings with his hands. It bothered her about how he had been up there all morning and ain't fucked her up or even cussed her ass out yet. That wasn't like him. Then she thought that maybe Nicole didn't say shit 'cause she was waiting to catch her somewhere and try to fight her. She smiled as she pictured herself beating Nicole's ass.

"Fuck you over there smiling at?" Mekco asked, knocking her out of her little daydream.

"Nothing, baby. I just was listening to the baby's heartbeat. It's so refreshing, and I feel so grateful that our baby is OK," Toya admitted to the guy she loved but knew was off-limits.

Toya did wonder why he hadn't gone off on her yet for sending that picture. Knowing how he got down, she told herself that either he was waiting for her to leave the hospital or maybe Nicole never said anything and was waiting to catch her ass outside somewhere.

Mekco sat there in his thoughts. He realized that he really wasn't shit. He played with both girls' hearts. Now, both were carrying his baby.

It hurt him to say it, but he was just like his dad . . . scared of commitment.

Just as Mekco was about to get up to leave, the nurse returned to the room. "I have good news for you, Ms. Morris. The doctors don't see any reason why they need to keep you any longer. Your vitals are good, and the baby is no longer in harm. The baby's heartbeat is strong, and everything else is good. We have your discharge papers coming."

Toya was happy; she hated lying up in bed all day. "OK, thanks."

"Someone gonna come in to unhook you from all this, and then you can get dressed and head home," the young nurse said before walking out of the room.

"Damn, I was about to bounce, but I guess I'll wait so I can take you home."

"You can go ahead and enjoy the rest of your day. I have a ride," Toya said as she continued to text on her phone.

Mekco noticed the change in her body language and wondered what the fuck she was up to. "You sure, Toya?" he asked.

"Yeah, Mekco, I have a ride," she finally said, putting down the phone.

Mekco stood up from the chair and began to walk toward the door. He had his own plan. One thing he didn't like was a sneaky ho.

"Call me later," he said as he walked out the door. Mekco knew Toya was up to no good, and that day, he had time to play with her ass.

Instead of leaving, Mekco went to the end of the hallway to the waiting area and just watched Toya's room. He saw someone come in to unhook her. Next, the doctor came in to give her the discharge papers.

So far, everything was going OK, but he stayed around to see if she was just as sneaky as he thought.

Fifteen minutes passed, and Mekco was tired of waiting. He didn't know why he thought he had the patience to sit and chill like that. As he stood up to really leave, he saw a nigga that he recognized from the hood walk into Toya's room. He shook his head as he crept back to her room.

"Damn, baby, I'm glad you and my shorty OK. I just wished you would have called me a little earlier. You know I would have been here before now," he heard the guy say.

"Daddy, I didn't want to scare you. I know how much you would have been worried about us. We OK, and I have my paperwork to leave."

Mekco stood in the doorway with a smile on his face. This bitch was lying about everything, trying to fuck up his life when he wasn't even the damn daddy.

Toya and Marcus finished their kiss. When Toya looked up and saw Mekco standing there, her jaw dropped, and she saw that Mekco hadn't really left, and she was now busted.

Marcus didn't know what was going on, so he spoke up. "Is there something we can help you with?"

Toya knew how wild Mekco could be, so she quickly tried to speak up before he showed his ass. "Umm, Marcus . . ."

Mekco knew he could have used this moment to expose her rat ass and go the fuck off, but for once in his life, he decided just to let the shit roll. Before Toya could finish whatever bullshit she was about to say, Mekco interrupted her. "My bad nigga, I got the wrong room."

Just like that, he walked away.

Toya was happy he didn't flip the fuck out, but at the same time, she was mad that she was really in love with a broke nigga, and her money train had just walked out of her life.

Mekco jumped into the car, happy as fuck. He had just dodged that fucking bullet. He was so happy that he wanted to call his wife and tell her the good news. He even thought about taking her on another trip. As he pulled his cell phone out and dialed her number, he watched as Toya and her lame-ass nigga walked to his car. He could tell that Marcus was in love, and she was feeling salty as fuck.

After not getting an answer for the third time, he drove off, clueless about where Nicole could be.

"Damn, baby, tell that nigga that you're mine now, and he need to stop calling you so much," Mercedes said as they watched his name pop up on her phone again.

Nicole giggled. "I wanna be far away from him when I let him know that I'm not fucking with him anymore."

Mercedes wasn't planning on staying around forever and knew she needed to speed things up. She was about to jump into action.

"Far away, baby? How far you trying to go 'cause I'm down for traveling."

"I'm not sure yet. How about we go back to Vegas?" Nicole suggested.

"Girl, if we gonna get the fuck on, we not about to be in Vegas. I was born and raised there. I wanna see something else."

"OK, baby, I'm looking at it your way, and I see what you talking about."

Mercedes rolled on her side and gave Nicole a kiss to pull her in even more.

"While we talking about bouncing, where we gonna get the dough to sponsor our new future together?"

Nicole took a second to think their plan through. How the fuck was she gonna raise a baby and move out of state with only $7,548 in her bank account?

Had she known that one day she would stop fucking with Mekco for real, she would have been saving money.

"Look, I only have a couple thousand dollars, and I'm not sure how far that would take us."

Mercedes took a mental note of everything Nicole was saying. She wanted to make sure she didn't fuck up their plan, meaning hers and Rodney's.

"Damn, I guess we're in the same boat. Shit, we ain't gonna make it far."

Nicole turned around so that her back was toward Mercedes. She was feeling down 'cause she wasn't sure how she was gonna be with Mercedes in Detroit without Mekco killing both of their asses. She felt trapped.

Mercedes shook her head behind Nicole's back. She was tired of this bitch already. She loved the way her pussy tasted and how soft her skin felt, but she was a li'l too slow for her.

Mercedes was about to see just how slow she really was. "I have an idea, but I need you to think about this shit. It has to be planned out just right."

Nicole turned back around. "What you have in mind, baby?"

"Your husband got some dough lying around the crib. Snatch that shit up, and we'll be good."

Nicole thought about how Mekco had the safe in his office and that she knew the combination. But her smile quickly became a frown as she pictured Mekco beating her ass and then killing her if she was ever to get caught.

"Bitch, he would kill me, you, and this baby. Are you fucking crazy?"

Mercedes saw she was scared, but she had to get that cash. She slowly started placing soft kisses on Nicole's face, neck, and chest.

"Baby, don't be scared. Once we get this bread, we're bouncing and never coming back. You don't have anything to worry about. This plan is flawless."

Nicole sat there looking worried, and Mercedes was trying not to get impatient with her. Mercedes climbed on top of Nicole and kissed her naked body, working her way down to her juicy center.

Mercedes knew what she was doing. She knew that if she made her feel like the only girl in the world, she would give in and do whatever she told her to do. It was crazy how she was using Nicole because her boyfriend told her to fuck her over and get Mekco's money, but she enjoyed pleasing Nicole.

Lying there with her feet to the ceiling and mouth wide open, Nicole was having the time of her life with Mercedes, but she wasn't sure about that shit Mercedes was talking about.

Mekco was a special kind of crazy, and she knew he would have either made sure her body was never found or sent her mother a different body piece every other month. It all depended on how he felt at that moment.

"Damn, baby, you get wet as fuck," Mercedes mumbled as she lay back down next to Nicole.

Nicole moved a little closer toward her and cuddled up like she would have done with Mekco.

"So, what we gonna do, Nicole? We can't stay here in the same city as your husband, and we don't have enough money to just bounce on our own."

"I understand that if I do this, we have to bounce right after I get the money. I know he would kill me and this baby if he caught me."

Mercedes felt bad 'cause she never planned on getting on a plane with Nicole. She was gonna leave that bitch high and dry. That was the only way she and Rodney could live a better life. Shaking her conscience away, Mercedes pretended to care.

"Baby, stop doubting yourself. You can do it. Didn't you say he was always drunk and shit? Snatch that shit when he gone or knocked out, and I'll be here waiting for you."

"OK, baby. When I leave tonight, I will get the money and return here as soon as I get it."

Mercedes smiled but quickly calmed down. "Damn, girl, I love you," she lied.

"I think I love you too," Nicole said with a big smile.

After sucking and licking on each other again, Nicole jumped in the shower and thought about how she was about to go home and fuck over the man that she thought she loved.

Mercedes was applying plenty of pressure to make sure she and Rodney would have the best future ever.

Mekco sat on the couch searching through the internet. He was looking for a special place to take his wife for

Christmas. Detroit was cold as fuck in the winter, so he was looking for a place where they could lie up on a beach with the sun shining in their faces. He knew Nicole would enjoy that too.

Nicole walked in the door, scared out of her mind. She had never gone against Mekco until she started dealing with Mercedes.

As Mekco sat on the couch, she walked in and sat on the love seat.

"What you been up to all day, baby?" Mekco asked.

"Chilling with my mom. You know we had to make up for old times."

"Baby, I got to talk to you about something. Last night, Toya texted me, letting me know that she was in the hospital and she was scared that the baby was harmed. So, this morning, I went to see what was up with them. Long story short, when I left, I ended up doubling back 'cause I forgot something, but anyway, that bitch's *real* baby daddy was in the room with her."

Nicole jumped up from her seat. "Are you fucking serious? I wanna beat that bitch's ass so fucking badly. I know you went off on that bitch, baby."

"To be honest, I didn't. When they noticed me standing behind them, I couldn't do shit but laugh and walk away."

"I'm glad you found out the truth because I was really hurt about you getting her pregnant. I really hated the thought of another bitch carrying your baby," Nicole admitted.

"Baby, I know, and I'm sorry for putting you through this shit. If I could change things, I would have never betrayed you like that. I felt bad about hurting you, and that's why when we got married, I was dead-ass serious about doing right by you. I've been a hundred percent faithful. I don't even entertain these hoes when I be out at the club. I was serious when I said from now on, it was all about us."

Nicole listened to Mekco and started to feel bad about what she had been up to. Then she started thinking about the picture that Toya's bitch ass had sent her, and she got pissed that Mekco was even playing in her face and lying about being faithful. He was still the same cheating-ass dog, and ain't shit change.

"Nicole, baby, I'm so sorry for hurting you, and I promise to do whatever to make things better between us. I wanted it to be a surprise, but I can't hold it in any longer. For Christmas, I wanted to take you on a trip somewhere out of the country just to show you how much I really love your ass."

Mekco watched Nicole's body language and could tell she wasn't impressed by his words. He needed her to realize he loved her and wanted his family to work.

Even though he was dead serious, she still took his words as a joke. Without saying anything, Nicole got up and walked to their bedroom. She was still tired from being with Mercedes and needed another nap.

Mekco sat on the couch, wondering what else he could do to improve things between them. He picked his phone up from the end table. Maybe his bro would be able to help him out.

Mekco was usually the ladies' man, but lately, he found himself turning to Pierre.

Mercedes grabbed her phone to call Rodney. She couldn't wait to share the good news with him.

"Hey, baby, what are you doing?" she asked.

"Shit, just came back to my room. I like these casinos in Detroit, baby. I won $400 at the tables."

"Yeah, yeah, yeah, enough of that shit. I just hit the jackpot, baby."

"What the fuck going on between you and that stupid bitch Nicole?" Rodney asked.

"Well, at first, she was scared to take Mekco's money, but I ate the dumb bitch's pussy and told her I loved her. Next thing I know, she was on her way to his house to get the money."

Rodney laughed at her story. "You told that bitch you loved her? Girl, you are fucking crazy for real."

"Baby, you said get that money by any means necessary. I'm just doing what you said to do. I still don't understand why you don't like that nigga Mekco," Mercedes said, hoping to get some answers.

"Look, just make sure that bitch got that bread for us, and let me deal with that nigga Mekco."

Rodney didn't give Mercedes a chance to respond. After hanging up in her face, he lay in bed and thought about why he really hated Mekco. From what he could remember from the stories he heard, his mom and Mekco's mom were pregnant by the same man.

Their dad was an original member of the Brick Boyz. He was a playa and didn't want to settle down with either. All he wanted was his kids. Mekco's mom let him grow up with his dad, and he became a Brick Boy and was making money at a young age. As far as Rodney's mom was concerned, she wasn't having that. She wouldn't let Rodney come over on the weekends or ever stay with them during the summer.

Once she got a new boyfriend, and he didn't like Rodney being a Brick Boy and making more money than him, he started complaining. Soon after, Rodney's mom moved them far away from Detroit.

Because of that, it had been years since the brothers had been together.

When Mercedes came home with $10,000 and bragged about her night, Rodney didn't even trip until she pulled out her phone and showed him a picture of the couple she got fucked by.

Growing up with his mom, they weren't living the good life like Mekco was. That one thing alone made Rodney hate his own brother for years. Now, finally, he was about to get the chance to live a good life like every other nigga.

Without telling her why he hated the guy, he devised a flawless plan that could benefit them both. For a few days straight, he talked Mercedes's ears off, repeating the plan to her repeatedly. He was determined to make sure she didn't fuck up anything, and they were gonna get the money that was due him.

Rodney got out of bed and walked over to the window. He then went to the dresser and pulled out a picture of his mom.

"Damn, Ma, I'm sorry you didn't make it long enough to enjoy this bread we about to get. Just know that I did this for you. I know you always wanted the best for me, and now I'm about to get it. I love you, Ma."

Rodney kissed the picture before placing it back on the dresser. His mother struggled to raise him and his siblings even though she was working two jobs. She had passed away eight years ago, and truth be told, she worked herself to death.

Rodney was now about to get the chance to live life the way he was supposed to.

Chapter 14

Pierre and Erica were just leaving the pastor's home. They got together for dinner and to talk about her wedding. Erica loved the man Pierre was becoming, even though she fell in love with the street guy. But she loved both sides equally. She also loved that her father was getting along with Pierre now, and it wasn't the fake stuff like before.

As they got into the car, Pierre's phone rang.

"What's up, bro?" Pierre said into his Bluetooth.

"I was thinking about taking the wife to Jamaica for Christmas, man. What the fuck you think about that?"

Pierre looked over toward Erica, who was in the passenger side, dozing off. He smiled as he thought about how she would be happy to wake up to a new scenery for a week or so.

"You know what, my nigga? I like that idea. I might have to bite off that idea. I know Erica would love that shit," Pierre said, taking a quick look at Erica, making sure she wasn't listening to his conversation. Luckily, that dinner at her dad's house had her knocked out.

"You know what? We should go together and make these girls squash all that bullshit," Mekco suggested.

"Yeah, I agree. But anyway, I'm gonna hit you up in the morning about this shit. Hopefully, she stay asleep long enough for me to take a look at this shit on the internet."

With that being said, they both hung up the phone. Pierre continued to drive home while Erica slept. He laughed as she began to snore softly. Snoring and all, she was still beautiful, and he loved her.

***

It was December 1st, and Detroit was colder than ever. Pierre sat at his desk, looking online at some buildings for sale. He planned on buying a building and closing by February if he could. He hoped everything went as planned. He wanted to get the building up and running before the summer came.

"Good morning, baby," Pierre heard from behind him. He turned around with a smile because he knew it was only coming from his beautiful future wife.

He pulled her down on his lap, then placed a kiss on her lips. "What's up, baby?"

Erica was so bust trying not to be nosy, looking over his shoulder to see what he was doing on the computer.

"E, that's none of your business, girl," he said jokingly. "You need to be on your laptop doing your damn schoolwork."

"I got all day to turn my paper in for my final. I got this, Mr. Miller," she quickly responded.

Pierre turned back around in his chair with her still in his lap. Although he said it wasn't her business, he wanted her opinion on what building would fit her idea.

"So, look, I've been looking at these buildings; these three are my final choices. Go ahead and look at these and tell me which one you think we should go with."

Erica laughed. "I thought you said this wasn't my business. Now, look at you running back to me."

They both laughed. It was something how those two together could sit around each other all day and just laugh and have a good time together. The two were meant to be together, and everyone could see that.

Erica took her time looking over the three buildings he had chosen. She liked them all, but she had to think about price . . . how much it was gonna cost to fix up and then property taxes. So, she couldn't judge just by the looks. Just like a true businesswoman, she looked over the fine print and everything.

Pierre loved how smart she was, and he didn't mind that it took her forever to narrow it down to just one building. He eventually got up to look at the news on TV in the living room. He left Erica alone so she could get everything together for them. He also knew that she was gonna be the perfect person to give his all to because she was what you would call a rider.

"OK, baby, after looking over this stuff, I need your input to make the final decision," Erica said as she walked toward the couch with some papers in her hand.

"I thought you was gonna come out here talking about you found the right place."

"Whatever, Pierre, just listen to this," she said as she separated the papers, placing them in individual piles.

"So, right off, I disqualified this building because the back taxes are too high, and the whole building has been gutted and scraped. It's gonna take too much money to invest in this building. Plus, it's the smallest; the bigger, the better."

Pierre took a look at the building one last time. Once he was done, he balled up the paper. "Next."

"Now, this one has back taxes, but it's only a few thousand dollars. There's only a few things that you would have to get work done on."

He picked up the last paper. "What about this one?"

"Dang, I'm getting to that now. This one was recently used, so it has no damage, but it has some back taxes. Now, this building has back taxes, and the other building has back taxes and some damage. They both are the same size and around the same amount to get running, so it all boils down to if you wanna be on the east or west side."

Pierre smiled. "Damn, I love your smart ass."

"I love you too, baby," she admitted.

"I'm ready to go downtown and see if I can get this building. Go get some of that bread out of the safe."

"You so silly, Pierre. How I'm supposed to do that? I don't have your combination. Plus, I think you should have my dad go with you. He knows all about that type of stuff."

"You know what? I'm gonna call him up. Maybe we can ride down there tomorrow or something. How you been staying here for so long and don't know the combination?" Pierre asked.

"Because I don't be watching you when you go into your safe. That's your stuff in there, and that's not any of my business."

Pierre stood up and took her by her hand. "Come here. Let me show you something."

They walked into the bedroom. Pierre walked them toward the closet, then pushed all the clothes hanging up toward the right. Most people would have the safe in the back, but Pierre had to be different. They walked into the closet.

"Now, what do you think my combination is?" he asked.

"I don't know, baby. Maybe your birthday or maybe your grandma's. It could be your mother's birthday. Baby, I told you I didn't watch you whenever you went in here."

"Look, I'm gonna tell you this because I want you to know that this shit in here isn't just mine; it's *ours*. If something ever happens to me, I want you to be able to take care of yourself and my babies."

Erica knew he was only speaking the truth, but she hated it when he talked about something happening to him. That scared her just thinking about him not being in her life.

Tears formed in her eyes as she tried to walk away. She didn't get a chance to go far because Pierre was right there behind her, snatching at her arm. "Baby, don't be like that, OK? You need to learn this, baby. I know it hurts just thinking about me not being around, but just let me show you this so you could at least survive, baby."

Pierre wiped her tears and placed a kiss on her wet cheeks. They walked back into the closet, where Pierre stood behind Erica and showed her how to open the safe.

Erica smiled as she saw that the combination was her birthday.

Pierre then opened up the safe and placed another kiss on her cheek and neck.

"You see all this in here?"

Erica was speechless but still managed to nod her head. She had never thought about how much money he really had saved that was lying around the house. She was impressed seeing that he was always out buying her something or even shopping online for himself.

Pierre hugged her. "I know just thinking about me not being here makes you sad, and I didn't mean to bring that shit up to hurt you. I want you to be aware that you and my babies would be well taken care of if some shit do pop off."

"I understand, baby. Can we get out of here now? I'm hungry."

"How did I know that was coming?" he asked, laughing at his love, rubbing her round belly. "Three more months to go."

"Yes, and I can't wait to go down to my regular size," she said as they walked into the kitchen.

"Whatever. I love that extra weight you put on. You juicy as fuck."

Erica laughed. "Baby, you so freaking silly. But if you act right, I might keep a little bit of it on me," she teased.

Pierre laughed as she pulled out a pack of bacon and the carton of eggs. He sat at the table while she hooked up breakfast for them. He also looked at some information that Mekco emailed him last night about the trip to Jamaica.

Nicole watched Mekco sleep as she put on her clothes. He was up all night on the internet planning trips she didn't plan on going on. Once he came to bed, she gave him some pussy and put his ass to sleep. She made sure to please him, seeing that it was gonna be the last time fucking him.

She watched him sleep for a minute, scared and confused, all wrapped up in one. After weighing her options, she decided that this was the best time to leave if she ever wanted to be free.

She silently got up from the bed and went over toward their walk-in closet. Putting in his combination, she opened the door to the safe. She was happy that cash was already stuffed in a duffle bag. In seconds, she grabbed the bag, shut the safe, then hurried out the door.

As she drove to her house where Mercedes was hiding, she called her.

Answering on the third ring, Mercedes spoke. "Hey, baby, I miss you. When are you coming back?" she asked, giving an Oscar-winning performance.

"I'm on my way now. I have the money, so be ready to leave."

Mercedes tried not to scream and dance, so she hurried and said OK before hanging up.

Nicole's heart rate tripled, and she cried as she drove to Mercedes. She prayed like hell that Mekco's ass was still asleep. She knew he would kill her, knowing that she crossed him. As she drove, she repeatedly checked to make sure she wasn't being followed.

After dancing around the house, Mercedes called Rodney. "Aye, baby, I can't stay on the phone for long, but she on her way with the money. We about to leave as soon as she gets here, so be at the airport and wait for my call."

"Damn, baby, are you fucking serious?" Rodney asked.

"Yeah, baby, but I gotta go. Love you, daddy."

"I love you too. See you in a minute."

As soon as Mercedes got off the phone and started to get dressed, Nicole walked in. She had the duffle bag in her hand. "Come on, baby, let's get the fuck out of Detroit."

"I'm almost ready, baby. Is that all you taking with you?" she asked, seeing that Nicole only carried that one bag.

"I got some clothes in my trunk that I'm gonna grab. I'll leave my car here, and we gonna take your car back to the rental. Once we're done with that, we can catch an Uber to the airport."

Mercedes was now putting on her coat. "That sounds like a good idea, baby."

As she gathered her belongings, she offered Nicole a shake she had been drinking. It was strawberry, her favorite.

Nicole didn't think twice before she drank it.

Mercedes took her time, allowing her to drink the shake at least halfway down. "OK, baby, let's go."

The two ladies jumped into the car and were on their way to a better life . . . or so they thought.

Rodney waited patiently at the airport for his baby mama and his bread. He was proud of Mercedes because she was about to bring them so much happiness.

It was freezing out, so he parked the car and entered the building. He grabbed a newspaper and took a seat. It wasn't more than twenty-five minutes when he spotted the two ladies walk in. He smiled as he watched them smile like they were in a real relationship. He couldn't wait to get his bitch back.

Mercedes and Nicole took a seat close to the restroom. "Look, baby, I'm gonna go get some plane tickets to whatever plane leaving the soonest. We can stay there until we decide where we wanna go."

Nicole smiled. "OK, baby. I'm down for whatever."

Mercedes passed Rodney as she walked away. She pretended to act like she was looking at the screen to see what plane was about to leave. She turned around to see that Nicole was reading a book, not paying her any attention.

Once Mercedes started walking toward Nicole, she stuffed what Nicole thought were the plane tickets into her purse.

Mercedes took her seat. "Baby, it looks like we're going to Florida. How do you feel about that?"

"As long as I'm with you, I don't care where we go."

Mercedes smiled as she waited for her final plan to kick in. She was ready to go home to see her son and lie up with Rodney.

"Oh shit," Nicole mumbled.

Acting like she gave a damn and didn't know what was going on, Mercedes once again gave another Oscar-winning performance. "Damn, baby, what's wrong?"

"My baby not feeling that shake or something. I need to go to the restroom. I'll be right back, baby." Nicole kissed her before she got up to go to the ladies' room.

Rodney watched as Nicole entered the bathroom. Then he saw Mercedes grabbing her bag and a duffle bag. He quickly got up and started walking toward the door. Mercedes followed him out the door. As the cold air hit them, they picked up their pace and ran to the car.

Rodney started the vehicle, then looked over at Mercedes. They both smiled at each other before sharing a passionate kiss.

"Damn, baby, we did it!" he yelled before driving off.

Nicole sat on the toilet, handling her business. That shake had her shitting for about fifteen minutes.

Once she was done washing her hands, she walked back out to the waiting area. She was surprised when she didn't see Mercedes sitting where she left her. As she took a seat, she looked around to see if she was nearby.

Nicole didn't get worried . . . until she finally looked down and saw that Mercedes's bag, along with Mekco's duffle bag, was gone. She felt her heart jump out of her chest.

She stood up. "Oh my fucking God."

She ran back to the bathroom to see if maybe Mercedes had gone in while she was in one of the stalls. She cried when she didn't see her. Pulling out her phone, she hurried and dialed Mercedes's number. She fell to the floor when she heard a recording saying the number was no longer in service.

That's when it really hit her that she had been played for the money she had stolen from Mekco.

Mercedes and Rodney drove back to his motel downtown. As soon as they hit the door, they took off their coats and rushed to sit on the bed.

"Now, before you pour out that dough, let me ask you a question. What the fuck did you do to have her running to the bathroom like that?" Rodney asked, trying not to laugh.

"You know I keep some laxative on me just in case I need to do some dirt, then bounce."

Mercedes and Rodney shared a kiss. "Damn, I'm ready to feel that meat in me, baby."

"I got you, baby, but let's look at our money first. Then we can fuck while planning our next move."

She slowly unzipped the duffle bag. "You already know we got to go to Vegas and pick up Rontae from my mom's house. I wouldn't mind going to Atlanta. What you think about that?" Mercedes asked.

"Shid, baby, I don't give a fuck. Just know once we get settled, I'm gonna marry your ass."

She smiled as she sucked up what he was saying.

Mercedes dumped the money out of the bag. Their faces lit up as they pictured what they would buy. When she was done, she threw down the bag. "Baby, do you understand how our life is about change?"

"Hell yeah!" he yelled as he picked up a stack of money. As he began to flip the money, his chest tightened as he realized the stack was stuffed with newspaper. He quickly started grabbing different stacks, finding out each stack contained the same thing.

"Fuck!" he yelled.

"What is it, baby?" Mercedes asked. His attitude scared her.

"Baby, did you look at this shit before y'all got to the airport?"

"When she came to get me, she opened the bag and flashed it, and that was the only time I saw it," she explained.

"Mercedes, that bitch played us. There's only a few real bills in this shit. We need to go back and beat her ass," Rodney yelled.

Mercedes looked through the money for herself. She couldn't believe that Nicole would play her like that. She thought Nicole was down for her and really loved her.

Mercedes grabbed the bag as if something real would be in it. She saw a note pinned to the inside of the bag. As she opened it, it read: *Got Your Dumb Ass.*

Mercedes sat on the bed and cried while Rodney sat there, shaking his head.

How does the playa get played? What part of the game was this?

Chapter 15

"Baby, I'm about to go meet up with your dad so we can look at that building with the realtor. It's cold as hell out, but if you wanna ride with me, get ready."

"Can we stop to get some tacos first?" she asked.

"Yeah, fat ass."

Pierre helped her get into the car, then went over to the driver's door. He drove to Taco Bell so they could go handle their business after eating.

They went through the drive-thru, and he ordered her tacos and a drink. After that, he drove to the building that he wanted to purchase. When he pulled up, the realtor jumped out of the car. Then Pastor Collins got out of his.

They all shook hands before walking in. Erica stayed in the car eating her tacos.

Pierre and Pastor followed the realtor, Mrs. Jackson, around the building. She was happy that someone was interested in the building before the city folks came to destroy the place.

Pierre made sure to take pictures of every room, especially the gym. He could picture the young boys in there playing basketball. He thought that Erica had really picked the right place. He loved that not only was the inside large, but the center had a large yard for outdoor activities. He couldn't wait to get this place up and running.

"OK, Mrs. Jackson, I wanna buy this building, but what's the procedure for purchasing it?"

As Mrs. Jackson broke down the steps he would have to take, Erica walked into the room. She stood there and listened. Once Mrs. Jackson was done, they all said their goodbyes and left. Pastor Collins hurried home to get ready for his date with Theresa. Erica and Pierre drove to the store to get his payment for the building in money orders. He had a meeting with the realtor the next day to put in an offer to the bank. After that, he just had to wait to see if they were gonna let him get the building or what.

After leaving the store, Pierre drove Erica home. She was now sleepy from the food.

"Baby, get my phone so you can see the pictures of the whole building. I can't wait to get this center up and running," Pierre said, full of excitement.

Erica was searching through the pictures when Pierre's phone rang. "Hey, baby, it's Mekco."

"Answer it, baby. Just put it on speakerphone for me."

Erica did as she was told. "Hello."

"What's up, Erica? Where my bro at?" he asked.

"Nothing much," she responded.

Pierre waited until she finished talking. "What's up with you, nigga? And why you ain't hit me back about that one thing?"

"Damn, nigga, calm down. I got a problem over here, and I feeling real fucked-up now," Mekco said sadly.

Pierre and Erica could hear the pain in his voice. By him being his boy, Pierre knew he had to go check up on him. "Aye, my nigga, I'm on my way over there now."

They ended their call right after that.

"Baby, I'm gonna drop you off so you can nap. Then I'm gonna go check on my bro."

"OK, I don't care as long as I can sleep," she mumbled. She was already half-asleep.

The bigger she got, the quicker she fell asleep after eating. Pierre couldn't help but laugh at his baby's fat ass.

As he drove toward their crib, P couldn't help but wonder what could be going on for his bro to call him while he was all in his feelings and shit. All P could tell was that nigga was trying not to cry over the phone. If a nigga about to cry and shit, there must have been some deep shit going on.

Mekco opened his door for P. He was hurt, and P was the only one in the world he felt comfortable pouring his heart out to. P followed him as he walked into his office and took a seat.

P sat across from him. "What's up, bro? Talk to me, nigga."

"Bro, since I've been married to Nicole, I haven't been fucking nobody else, and I thought everything was good between us. I was being faithful, even started planning trips with this bitch and everything."

"What the fuck happened, nigga? Don't tell me you caught her cheating, and you fucked around and killed her ass."

"I wish shit was that simple, but it's not. Bro, this bitch finally left my ass for real. I mean, she actually went in my safe and took that duffle bag with that money in it."

They both looked at each other, then burst out laughing. "Mekco, please tell me you're lying."

"I swear, man. I went in there this morning to get the money for the Jamaican trip, and the bag was gone, but she did leave a note saying that she couldn't continue to deal with my cheating ass."

P looked at him like he was crazy. The whole situation was confusing to him. "Didn't you say you hadn't been cheating? What the fuck you talking about then?"

"P, I guess she thought I was still cheating on her, and to get away from me, she decided to take my money. The crazy thing is that bitch did all that just to walk away with the bag I got from Brandon and Brian's snake asses."

P started to laugh harder than before. "Bro, how the fuck you get that shit back? I remember taking it from you to give to that ho-ass nigga that kidnapped Erica."

"Boy, you been asleep. Remember when you left to take Erica home that night we found her?"

"Yeah, I'll never forget that shit," P answered with a slight attitude because he hated thinking about that night and what happened to her.

"Well, I don't know what was running through my head that night, but something told me to grab it, so I did. I kept that shit in the safe, and this morning when I was asleep, she left with the bag. I'm willing to bet any amount of money she somewhere crying and wishing she never crossed me now."

"So if she come back, what you gonna do?" P asked. He couldn't imagine Erica doing some shit like this. He wouldn't wanna just leave her out in the cold, but at the same time, she wanted to leave, and with his bread.

"That's the fucked-up part. You know I don't fuck with no snakes, and what she did was beyond disloyal. I would never be about to trust her again even though she really ain't steal my dough. She thought that she was getting over on me, so she betrayed me. I'm at a fucking stand-still, and it's not because I still love her. It's mainly because she carrying my baby, and it's only right that I take care of my child."

At first, P didn't know what to say. He sat there trying to put his foot in his homeboy's shoes. This was a fucked-up situation, and he really didn't know what to tell his boy.

After a few seconds of quiet, P finally spoke up. "Bro, look, she crossed your ass, and thankfully, she wasn't smart enough to check the money before she left. She is carrying your baby, so you can't just cut her off for good. If I was you, I would fall back and just deal with her for doctor's appointments. Then when she has the baby, I'd make sure my seed have whatever they need. You not fucking with her heavy like before is gonna kill her, so you don't have to."

"You right, nigga. I was pissed and hurt behind this shit, but I'm just gonna have to deal with her the way I had started dealing with Toya's ass."

P couldn't help but ask about Toya. "Whatever happened to that Toya situation anyway?"

Mekco started laughing. "Bro, I was at the hospital with her one day, and she started acting funny. So, I acted like I was about to leave. Then another nigga came in the room with her. I snuck back into the room and come to find out that was her *real* baby daddy. Bro, I didn't even go off on her ass. I just walked out laughing."

They both shared a laugh about the women in Mekco's life. P thought it was crazy how they used to be able to share wild stories about bitches they were fucking, and now, he just was there to support his homie.

"Damn, nigga, I forgot to tell you I found the building for the center today. I just gotta meet up with this lady tomorrow to put in my offer. I'm praying I get it. I'm ready to do something positive."

"That's what's up, bro. You know I'm gonna have to come up there and show those li'l niggas how to play basketball 'cause I know you ass ain't even trying to embarrass yourself like that," Mekco said, joking around.

"Whatever, nigga. You know what? I forgot how your ass always thought you could ball better than everybody in the hood. Soon as I get everything in order, we gonna do the damn thing, and we can place a bet on that shit too."

Mekco stuck out his hand. "Bet, nigga. I can't wait to dog your ass all on that court."

Mekco was still in his feelings about the whole Nicole situation, but while P was there, he was able to think about other things.

"Damn, Mekco, this shit just fucked up the Jamaican plan. What we gonna do now? I had already told you my plan."

"Look, I'm not trying to fuck that up. You sitting there like you don't know who the fuck I am. I will make sure I have somebody on my arm in Jamaica."

After tossing back a few more drinks and just running their mouths, P got up to leave. He had been wanting to chill with his baby.

Once P was gone, Mekco pulled out his phone and dialed Nicole's number again. He prayed that she would answer. He was ready to punch the fucking wall when she didn't answer. After four more calls with her not answering, he finally left a message.

"Nicole, baby, we both know you fucked up, but I'm worried about you. Just come home. I promise I'm not trying to kill you. I promise I just really wanna know what the fuck you was thinking, leaving and taking that bag. Baby, if you really just wanted to leave, that's all you had to say. I love you, baby. Come home." Mekco managed to squeeze all that in before the beep went off.

Mekco was feeling like he had drunk a little too much, so he lay on the couch to sleep off some of the liquor. The last thing he wanted to do was hit the streets and end up regretting everything that he did that day.

As the TV watched him, he slowly began to drift off.

"So, where is she at now, baby?" Erica asked, sounding concerned about her ex-best friend.

Pierre had come home from Mekco's house and had a whole story for her ass about how Nicole had robbed Mekco and shit.

"I told you that bitch wasn't shit. I knew she wasn't shit from jump," Pierre yelled.

"Baby, shut up; you don't know the whole story. Stop talking about her," Erica said, trying to protect her friend.

Trying not to laugh, he finished telling her what had happened. "E, don't tell me you on that THOT side. She robbed my bro, but the crazy thing is, the stupid bitch stole the duffle bag with that fake money."

Erica didn't find anything funny, and she didn't like how Pierre was calling her all out her name. And the fact that Nicole had crossed Mekco for some play money was a sign that she was desperate. She felt a little bad for her.

"Look, baby, I don't mean to make fun of your dumb-ass friend. I'm sorry, now come give me a kiss."

Erica tried not to laugh at the situation, but Pierre had a way to make even the smallest thing a joke. She got up from the recliner in the living room and walked over toward the couch he was lying on. She giggled at him because she could tell he was drunk and looking all weird. When he was drunk, it was like he became even sillier.

"What you want, Mr. Miller?"

At first, Pierre struggled to stand up, but he grabbed Erica around her waist once he got his balance together.

"Stop playing with me, Mrs. Miller. You know I want your beautiful ass." Pierre smiled, showing his platinum slugs in his mouth. "Damn, that shit sounds sexy as hell. I can't wait to make that shit official."

Erica smiled as well. She couldn't wait for them to decide on a wedding date finally.

Pierre started dancing to his own little beat in his head. He pulled Erica in closer while doing a little slow dance.

Erica didn't mind because she loved when their bodies touched each other. Then his cologne made her fall in love all over again. She was happy that she had given him a chance because she wouldn't know how her life would have turned out otherwise.

"Baby, stay right here. I got the perfect song for us," Pierre said as he walked over to the sound bar to hook up his phone.

Erica patiently waited as he tried to turn his drunkenness down to turn on the music.

"I know you like this song because I heard you singing it one night while you were in the shower. *Bam*, here we go, baby!" he yelled as a Leela James song came on.

Erica smiled as Pierre pulled her in for another dance. She was impressed that he could do something with the music. Being drunk, Pierre sang loudly and off-key as they danced. She smiled from ear to ear. Erica loved everything about that man, from his thuggish ways down to the silly guy who would have you laughing until you cried.

The couple danced and laughed until the song went off.

"You know I'm gonna perform that at our reception, right?"

Erica continued to laugh. "Boy, no, you not. We can have someone play that, but you're *not* singing. Let these folks find out you can sing, and them church women *really* gonna be on your head," she jokingly teased.

"I love you, baby. I put that on my mama."

"I love you too, baby, but you don't have to put anything on her. I know how you feel."

As another slow jam came on, they continued to dance to the music. It wasn't long before they were lying on the pallet of soft blankets on the floor, making love, all while the fireplace was lit. Between the lovemaking and the warmth from the fire, nothing in the world felt better.

***

Nicole had done so much crying over what had happened that she finally hit the point that not one single tear could roll down her cheeks any longer. Mekco had been blowing up her phone, and with every ring, she got frightened. She couldn't understand how she could be so dumb to allow a bitch to talk her into betraying him.

She knew he was looking for her because even Erica had called her. Instead of thinking that maybe Erica was worried, she thought that she was trying to be nosy and just wanted some information to report back to Mekco.

Nicole held her phone, staring at the screen. She contemplated if she should listen to the voicemail that Mekco had left. One side of her wanted to hear it, but the other half was so scared that he could kill her over the phone.

Finally letting her curiosity take over, she listened to the voicemail. She was surprised to hear Mekco begging her to come home and not flipping out on her. That gave her some hope.

Finally, it was time to face the music. During the ride, she sat back and silently prayed that he didn't kill her as soon as she walked through the door.

Nicole knocked on the door and stepped inside when he opened it. The TV was still on.

"What the fuck was you thinking? You actually was gonna take my fucking money and leave me?" Mekco yelled as he jumped off the couch, scaring her half to death.

Nicole instantly began to cry. "Mekco, I'm so so so sorry. I made the biggest mistake of my life. I'm sorry, baby."

"You damn right your dumb ass did. What the fuck was you thinking?" he yelled again, walking up to her, making her back up to the wall.

She was scared of him but silently prayed that if he decided to beat her ass, he might at least let her live.

Standing before the woman he loved, he gazed into her eyes, trying to figure out what or who would make her do him like that. He was pissed, and it hurt knowing that he knew he couldn't be with her anymore. He wanted to hug her and slap the fuck out of her all in a short minute. He was just as confused as Nicole was.

Fearing that he might go against what he told her over the phone, Mekco stepped back. He then walked over to the couch and took a seat. Nicole followed and sat beside him.

After a minute or so, Mekco decided to hear what she had to say. "Go ahead and tell me what was going through your mind when you thought it was a fucking good idea to steal my money. Do you realize that you should have just left if you wanted to leave me? What tip was you on?"

Nicole cried, not because she was scared anymore, but because she felt stupid. Mekco waited for her to respond to him. He wanted to know the story behind her shit before he told her about the money being fake.

"Go ahead and talk. Fuck all that crying shit. I know your ass wasn't crying when you ran off with my shit."

Nicole wiped her wet face with her shirt. "Remember when we were in Vegas, and we messed around with that bitch Mercedes?"

"Yeah, I remember that bitch, but what the fuck that got to do with you being disloyal?"

"I'm getting to that. She started texting me when we got back to Detroit, and we began liking each other. Well, she was feeling me, and I kept telling her that I was happily married, but she wouldn't give up. So the night I found out you were still fucking with Toya, I cried to her. I told her how much I hated that you constantly hurt me and how you were forever cheating and lying."

"What the fuck, Nicole? I told you I hadn't been with that bitch since we got married, and I put that shit on whatever."

Nicole quickly pulled out her phone and went to her messages. Then she put the phone in his face. "What do you call *this*, Mekco? You say you weren't cheating, but your dick was in that bitch mouth."

Mekco stared at the picture hard, trying to remember when this picture was taken. He had on his wedding ring, so he knew it was after they got married. After another minute or so, he finally remembered what day that was. "Damn, Nicole. Look, this was the night we all went out, and she called saying she needed some money because her job had laid her off. I didn't want her on the fucking streets while carrying my child."

Nicole cut him off. "That's *not* your fucking baby."

"We know that now, but let me finish my story. That bitch called me over, and I went, even though I was pissy drunk. I remember taking a nap on her couch to bring down my high. When I woke up, I gave her some money, then dipped."

"So, are you telling me that while you were asleep, she stuck your dick into her mouth, and you didn't know?" Nicole asked.

"Hell yeah. But right now, you need to be telling me what tip *your* dumb ass was on earlier."

Nicole's whole attitude changed now that the heat was off Mekco and back on her.

"She came to Detroit to make sure I was OK. Mekco, she made me believe that I was better off without you and with her. She promised me that she would treat me better by not cheating on me. Mekco, that bitch even told me that she would help me with the baby."

Mekco couldn't do shit but laugh at Nicole. Over the years, he had called her so many stupid bitches and dumb hoes that she actually went out of her way to prove that he was right.

Nicole ignored the fact that he was laughing and continued her story. "We planned to leave town and start a life together. I didn't know it then, but I now know that she must have put some laxatives in my shake so I would be in the bathroom for a long time. We were waiting for our plane at the airport when I entered the restroom. When I left to go to the restroom, that's when she grabbed the bag with the money and ran off."

Nicole cried while Mekco looked at her strangely. It was hard for him not to laugh at her. It was crazy how she fucked him over just to be fucked over herself.

"Baby, I'm so sorry for taking your money just to let another bitch take it from me. I know I fucked up, and I just want us to be able to move on from this," she said, trying to convince him to look at things her way.

"Damn, Nicole, how could you be so fucking stupid?"

"I'm sorry, baby. I swear, everything in me didn't want to do it, but when she told me she loved me, I just fell for it," she cried.

Mekco stood up from the couch. "Look, let me tell you something since you think you smarter than a muthafucka. That bag of money that you took was the shit I got from them ho-ass niggas Brandon and Brian."

Nicole's whole face dropped. Now, that was something that she didn't expect.

"Oh, well, let me put you up to date on some other shit too. Remember how I told you about my pops and how he had another child who was never around because his mom moved out of town?"

"Yeah, I remember," Nicole mumbled.

"A few years ago, I found him on Facebook. I sent him a friend request, and he flipped the fuck out on me. This disrespectful bastard told me to suck his dick. Well, since then, I've been peeking at his page from time to time. Last year, I see that he had a child. When we got married, I saw his baby mama, and that night, I thought about what my brother said to me. To get even with him, I had you help me fuck his baby mama," he explained with a sneaky smile on his face.

"Oh my God, Mekco."

"See, that's why I always tell you to pay attention to everything, or you'll get fucked over. The way I see it, they worked together to fuck you over to get back at me."

"I'm sorry, Mekco. I swear I'm so sorry." Nicole began to dry out.

"Look, I loved the fuck out of you, girl, and I was happy about us having this baby. The problem is, I can't trust you anymore. I now know that anybody who pays you any attention could talk you into betraying anyone you supposed to love."

Nicole continued to cry again. "What about us, Mekco? I want us to work it out and get through this, baby."

Mekco shook his head. He couldn't believe she thought she could go back to how it used to be. "I know you still got your crib and shit, and I'll help out with your bills. And you already know I'll be there when you have the baby. As for us, I'm done with this shit."

"Wait, Mekco, no. We have to make things right. You can't just leave me like that. I forgave you plenty of times for cheating on me," she yelled.

Mekco pulled out his phone and dialed Toya's number.

"Hey, Mekco, what's up?" she asked, surprised that he even called.

"Look, you already know I'm not calling to be friendly. I just got a question to ask your sneaky ass. Did you send my wife a picture?"

She tried not to laugh, but the situation was funny to her. "Man, that was so long ago. Why you just now asking me about that?"

"Bitch, don't make me come pay you and that bum-ass nigga a visit. How the fuck did that picture come about?"

"You was drunk and fell asleep. I took the picture and sent it to her, thinking y'all would break up and I could be with you."

Mekco didn't say shit. He just hung up the phone. Nicole had a stupid look on her face as he placed his phone down.

"Mekco, please, give me another chance. I promise to make it up to you."

"Just get the fuck out of my house. I'm done with your ass."

Nicole cried as she dropped down to her knees. She knew giving him some head would bring him back down to earth.

As good as her head be, Mekco had to decline her offer. In the past, that shit had him acting like a little bitch, but not this time. He couldn't trust that bitch.

He pushed her hands off his pants buckle and then stepped back. "Look, Nicole, it was fun while it lasted, but there's no point of us trying to make shit work. Like I said before, I will never be able to trust you. The only reason I didn't beat your ass and gave you a chance to explain yourself was because of the baby."

Nicole stood up. "Mekco, please, please, tell me that you'll forgive me, baby."

"Get the fuck out of my fucking crib before I call the police on your ass for trespassing."

Nicole didn't wanna test him and end up in jail, so she grabbed her coat. As she started walking toward the door, Mekco called her. She thought he had changed his mind that fast.

"What?"

"You be careful out there and pay attention to every-thing."

With that being said, Nicole walked out the door with a face full of tears. She wasn't sure how she was gonna survive without him, but she was gonna try to do whatever she had to do for her baby.

Once she was gone, Mekco sat on his couch. He couldn't believe how shit went down. He felt like he did get the last laugh just because the money was fake, but he had to let his brother know that he was not the one to fuck with.

Mekco got up to grab his laptop. After going on his brother's page, he sent him a friendly message asking him if he enjoyed the money. As Mekco was about to get off the site, something made him look at his brother's page. He strolled through his timeline, just being nosy like most folks. That's when he saw a bitch that pissed him off, but at the same time, it gave him a better understanding of things.

For ten minutes straight, he looked at a picture of his brother, Rodney, and his childhood friends, Brandon and Brian. There was a caption on the status that said, Missing the homies. This trip to the D would have been so much better if these two were still around.

That shit had him fucked up, but now he knew who was behind everything. Mekco smoked his blunt, thinking about taking a trip to Vegas. He knew he had to take his brother out before that muthafucka came up with another plan to take him out.

Rodney and Mercedes woke up early to make their way back home. They were bitter about the whole money situation, even though they were both wrong. Neither knew the truth behind the whole money bag, but both knew that it was time to face the fact that living a better life off another's man expense was out of the question.

Later that day, while they were on the road, it had finally hit him that the money they got from Nicole just might have been the bag he told Brian and Brandon to make when they were gonna come back to Vegas.

Chapter 16

"Erica, come on, baby. You gonna make us late for the program," Pierre yelled to Erica, who was still in the bathroom.

Erica walked into the living room, looking beautiful, as always. Her pregnancy gave her face a glow. Pierre was gonna fuss at her, but he was speechless once she stepped into the living room. She was so beautiful in his eyes that he now understood exactly why she took so long.

Even though she barely wore makeup outside of lip gloss or lipstick, that night, she added a little more, and Pierre couldn't complain.

"Damn, baby, you so fucking beautiful. I appreciate you giving me a chance to be in your life," Pierre said, kissing her forehead. She had on some lipstick, and he didn't want to mess it up or have the shit on him.

"You're so sweet, baby. Now, let's go before my daddy be calling."

The couple made it to the church just in time to get a good seat for service. Around Christmastime, the church was filled up with more families and guest speakers. Erica was surprised to see Nicole sitting next to her mom since it had been a minute since she had attended church.

As Pierre helped Erica take a seat, he noticed how Nicole made it her business to keep looking at Erica. He wasn't sure what her problem was but did know that even in a church, he would go the fuck off.

Once Erica noticed that Pierre wasn't paying attention to her dad but was looking at something else, she tapped his leg. "Baby, what's wrong?" she asked.

Pierre moved a little closer to whisper in her ear. "I was just trying to see why that girl keep looking over here."

Erica whispered back, "Don't worry about her because I'm not worried about her. Now, pay attention to the service."

For the next hour and twenty minutes, Pierre did exactly what Erica told him to. He chilled out and listened to the service. As always, the service was excellent.

When everyone got up to leave, Pierre did what he always did after service. He helped Erica clean up and make copies for the following week's service. Pierre watched the time on his phone; he had a surprise for Erica. This was gonna be one of the best Christmas gifts she would ever receive, and he was willing to bet any amount of money on it.

As they were getting ready to leave, Nicole popped up in the doorway. "Erica, can I talk to you for a minute?"

Erica was surprised but said, "Yeah."

Pierre gave Erica a hug and kiss while whispering in her ear, "If she try anything, you better mace her, then beat her ass."

They both laughed. "Aye, I'm about to be out in the car waiting for you," he said before walking out the door.

Nicole walked a little closer toward Erica. Erica thought about what Pierre had said, but at the same time, she wasn't worried—not one bit.

"What's up, Nicole? What did you want?"

Nicole could tell that Erica had her defenses up, and she couldn't blame her. Her being a bitch had caused her to lose out on having a best friend. She took a seat to make Erica feel comfortable in the same place as her. Erica did the same.

"Look, Erica, I was so wrong for pushing you away. I allowed my jealous ways to take over, making me hate you. Just know that I don't hate you for real, and to be honest, I still love you. I mean, we weren't just best friends; we were more like sisters. Erica, can we get that back?"

Erica saw that Nicole was becoming emotional, and she too was getting teary-eyed.

"Nicole, I just don't understand why you were jealous of me in the first place. We both had great guys in our lives, and we dang near was living the same life."

"To be honest, your life was better because what you and P have is real love. I knew Mekco's and my relationship wasn't real like y'all, and it killed me to watch y'all two all happy while me and Mekco faked it."

"Aww, Nicole, don't ever feel like that. Every relationship won't be the same. Me and you both love our guys differently, and our guys love us differently. At the end of the day, we both are getting loved on by wonderful guys. There wasn't no reason to be jealous."

"Girl, Mekco and I are not fucking with each other anymore."

Erica looked at Nicole, confusion all over her face.

"Listen, I need time to digest everything. I'll explain in due time. I'm coming to you asking for your forgiveness."

Erica couldn't stand not having Nicole in her life, and that's why it was so easy to forgive her. "I forgive you, Nicole."

The girls cried while hugging each other. Erica was happy that they were friends again, even though something deep inside told her that things would never be the same.

"OK, I have to lock up the church, and I'll call you later," Erica said, pulling back from Nicole.

"OK, girl. I gotta go anyway. I have to work."

"Where you working at now?" Erica asked.

Nicole laughed. "Girl, believe it or not, I'm working at a CVS."

"Oh, OK. Well, call me when you can," Erica yelled while walking toward Pierre's car.

Pierre saw that Erica was on her way to the car so he got out to open her door. Before she got in, he wrapped her up in his arms, placing a sweet kiss on her lips.

"I love you, baby," he whispered in her ear.

"You better, Mr. Miller," Erica jokingly said.

Pierre gave her another kiss. "You better stop playing with me, E."

"Dang, baby, I love you too. You know I was just joking with you," she said before getting in the car.

Nicole was in her car watching them showcase their love and slowly began to cry. She thought she could deal with not being with anybody, but seeing that made her jealous all over again.

"Fuck!" she yelled, hitting the steering wheel.

Nicole watched as Pierre and Erica drove off. She sat there for a moment, crying her eyes out. "I fucking hate that bitch," she mumbled.

"Baby, where are we going? You done missed our exit."

"Go ahead and sit back and let your man handle every-thing," Pierre replied, all cocky and shit.

"Whatever, but I still wanna know where we going."

"Look, I got a surprise for you, baby. It's an early Christmas present, and I know you're gonna enjoy it."

Erica smiled. "I love surprises, baby."

Pierre continued to drive toward the airport. Erica sat back in her seat and soon was knocked out asleep.

Finally arriving at the airport, Pierre woke her. "Baby, it's time to get up," he said, giving her a little shake.

Erica woke up and then allowed Pierre to help her out of the car. "Pierre, why are we here?"

"It's all part of one of my surprises for you. Just chill for me."

Erica didn't say anything else, but she kept a smile on her face. She knew she was in for a good time, knowing he had planned something special.

***

Erica stood on the balcony, letting the sun hit her face. She loved being out of Detroit, especially in the wintertime. Pierre walked onto the balcony and held her from behind. As he placed kisses on her neck, he whispered in her ear.

"So, when you gonna tell me how much you love me and how you love one of your Christmas presents?"

Erica turned around and didn't hesitate to show Pierre some love. She placed a thousand kisses on him before she started to cry.

"Baby, what's wrong? Why the fuck you crying?"

"I'm just so happy to be here. Thank you so much, baby. I swear I love you so much."

Pierre hugged her again. "Baby, don't cry. And I love you too, just know that."

Erica wiped her face, then smiled to show Pierre she was now OK. "It's so beautiful out here in Jamaica."

"Not as beautiful as your ass. It's just all right compared to you," he said, leading her back inside.

"Come on, it's late. Let's eat something. After that, we can just chill for the rest of the night," Pierre suggested.

The couple got comfortable on their California king-size bed and ate their food. Erica wasn't sure what she would like, so Pierre ordered a mix of several things.

"Here, try this right here, baby. I swear you gonna love this jerk chicken and rice."

Erica stared at the food for a minute. She was always the one who judged the food by how it looked and smelled. Since she was a child, she has always been a picky eater.

"Go ahead, baby. My kids want to taste it."

Erica laughed before placing a forkful in her mouth. Pierre watched as she chewed the chicken and rice.

"So, what you think, baby?"

"It was all right, baby," she said before taking Pierre's plate and stuffing her mouth.

Pierre laughed as she ate most of the food. "I thought it was just all right, but I see your greedy ass done ate almost all of it."

"It was good, baby," she said while giggling.

Pierre woke up early, making phone calls and taking care of his business. He needed everything to be in order for Erica.

After getting off the phone, he returned to the room to wake Erica, but just like magic, she was just now sitting up in the bed.

"Pierre, this has been the best two days of my life. I love being here."

"Why don't you go take a shower and get our day started? I got a major surprise for you today."

"Baby, you have already done so much already. I don't need any more surprises in my life. Just being out here is the best surprise ever," she said with a huge smile.

"I'm not trying to hear that shit, girl. I got one more surprise for you. After that, I'll be quiet for a while," Pierre announced, knowing he wasn't telling the truth. He planned on spoiling Erica and his babies until the day he died. Even then, they would still be taken care of.

Erica climbed out of bed and made her way to the bathroom. She smiled as she picked up the bathing suit she wore the night before when she and Pierre made love on the beach. That was a memory that she would never forget.

After getting out of the shower, Erica saw that Pierre had already laid some clothes on the bed for her. Next to the dress was a note that read, *Baby, put this on and go downstairs. Your ride is waiting for you.*

"This dress is beautiful and my favorite color," Erica said while pulling the lavender dress out of the box.

As she dressed, she kept wondering what he had planned and where he disappeared. Once she was dressed, she looked at herself one last time before walking out the door.

Finally getting downstairs in the lobby, she saw a guy holding a sign with her name on it. She slowly approached the guy.

"Good morning. Are you Erica Miller, ma'am?"

Hearing him say Erica Miller and not Erica Collins put a grin on her face. She couldn't wait until the day her last name would officially be Erica Miller.

"Yes, sir, good morning. I'm Erica."

The driver opened the door, then allowed her to step into the limo. As she sat back in her seat, she smiled, knowing she had picked a winner. She had heard a lot of crazy stories and knew that sometimes, females would go through a lot trying to find real love, but she was the 5 percent that found it and was gonna have it for life.

Soon, the partition rolled down, and the driver began to talk, which knocked Erica out of her daydream.

"Ma'am, there's a blindfold on the seat. Your husband would like you to put it over your eyes for his surprise," he told her as he rolled up the partition again.

Even though Erica didn't trust him, she slowly tied the blindfold around her eyes. She had watched the ID channel too much and believed everyone was a suspect.

After riding for another fifteen minutes, the driver finally stopped the car and opened the back door for Erica.

"Ma'am, I'm gonna help you enter a building. Just hold my arm."

The driver stepped back as Pastor Collins stepped up, allowing Erica to wrap her arm around him. Pastor Collins smiled as they walked into the chapel.

As soon as they stepped into the chapel, Erica heard the instrumental of "Here Comes The Bride." She snatched the blindfold off and looked around. Seeing her dad standing next to her made her break down and cry. Sitting down, waiting for her to walk down the aisle, were

Theresa, Mekco and his date, her uncle Cross, and Nicole. Seeing everyone that she loved made her cry even harder.

"Come on, Erica, this what you wanted, ain't it?" her dad whispered.

Erica tried her best to pull herself together once the music started to play again. As she made her way to the front, she looked at Pierre, who looked like he had also shed a tear or two. She mouthed out, "I love you so much."

He smiled before mouthing out, "I love you more."

The wedding was beautiful and everything that Erica wanted it to be. Having everyone show up was a bonus. Everyone saw that she was enjoying her surprise.

For the reception, Pierre had someone set up a nice spot on the beach. Erica and Pierre were on the dance floor acting a fool. Erica looked around and saw that everyone was enjoying themselves. She even caught her dad and Theresa slow dancing to the music.

Erica was getting tired so she walked away from Pierre and allowed him to talk to some of his Brick Boy buddies. She went over to where Nicole was sitting. "Hey, Nicole, are you all right? You sitting over here by yourself. Come make you a plate of food and talk to me."

Nicole got up and walked over to the table where the food was. She was trying so hard not to spazz out on Erica. She knew it was her big day, and she couldn't get mad that she wasn't happy or the fact that Mekco had come with another female. Erica had nothing to do with that. In fact, she didn't have anything to do with the whole Jamaican trip. She was just as surprised as Nicole.

The two girls took their seats so they could feed their babies.

"So, I guess this is why I'm still waiting on that phone call," Nicole said, being petty.

Erica laughed. "I'm sorry, girl. I swear I didn't know nothing about this trip. It was all a surprise. When we left the church, he drove us straight to the airport. We've already been here for two days."

"It's OK, boo. I'm so happy for you and Pierre. You guys seem so happy with each other."

"Nicole, you just don't know how happy I am with him. Sometimes, I have to pinch myself just to make sure that it's real. It's like sometimes I feel like I'm living a fairy tale or something."

Nicole didn't say anything, but for a moment, Erica could have sworn that she saw her rolling her eyes. She was happy to see Pierre coming their way because she could tell that Nicole was still on some other stuff, and she wasn't gonna let that girl ruin her day.

"Y'all good over here?" he asked.

"Yeah, baby, we good. I'm done eating. Can you walk with me to the restroom?"

Pierre tossed her plate in the trash, then took her by the hand to lead her to the restroom.

"Baby, I really appreciate you doing all this for me. Everything is so perfect. I don't know how to make this up to you."

"Listen, you done enough already. You gave a nigga like me a chance, you trusted me with your heart, you married my ass, and soon, you gonna have my babies. You giving a nigga two babies at once. The way I see it, I'm paying your ass back."

Erica kissed Pierre before entering the restroom.

"Now, Nicole, we on a nice little vacation, and I'm not about to let you sit around looking all crazy because that man is with somebody new. When y'all was together, all y'all did was party and fuck, then, from time to time, he fucked someone new. That boy is no good for you. The sooner you get that through your head, the sooner you can move on with your life. I'm begging you not to sit around and mess up this girl wedding," Theresa said after seeing her daughter looking at Mekco and his girlfriend with death in her eyes.

"It's not fear, Mama. I wanted to live this life. I gave Mekco three fucking years, and Pierre and Erica ain't even been together for a whole fucking year yet. It's not fair!" she yelled out, hitting the table.

"Nicole, your relationship with Mekco consisted of fucking and drinking, and that's how Mekco treated your ass—like a fucking fuck buddy. Now, Erica carried herself on a higher level, and she found a man who was up to the challenge to prove his love to her. You got what you wanted, you damn fool. Now, go to the hotel and get your life."

Nicole stood there for a minute, deciding if she wanted to go off. Something inside of her told her to speak her mind. "You think you that bitch mother because you been fucking her daddy since before her mom died? Is *that* the reason you all on her dick now?"

Nicole was doing all that yelling, and before she could say anything else, her mom slapped the shit out of her.

Neither saw that Erica was standing behind them. She was shocked by what she had just heard. "What? Nicole, what did you just say?"

Nicole and Theresa turned around and were shocked to see Erica standing there. Theresa didn't say anything, but Nicole was ready to spill the tea.

"You heard me. Your daddy and this lady right here been fucking around since your mom was alive. When your mom was on her deathbed, your daddy was out fucking this whore right here."

Erica charged at Nicole, ready to lay her ass out, but before she could get to her, Pierre came from nowhere and grabbed her. "Let me go, Pierre!" she yelled.

"Hell nah, not with my babies in your stomach. Catch that bitch in a few months," Pierre said, holding her back.

"That's right. Hold that scary bitch back. You standing over there protecting her, and you don't even know if them your fucking kids with your dumb ass," Nicole teased.

Pierre knew that little statement was enough to piss off his wife. As bad as he wanted Erica to beat her ass, he knew she couldn't do it because of the babies.

"Bitch, shut your retarded ass up before I slap your ass," Pierre yelled.

Just then, more guests from the party were walking toward them. The bigger audience gave Nicole more motivation to be disrespectful. "Fuck both of y'all and those babies that *might not be yours.*"

Pierre was pissed that she had the nerve to repeat that shit. He always knew the bitch was foul. Without warning, he grabbed Nicole by the neck. If Mekco hadn't jumped in his face, he would have chokeslammed that bitch on the fucking ground.

"Bro, what the fuck you doing? That's still my baby mama," Mekco yelled as he pushed Pierre, making him drop Nicole.

"Man, fuck that stupid bitch. How the fuck she gonna come here trying to fuck up my wife day?" Pierre yelled.

Best friends Mekco and Pierre stood in front of each other, ready for the next to make a move. Erica stepped by Pierre's side. "Pierre, let's go. We can't let this ruin our day."

Pierre was pissed off, but just like any other time, her touch warmed his heart, and he calmed down just a little.

The bitch who Mekco had arrived with was pissed that he had even stood up for Nicole. Especially how he made it his business to tell her how Nicole tried to get down on him. Seeing him holding Nicole in his arms, Remy quickly walked off. She wasn't for his shit.

Cross stood in between his best workers. "Y'all two better cut this bullshit out. I don't give a fuck who did what. Cut this shit out now!" he yelled.

Mekco and Pierre both took a step back from each other. They hadn't really gotten into it since they were kids, and Cross hated to see two young niggas that he watched grow up fighting over bullshit.

After everything was all said and done, everyone went their separate ways. Theresa and Eric went to their rooms; neither knew what to say to the other. Their little secret was out of the bag, and they couldn't blame anyone but Nicole.

"Look, Eric, this whole thing between us has been great, but I don't know how we are supposed to move on after what that child of mine did."

"Look, Theresa, I love you and will talk to my daughter, just not today on her wedding day. I love you, and I'm not ready for this to end."

"Eric, I love you too and want us to be together. I know Erica is hurt, and I don't want her to hate me for loving you," Theresa cried out.

The couple hugged each other. Over the years, they had grown so tight, and now that their secret was out, they weren't sure if they could survive.

"Let's get our bags and just go home," Theresa suggested.

"For once, lady, you got a great plan," Eric said, laughing.

The two kissed each other before gathering their belongings. They enjoyed being away from Detroit, but there was nothing like being at home.

Once Mekco entered the room he shared with Remy, she was already zipping up her luggage.

"So, you was just gonna leave without saying anything to a nigga?" he asked.

"Look, Mekco, I appreciate you inviting me out here, but I don't play second to no bitch. I told you from jump that if I felt like you wanted another bitch, then I was gone. It's been real, but I'm gone, and please don't call me when you make it back to Detroit."

Just like that, Remy was out the door.

Mekco wasn't even mad. He had really just met the bitch, and since he didn't wanna come alone, he allowed her to tag along.

Sitting on the bed, he thought about everything that just happened. Nicole was dead-ass wrong, but at the same time, Pierre shouldn't have put his hands on her, especially while she was carrying his baby. He hated that his friendship was probably over because, once again, Nicole was jealous of Erica.

He decided to go ahead and get his shit together too. He was ready to go back home. At least, there, he ain't have no real problems.

Erica lay across the bed, crying. Nicole had ruined one of the most important days of her life. Erica really wanted to punch her in the mouth, but she just couldn't do it for some reason.

Pierre was smoking in the living room area. The whole situation had him fucked up. He wasn't even mad that Mekco got in his feelings behind a bitch. He was angry because Erica was hurt. He once made a promise that if someone were to hurt her, he would kill them. Now, he was sitting back, wondering if he should do it in Jamaica or wait until they returned to Detroit.

After smoking his blunt, he was calmer. He went into the room and saw that Erica had taken off her dress and cried herself to sleep. He knew she was hurt by that shit Nicole had said. Then to find out your pops had been fucking around with another lady while her mother was sick and dying, that shit was fucked up.

Once Pierre slipped off his clothes, he joined her in bed. He pulled her in closer to his chest. "I love you, Mrs. Miller," he whispered in her ear.

Erica was only half-asleep and heard him. She turned around to face him. "I love you too, Mr. Miller," she said sadly.

"Aye, look, don't let that shit get to you, OK? Just say the word, and whoever you point out, that's who I'm gonna kill. I can't have muthafuckas hurting my baby."

Just like any time before, Pierre made her laugh. "Baby, I don't need you to kill anyone. Me not dealing with Nicole and just being happy with you is gonna kill her. Besides, I been told you that you were my best friend."

"I love you, girl, and I do whatever to make sure you are happy."

Erica began to cry. She was trying to be strong, but Nicole had really hit her below the belt.

"I just can't believe she would say that shit about me not knowing who my kids' father was. That was just wrong."

"E, don't cry about that shit. Fuck that bitch. We know them my babies, so whatever the fuck she talking about, she can just shove it up her ass."

Pierre gave her another kiss. "Let's enjoy the next two days here. Or was you ready to go home to the cold?"

"Baby, I don't care. All I know is I wanna be with you. You is what makes me happy."

Pierre couldn't resist kissing all over her body. He took his time sucking and flicking his tongue on her pretty black nipples. Then he took his time making it down to her juice box. Just how he liked it, she was dripping wet. Erica lay there enjoying the way Pierre pleased and teased her private area. She always told him he was the best, even though she had nothing to compare him to.

"Damn, baby, ease up a little. I'm not ready to come yet."

"Shut that shit up. You already know how I get down. This only the first of many that you gonna be releasing."

With that being said, he buried his face deeper in her pussy. He loved how sweet she tasted, and it was a bonus that he was the only nigga who had a chance to taste her sweet stuff.

Erica's mind cleared as Pierre took his time to make love to her. He had a way of taking her mind off everything.

Erica and Pierre had a ball in Jamaica for the next two days. Her dad and Theresa called to apologize and ask for her forgiveness. Eric explained that when she was younger, and her mother became ill, she had told him to leave her and find someone who was gonna treat him with the same love that she gave Erica. Erica kindly told them she forgave them and wasn't mad at them. She even thanked Theresa for being in her father's life. In her eyes, Theresa was a good woman, and if her dad hadn't moved on, he probably would have killed himself after her mom had died.

They loved the hot sun, but stepping back to the D was everything. They were tired, so when they entered the house, Pierre set their luggage right by the door.

"Damn, E, look at all this mail that piled up. It better all be something good because I swear I paid all the fucking bills."

Erica laughed. "You want me to help you see what's going on?" she asked with her hand out.

Pierre handed her a few envelopes. "I hope you not gonna deliver no bad news."

"Be quiet, boy, with your crazy self."

"But you love my crazy ass, don't you, Mrs. Miller?"

While giggling, she managed to answer him. "That's right, Mr. Miller."

Erica took her time looking over the mail, but one letter really caught her attention. "Oh my God, baby, look at this."

Pierre went over to her side of the dining room table. "What's this shit?" he asked as he took the paper out of her hand.

"Man, what the fuck? Is this shit real, E?" he questioned.

"Baby, this *is* real. Did you know you were getting this?"

"Fuck nah, E. You know what? Merry Christmas and a Happy New Year, baby."

"Are you freaking crazy? I can't accept this, Pierre." Erica had to yell out because Pierre refused to take the paper from her. Instead of taking the paper, he got up from the table and went to the living room.

"Pierre, do you know what this is? I can't take this, baby. Your mom had this set up for you."

"Look, I don't need it. Put it up in a bank for the kids."

Erica looked at the check that was $35,635. Come to find out, his mom had life insurance on her that his grandma had paid up. Pierre never knew about it.

"Baby, I'm not gonna throw it away because that would be stupid, but I will put it up for the kids. Just think about it this way. They already got money put up for college," she explained.

"Yeah, that's a good idea, but I was just thinking that I'm not sure I want them in a public school. We could use some of that money to put them in a private school. I want my babies to have the best education they can get."

"The best education would be homeschooling, baby."

Pierre looked at her like she was crazy. "Hell nah, that shit might make them weird and shit."

They both laughed before getting back into the TV.

Chapter 17

"Baby, I'm about to get me some juice. Do you want some?" Nicole asked Mekco as she climbed out of bed.

"Nah, I'm good. Just hurry up and get back in here with me."

It was the night before Valentine's Day, and the couple decided to spend their first Valentine's Day together as a married couple in the house. They planned to spend the whole weekend in bed, making love and watching movies on the TV. Neither left the bed for anything other than to use the bathroom or to answer the door when the delivery guy was outside.

Since the trip to Jamaica in late December, when they ended up on the same plane, they decided to work out their problems. Mekco truly loved her and couldn't see himself moving on without her and his baby not in the same household as him.

Nicole was also happy that they were back together. She loved him to death. When she got back home from Jamaica, she actually thought about killing herself. The only thing that stopped her was the fact that she thought about how she and her baby would die, and Mekco would have been able to move on quicker since he had nothing attached to her. But she quickly decided against suicide. She wasn't going to let him off so easily.

Neither had talked to Pierre or Erica since that day they had fallen out in Jamaica. Even when Mekco had a meeting with Cross and Pierre had to be there, they never talked to each other. Cross tried his hardest to stay out of their business, but at the same time, he constantly reminded them that they were brothers and needed to squash all that bullshit.

Both guys were so fucking stubborn that even Cross couldn't get them to act right. He couldn't get them to speak, even at his New Year's Eve party. Pierre had thought about being the bigger person and talking to Mekco . . . that was, until he saw Nicole hugged up with him. Once he saw that his boy was back with that bitch, he didn't give a fuck if they ever spoke again. That bitch liked to start shit, and he would have hated to put one in that bitch's head if she ever came at him or Erica again.

Nicole came back into the bedroom. "Here, baby, I brought you a bottle of water just in case you changed your mind."

"Thanks, baby."

The two spent their weekend making love like never before. Nicole thought about the shit her mom had said about all she had to offer a man was sex, and that was why Mekco treated her just funky. Even though she knew her mom was right, she just couldn't leave him alone. Plus, she liked living without having to work or do anything.

The next afternoon, they cuddled in the bed, and Mekco rubbed her belly. It was all new to him, and he loved how his baby was putting on some weight. It was hard for him to keep his hands off her.

"So, do you want a baby shower?" Mekco asked.

"Hell no. You should already know that. Don't nobody fuck with me like that. You can just buy whatever the baby needs."

"Man, that's your fault, Nicole. I'm not trying to be funny, but you be bugging out sometimes, baby."

"Fuck you, Mekco. I'm starting not to like your ass anymore. You just like everyone else, and you never have my back on shit," she yelled as she jumped out of bed and started to pull her clothes out of the closet.

"Where the fuck you going, Nicole?"

"Away from your stupid ass. I fucking hate you. I bet any amount of money you on that bitch side, and you probably wanna fuck her too. I bet you and P took turns on that ho. You might just be her baby daddy, ho-ass nigga."

Mekco was fed the fuck up with Nicole's mouth. He jumped out of the bed and slapped her upside her head. "Stop talking like you fucking retarded. You know damn well you talking a bunch of bullshit right now."

Nicole raised her head with a smile on her face. "So, you just gonna keep hitting me while I'm pregnant with your baby, muthafucka?"

"You so fucking crazy, Nicole. I don't know what I got myself into," he said, walking away.

Nicole being crazy was driving him crazy. Instead of leaving him alone, she followed him back into the room.

"You such a pussy-ass nigga. You stay putting your hands on me, but I ain't never saw you fight a nigga before, and you say you the man of the streets. I say you a fucking joke."

Mekco wanted so badly for her just to leave him alone, but he fucked up when he put a baby in her stomach and a rock on her finger. "Look, crazy bitch, get the fuck out of my face," he yelled, pushing her away from him.

Nicole was on some other shit, and his rejecting her only excited her. She really got pissed when she saw that he was putting on his pants and shoes. "Mekco, where are you going?"

"Man, listen, I don't know what the fuck wrong with your crazy ass, and I'm not about to try to figure the shit out. I'll be back later."

Nicole chased after him until they reached the front door. "Mekco, you said you weren't going nowhere tonight and was gonna chill with me."

"Look, you nutty-ass muthafucka, I'm not about to be in here while you acting all looney and shit. What the fuck wrong with you? Are you acting out because you done let a bitch turn you the fuck out and then played your ass? Because I can't see no other reason why you acting out."

Those words hit Nicole like a brick to someone's head. "So, you really trying to throw that shit in my fucking face? Yeah, you right. I did fuck with a bitch, and she ate my pussy ten times better than your punk ass."

Mekco laughing at her pissed her off even more. She jumped closer in his face, ready to continue the argument, but he wasn't having it. He pushed her out of the way. "Look, I trying to get the fuck away from you because I don't wanna beat your ass for real. I been locked up in this house giving you this good dick, and you still acting crazy and shit. Why don't you go lie down, and I be back later?"

Nicole stood there thinking of something clever to say but came up short. "Fuck you, Mekco."

"Nah, fuck your crazy ass. I swear I should have left you at the altar so I wouldn't have to deal with you no more. I don't know what the fuck I was thinking marrying your ass."

"Really, nigga, that's how you feeling? So, it's fuck me now? Guess what? Fuck your whack ass," she yelled.

Mekco wasn't expecting it, but Nicole slapped his ass first this time. He stood there holding his face. He was shocked that her little ass had any force behind her hit. He said a silent countdown, trying to calm down. The way he was feeling, he didn't want to fuck around and kill her.

"I'm tired of saying the same shit over and over. Take your ass home and stay the fuck away from me."

"Wait, Mekco, how you just gonna break up with me? I'm your fucking wife."

"All that's gonna change come Monday morning."

Seeing that Mekco wasn't playing with her ass, she grabbed some clothes to put on. Instead of crying, she gathered the shit that she wanted and threw it in a bag. She wasn't even gonna trip about him sending her home. What he didn't know was that she had what she really wanted at her house anyway.

Mekco watched her get her shit together. He didn't know how the fuck he married her crazy ass in the first place. Truthfully, he was feeling like he fucked up begging her to keep their baby. He just knew she was gonna be a problem, which was why he sent her away. She was the type of bitch you would have to kill just to make her shut the fuck up. As Nicole got ready to leave, Mekco sat there watching her. He couldn't think of what triggered her to act all crazy and shit.

Nicole didn't even say shit as she threw his keys at his face and stormed out, making sure to slam the door.

Mekco walked over to the door to make sure she at least got into the car safely. She had really pissed him off, and he needed a drink. Finally, Mekco got dressed to go to his favorite bar.

Pierre woke up with Erica sitting on the side of the bed. She was holding her stomach, rocking back and forth. For a minute, she had him scared. Jumping up and rushing to her side, Pierre sat beside her. While rubbing her back, he said, "Baby, you OK? Do you need me to do anything?"

Erica looked up with tears in her eyes. Pierre was really concerned now.

"Baby, talk to me. Tell me what's going on," he begged.

"Pierre, I just got up, and I'm so hungry, and I called your name twice, but you didn't get up," she cried.

Pierre couldn't believe what the fuck he was hearing. He tried his best to hold it in, but he couldn't any longer. He busted out into laughter. "Are you fucking serious right now? Here I am, thinking you in pain or something, and you up crying 'cause you hungry."

"It's not funny. Stop laughing at me," she ordered.

Pierre planted a kiss on her forehead. "I'm sorry, baby. That was just some fat-ass shit you were doing. What you want me to get you?"

Erica wiped away her tears. "I really just want something sweet, like some gummy bears or something."

Pierre stood up from the bed, laughing at her cravings. He was surprised that she didn't say she wanted some damn tacos. "Let me see if there's still some of that big bag we got from Walmart the other day."

Erica sat back in the bed, rubbing her stomach. The twins were so active whenever they got hungry. Sometimes, their kicks felt like they were in there playing soccer.

Pierre returned to the room with the bag of gummy bears. "Baby, I understand that you're pregnant, but you can't wake up crying and shit 'cause you hungry. I mean, you got like six weeks left in this pregnancy, and that shit scares the fuck out of me. I thought you were about to have the babies."

Erica got emotional and started crying again. "I'm sorry, baby."

Pierre climbed back into bed with her. "It's OK, E. I just was worried, that's all. You don't have to cry, OK?"

Erica wiped her face again before eating her candy. She looked at Pierre, who was watching her. She could tell he was still feeling some type of way about waking up to her crying. She placed the bag of candy on the nightstand and scooted over toward him. "I'm so sorry for scaring you. These kids just got my emotions all whacked up."

Pierre smiled and kissed her again. "It's OK, baby, and I love you and them babies."

"And we love you too."

Pierre looked at the time on his phone and realized it was only 11:45 p.m.

"Damn, baby, you be having me in the bed early as hell. I just knew it was about 3:00 a.m."

"When I get sleepy and get in the bed, you the one who is always following me," Erica said, laughing.

"Aye, baby, would you be mad if I leave out for a few? I wanna go get some fresh air."

"You know that I don't care. The way I look at it, you better go ahead and do you before these babies have your ass on lock next month."

Pierre stood up and kissed her on her lips. "I swear that's why I love the fuck out of you. You don't never trip about shit."

Erica smiled. "I don't have no reason to trip. You do so much for me, and you're just the best person in the world. I don't see no reason for me to trip 'cause you wanna leave. Just bring me back some tacos."

P went straight to his favorite bar. His father used to be friends with the owner before he got locked up and died. Even when he was underage, Sam would allow him to come in and drink as much as he wanted.

After ordering his drink, P turned away from the bar to go sit in his favorite booth. He wasn't a bit surprised to see that Mekco was already sitting there. For a minute, he debated his options. He wasn't sure if he wanted just to drink his drink and leave or see if Mekco wanted to rumble.

Mekco saw his old friend standing across the room. They both stared at each other with a mean mug on their faces. It was a damn shame how two people could be friends since wearing diapers, then not even speak to each other after a slight falling out.

Mekco knew how P got down, and he never was known for being a ho, either. Mekco stood up ready to fuck up a nigga if he jumped stupid. Pierre started walking toward him. He was somewhat sorry for the sin he was thinking about committing, but he stayed ready.

As the two came face-to-face, neither wanted to really be the one to make the first move. But truthfully, somewhere down the line, they were fucking brothers. They stood there for a minute, thinking about how they wanted the night to end. Then simultaneously, they put down their guard and gave each other dap.

"You know you my fuck mans, nigga?" Mekco said, taking a seat.

Pierre sat across from him. "Yeah, you my nigga too, but shit did get a little crazy on my wedding day."

"Bro, I really don't know what's wrong with Nicole's ass. I don't know what to do with her ass."

"Yeah, bro, you know I don't really put my hands on females, but she said some disrespectful shit and was cutting on our fucking wedding day. She was out of line for that shit."

Mekco understood why Pierre was mad at Nicole, but at the time, he wasn't really protecting her; he was really thinking about his baby. "Man, I'm not sure what the fuck wrong with that girl. She just tried to fight me and shit. I had to put her ass out of my fucking crib. Then when she was about to walk out the door, she threw the damn keys at my face. That's how I ended up here. I needed a fucking drink bad dealing with her ass."

Pierre laughed at his boy. "Dog, I swear I'm happy I don't have those problems in my marriage."

"Yeah, bro, you lucky-ass fuck. But I got some shit I need to tell your ass."

Pierre sipped on his beer before saying, "What's up, nigga?"

"Remember how I told you about that bitch me and Nicole had a threesome with on our wedding day?"

Pierre nodded. Yeah, he remembered that story well. His boy was a fool for that shit.

"Well, you know how I told you that Nicole was fucking with that bitch, and it was her idea to run off with my money? Tell me why that bitch is Rodney's baby mama."

Pierre looked confused as he thought about the name Rodney. "Wait a fucking minute. Who the fuck is that nigga? The name sounds familiar, but I don't have a face with the name."

"You don't remember Rodney, my fucking brother?" Mekco asked.

"Oh shit, my nigga. You know the old saying, out of sight, out of mind. I haven't heard his name in years."

"Well, listen to this shit. I found out that he was still fucking with them niggas Brandon and Brian. Plus, he sent his bitch all the way here from Vegas to get my bread."

"Damn, nigga, so how we gonna play this shit out?"
Pierre asked.

"Brother or not, he gotta go. This nigga been coming at
me for a minute now. And the crazy thing is, I didn't even
know it was him behind all this shit."

"Look, bro, you my mans and shit. I'm down for whatever, but Erica due in the next couple of weeks, so I'll be
ready to take that flight after she have the babies," Pierre
said, thinking about how Erica probably would kill him if
he weren't there in the hospital with her when she gave
birth. And with her dad being plugged in with the Lord,
whatever she wanted his fate to be in his life, she had the
call on that.

"I feel you on that shit, so I'm gonna chill for a minute.
Only thing I can do is watch my fucking back, especially if
he ain't succeeding in taking my ass out yet."

Mekco and Pierre chopped it up for about two and a
half hours. Both had really missed each other, and them
not talking was somewhat fucking up business. By the
time they finished talking, it was like nothing ever happened between them.

Pierre came home with his wife's tacos in his hand.
As he walked to the room in the house, his phone began
to vibrate. He set her food on the kitchen counter, then
pulled the phone out of his pants pocket. He was wondering why Erica was calling him. Pierre pulled out his strap
and slowly walked to their bedroom. He was ready to pop
whoever was in his house fucking with his wife.

As he got closer, he could hear crying, and she started
talking, "Oh my God, Pierre, please answer your phone."

Pierre put the gun in his pants as he realized she was
by herself, but something might have been wrong with
her. He pushed open the door to find her crying her eyes
out.

"Baby, what's wrong? I'm here now," he said, wrapping her in his arms.

"My daddy, it's my daddy," she cried out, holding tightly to Pierre.

The first thing Pierre thought was he had passed away, so his heart stung a little. The pastor had just started fucking with him a few months ago. He rocked Erica in his arms, trying to calm her down so she could tell him what happened and where they needed to go.

"I got you, baby; tell me what happened."

"Theresa called. She said he had a heart attack. Baby, they're at Henry Ford Hospital now. I'm so scared, baby. I don't wanna lose my dad," she cried out, barely making it easy for Pierre to understand her words. But he knew he never heard her say that her dad had passed away.

"Baby, he gonna be OK. I promise you that. Sit down. Let me get you some clothes, and then we gonna head to the hospital."

Erica didn't say a word. She let him take charge as he helped her put on her clothes and shoes. As he picked up her purse, he placed her gummy bears in the bag in case she needed them.

Pierre helped Erica into the car before he got in. She still hadn't said anything, and he was all right with that. He knew her mind was going crazy thinking of her dad, and he didn't wanna upset her.

Arriving at the hospital in no time, Theresa greeted them. She pulled Erica into a big hug. "They got him as quick as possible, baby. The doctors have him in the back now and are working on him. I know God is gonna help him and see him through this. The devil will not win this battle."

Erica took the Kleenex from Theresa and wiped her face. "I'm so scared right now," Erica admitted.

"He gonna be OK, baby. Go ahead and sit down. You don't need to be on your feet."

Erica listened to her husband and sat down. Pierre bent down and placed a kiss on her forehead. "They working on him, baby, and everything is gonna be all right."

Pierre and Theresa walked to the vending machine at the end of the hallway.

"Pierre, thanks for getting here so fast and calming her down. I believe that Eric is gonna pull through, and everything will be just fine."

Pierre got Erica a bottle of water from the machine, and then they walked back to the waiting area. Erica was just sitting there spaced out. Pierre handed her the water. "Here, baby, drink some of this water," he ordered.

After Erica drank some, she spaced out again. Pierre sat beside her and held her hand.

Theresa sat two seats down from the couple spaced out herself. She couldn't see herself without Eric in her life. Even though they tried their best to keep their personal business on the low, she really loved that man, and it had been that way for almost twenty years.

After waiting two hours, Erica was leaning on Pierre, knocked out asleep. She couldn't deal with the wait and ended up crying herself to sleep. Theresa was leaned up on the wall, asleep herself.

Pierre watched as a doctor walked into the waiting room. He prayed that it was for them, and he had only good news.

"Family for Eric Collins," he called out.

Pierre shook Erica. "Baby, get up. The doctor's out here."

Erica looked up at the doctor. She couldn't read his face, so she wasn't sure what to think. She was scared, so she slowly got up. Pierre woke Theresa, and she started walking toward the doctor. Pierre could see that Erica was frightened, so he held her hand and walked with her toward the doctor. She squeezed his hand tight as the doctor started to talk.

"OK, the good thing about this is that the EMS got him here promptly so we could stabilize him. Now he is stable, and his vitals are slowly becoming normal. He will be here for a few days for observations."

Erica, Theresa, and even Pierre smiled at the good news.

"Can I see my daddy?" Erica hurried and asked.

"He's recovering from surgery right now and isn't awake, but you guys can see him for a minute or so."

Walking into his room, Erica started to cry a little. She and her dad had their fallouts, but at the end of the day, she thanked him for helping her stay on a straight track. Theresa walked in and went straight to Eric.

She placed a kiss on his chapped lips. "Don't ever scare me like that again," she whispered in his ear.

Knowing he was gonna be OK made everyone's mood a little better. They sat around his bed, having random conversations to cheer each other up. After a good hour, the nurse returned to the room. "OK, guys, it's already late. Is anyone staying?"

Before anyone could say anything, Erica spoke up. "We're gonna leave," she said, pointing to Pierre and herself, followed by, "His wife is gonna stay."

Theresa looked at Erica, and tears instantly formed in her eyes.

The nurse said, "OK," then left the room.

Theresa hugged Erica and Pierre. "I'll call you guys in the morning. Go ahead and get you some rest, baby."

As soon as they got home, Erica took off all her clothes and fell asleep. Pierre wasn't too far behind her. He climbed into bed, pulling her closer to his chest like he did all the time. It wasn't long before he was knocked out too.

The following day, Theresa called, letting them know that Eric was up and actually doing fine. He even got on the phone and talked to Erica, making sure that she was OK even though he was the one who was in the hospital.

Erica was happy that he was doing fine 'cause she wouldn't know what to do without him.

Later, Pierre and Erica went to the hospital to visit him.

"Daddy, please don't scare us no more. I can't take all that," Erica said, hugging him.

"Baby, you know better than that. If the Lord ready for me to come home, there's nothing anyone can say."

Erica sat down. She didn't even wanna start with all that. He might have been speaking the truth, but when something like this hits close to home, you gonna hurt no matter what.

Seeing that things were about to go left, Theresa stood up. "Well, since you guys are here, I'm gonna go freshen up. I'll be back later. Eric, do you need anything from home?"

"Nah, I really don't feel like doing anything but lying here catching up on TV," he said.

Theresa said OK, then left.

"Pierre, you know if my Father ever call me home, I expect you to take over as pastor at the church."

Pierre looked at him like he had lost his mind. "That's nice and all, but I don't think I can do that."

Eric laughed lightly. "Sorry, son, but that was a bad joke."

While her dad laughed, Erica sat there upset.

"What's wrong with you, Erica?" Pastor Collins asked.

"Dad, you joking about you dying, and it's not funny. Do you see how hurt I am?" Erica said, trying not to yell or cry.

"I'm sorry, baby girl. That was a bad joke. You know the saying, sometimes you got to laugh to keep from crying."

After an hour, Theresa returned, and Erica and Pierre were on their way home. She was tired and wanted to go straight to sleep.

Nicole woke up on the living room floor feeling sick as hell with a slight hangover. Lately, she had been fooling everyone, but no one understood her. Mekco thought she was acting out because she needed to be constantly dicked down, so he made sure to keep his dick planted in her pussy. She loved it at first, but that wasn't what she wanted. She wanted something else that he had turned her on to. She had tried so hard to stop drinking because of the baby, but not drinking made her cut up on every-body. Now, she didn't have nobody, and she was OK with that. She could now be at home and drink all she wanted without hearing shit.

Looking at her phone, she saw that her mom had been calling her. Instead of calling her back, she tossed the phone on her bed before stripping. Nicole went into the bathroom to take a nice warm shower. She really didn't have any plans for the day. All she knew was she was gonna sleep most of the day away.

As the warm water flowed down her body, Nicole started thinking about Mekco and then that bitch Mercedes. She wasn't sure why she thought about that bitch, especially after she played her and had her looking stupid.

After drying off and throwing on a T-shirt, Nicole picked up the phone to call Mekco.

"What do you want?" he said, answering the phone on the fourth ring.

"Baby, I need some money for some groceries."

Mekco shook his head. He didn't mind helping her out because of the baby, but she was just acting an ass, and here she go on the phone trying to act like she got some fucking sense.

"Where you at, Nicole?" he asked.

Nicole had never told him where her spot was, but she knew that if she wanted anything, she was gonna have to tell him now. After giving him the address, she jumped up to clean up her mess from the night before. Because she was still a little woozy, she had decided to blame it on the baby. It was a shame that she was gonna lie, and she was really wondering why she didn't get the abortion earlier. She wasn't ready to be locked in the house raising a crying-ass baby.

After a good two hours, Mekco finally pulled up. It was a damn shame how her panties were getting wet just from him stepping through the door.

"I see your ass calmed the fuck down."

"Don't start with me, Mekco," she said as she started to walk to her bedroom.

Mekco didn't have time for her bullshit, and it wasn't in his plan to stay long, either. "Nicole, where the fuck you going? Come get this money, girl," he yelled.

Nicole didn't answer, so he took it upon himself to walk to the back to see what the hell she was doing. As he reached the room, he saw that she was in bed. "What's wrong with you, Nicole?"

"Mekco, this baby got me sick as hell today," she answered.

Mekco was familiar with her being sick from the baby. He took off his coat, then his boots. He climbed into the bed with her and held her like always at his house. Nicole lay in his arms, and at that moment, she felt like Mekco was the only guy who would ever love her, and she would forever love him.

"You feeling any better, baby?" he asked.

"Just a little. I don't know why it seems like when you're around, it acts right."

Mekco laughed. "What the fuck you be doing to my baby when I'm not around?"

Nicole turned around to face him. Now, she was laughing. "I swear I don't be doing nothing."

The two of them locked eyes for a second, and that was all they needed to start making out with each other. Mekco didn't know what it was about her that kept him running back to her. He still loved her, but she was crazy and a fucking headache at the same time.

In a matter of seconds, they both were naked and making love. Their relationship was a little strange, and nobody else in the world could understand them.

"Damn, Nicole, this shit be feeling so fucking good," Mekco moaned in her ear. He was making her feel so good that she couldn't even talk. All she could do was moan out loudly as her legs began to shake while wrapped around his waist.

Mekco sped up his pace as he felt her come all over his dick. It wasn't long before he released inside the place he called home.

The way Mekco looked at things, he and Nicole were gonna be together for life. No matter what they went through, something always pulled them back to each other. It was like the Chingy and Tyrese's song "Pullin' Me Back."

The sound of his phone going off woke Mekco from his sleep. He softly removed Nicole from his chest and got out of bed to get his phone from his pants pocket. He shook his head, seeing that it was Toya's sneaky ass.

"What the fuck you want, girl? Why the fuck you calling me? Where the fuck your man at?"

"Damn, Mekco, hello to you too. Anyway, I thought I should be the bigger person and call first to straighten out some things."

"Bitch, what the fuck I need to do to get straight with you? I know all I need to know. That baby not mine, so what the fuck you calling me for?"

"Look, Mekco, yeah, I got a nigga, but there is a chance that you could be the father. I was fucking both of y'all nigga at the same time," Toya explained, feeling embarrassed by the choices that she had made.

"Man, get the fuck outta my life with that bullshit." Mekco hung up the phone, then got back in bed with Nicole. He wasn't about to let Toya fuck up what he had going on.

Erica set the table for dinner while Pierre and Theresa went to pick up her dad from the hospital. She was happy that he was finally coming home after a long six days.

As she returned to the living room to have a seat, she could hear Pierre's truck pulling into the driveway. She got back up, ready to greet her dad at the door.

As they walked in, Theresa helped Eric sit in his favorite chair.

"Welcome home, Daddy. How are you feeling?" Erica asked.

"I'm good, just starving. You know those hospitals don't be feeding us folks the right way," Pastor Collins said, laughing at his own joke.

"OK, dinner is ready, so come on. Let's get to this table. I hope everyone enjoys 'cause I am tired."

Everyone followed Erica's orders and hurried off to the dining room table. Her dad was the last one to sit. "I'm sorry, Dad, I should have brought your plate out to you."

"It's OK, my sweet daughter. I'm never in too much pain to enjoy your cooking."

Everyone ate their dinner and was full. Theresa offered to do the dishes since Erica had cooked, but Erica said she wanted to do them. Pierre was in the kitchen helping his wife. He really wanted her to go sit her round self down, but she felt like she had to be the one to do something for her dad.

"OK, sir, the dishes are washed and dried. I put the leftovers in the fridge. Do you need anything else before we head out?" Pierre asked.

"No, I should be OK. I just have to take my meds, and then I'll be knocked out soon. Plus, with Theresa here, I should be fine. Where's Erica?"

Pierre chuckled a little. "She had to use the bathroom before we head to the crib."

"Oh, OK. Make sure you take her straight home. She was looking a little funny tonight."

Pierre was confused. As much as he stared at her that day, he hadn't noticed anything. When she finally came out of the bathroom, Pierre watched her closely. He didn't see anything out of place, so he brushed it off.

After saying their goodbyes, Pierre drove Erica home. She was a little too quiet for him, which worried him a bit. He tried not to think about what her dad had said before they had left.

"Baby, you OK? You mighty quiet over there. You OK, baby?" Pierre asked, showing his concern.

"I don't know, baby. I'm just tired and sleepy, I guess."

Pierre used one hand to drive while his right hand rubbed her stomach. He could feel how hard her belly felt and could tell that she was very uncomfortable. "It'll be all right, baby. We almost at the crib. I'll run you some nice bathwater, and you can just soak your body, then go to bed."

"OK, baby."

Pierre got them home in no time. He helped his wife into the house and over to the couch. "Just sit right here and let me run this water for you."

Erica tried to get up. "Wait, baby, I need to find my nightclothes."

"Sit your ass down, E. I told you I got you. I want you to chill. After that, go to bed," Pierre ordered.

He now could see how miserable she was looking. She was something else. She had been smiling like everything was all good, but them babies were draining her, and it was finally starting to show.

Pierre went to take care of everything for his wife. She had about a good three weeks to go, and for those three weeks, he didn't want her to have to worry about shit. Fuck whatever she thought was going to happen. He was putting her ass on bed rest until her appointment the following week.

It wasn't long before Pierre was helping Erica into the tub. "Just relax, baby."

Erica put her head down and started to cry. Her emotions were at an all-time high, and she could no longer hold in her feelings.

"Damn, baby, what the hell you crying for? What's wrong now?" Her crying usually worried him and shit, but nowadays, she would cry if she ate the last piece of chicken and wanted more. So, there was no telling what she was crying about now.

"I'm just so fat and tired, baby. I'm not trying to be mean, but I want these kids out of me."

Pierre kissed his wife. "In due time, my love. These next couple of weeks are gonna fly by so fast."

Pierre walked toward the door, but before stepping out, he turned the Bluetooth speaker on so she could listen to some music. Then he turned around and told her, "Just chill for me, baby. Everything is gonna be all right, I promise you that."

Erica smiled to show that she was feeling a little better. After he left, she lay her head back and allowed the warm water to do its job.

Pierre went into the living room to watch the news. That was something he did every night. Watching the Detroit news sometimes surprised him with all the crimes being committed. After a while, shouldn't shit surprise him, but it did. Detroit was a wild city to live in, with all the murders happening left to right. He owed Erica the world for keeping him off the news for committing a murder.

Mekco walked into Nicole's room. He had been calling her all night and was pissed that she wouldn't answer. Lately, she had been acting a little better, and he had come to the conclusion that they just needed their space. So, some nights, she would go home instead of being up under him all the time.

"Nicole, get your ass up. You ain't hear your fucking phone ringing?" he yelled, walking closer to the bed.

Seeing that she was knocked out, he began to shake her. "Nicole, Nicole, get up. Where my shit at?"

Nicole started mumbling in her sleep, and that's when he knew he was about to fuck her up.

"All this time, I thought you had stopped drinking, and here you go, drunk and shit. Bitch, get your ass up before I fuck up your stupid ass."

Nicole was trying to push his hands off her. She wasn't ready to get up, and that yelling only made her more aggressive.

"Leave me the fuck alone, Mekco," she yelled as she hit him.

Without thinking about his actions, he pulled her out of bed by her hair, making her hit the floor. Unable to control his temper, Mekco kicked her in the head.

Nicole screamed out in pain. "Mekco, stop, please. I'm sorry."

"You right. You is a sorry-ass bitch. How the fuck you carrying my baby and drunk as fuck? I'm not about to deal with this shit."

Nicole pulled herself off the floor as Mekco started walking toward the door.

"I'm sorry, baby. Please don't leave me."

"Bitch, fuck you and your drunk-ass pussy."

Nicole wasn't about to let him walk away from her without a fight. She jumped on his back while scratching at his face and neck. "You not about to leave me, nigga," she yelled.

Not even thinking about his child, Mekco somehow managed to toss her ass on the floor. "Get the fuck off me, bitch."

Nicole still wasn't having it. She got up, charging after him again with her fists swinging like she was crazy. Mekco was trying to avoid getting hit and ended up punching her ass straight in the eye.

While Nicole screamed out in pain, holding her eye, Mekco didn't even stick around to see if she was hurt. He hurried and jumped into his car. As he pulled off, he told himself that he was done with her nutty ass.

Nicole sat on the couch, crying her eyes out, but she wasn't tripping about her swollen eye. She was more hurt that her cover was blown about her drinking and that he left her. She was pretty sure that he was gone for good.

She picked up her phone and dialed his number. She was getting pissed that she had called him five times, and he wouldn't answer. Nicole decided to call one last time and was happy that he answered.

"Look, stupid bitch, stop calling me. I'm done with you."

"Mekco, we can't be over. We married, nigga. Or did you forget?" Nicole yelled into the phone.

"Not no more, bitch. I'm filing for a fucking divorce in the fucking morning. I hate your ass and wish I never stopped you from getting that fucking abortion," he yelled right before hanging up.

Nicole sat there thinking about how to get back at him since he didn't want her. "Bingo," she said as she picked up her phone.

"911, what's the emergency?" the female operator asked.

Nicole put on her best Oscar award act. "My husband just beat me up, and I'm pregnant. Please send someone out to help me," she cried into the phone.

"OK, ma'am, is your husband still in the home right now?"

"No, he ran away," she answered.

Nicole stayed on the phone, playing her role. She gave the operator her address and held the phone, crying as she waited for the EMS and police to show up.

"Pierre, let's go get some tacos," Erica suggested with a huge smile.

Pierre laughed. "You not getting out of the bed unless you have to fucking pee or shit. You lucky I didn't buy your ass some diapers."

"I've been in this bed for almost two weeks now. I'm tired of being in it."

"Well, it wasn't just my decision, E. Your doctor even put your ass on bed rest. You can get up when it's time for you to lie in that hospital bed and push out my babies."

Erica sat up a little more in the bed, then grabbed her gummy bears off the nightstand. "It's OK. I'm gonna pay you back; just watch. You know how some couples wait their six weeks after giving birth before having sex? I might have to triple that number on you, Mr. Miller."

"I see your ass got jokes. Don't make me take that shit, Mrs. Miller."

They both laughed. "I swear you so freaking crazy, baby."

Pierre moved in closer to Erica, and they shared a passionate kiss.

Erica suddenly grabbed her stomach. The pain that she was feeling was nothing that she had felt before. She honestly thought she was gonna die. "Baby" was all that she could scream out.

Pierre jumped up from the bed. "E, you OK?"

"No, baby, it hurt so badly. I think it's time."

Pierre stood there frozen for a second. He thought he was ready . . . until it was time to be ready.

"Pierre, baby, we got to go," she managed to say between her labored breaths.

Finally snapping out of the daze, Pierre gathered her bag and everything they needed before helping her in the car. He drove like a bat out of hell to make sure she didn't have his babies in his vehicle.

After being admitted and given some drugs, Erica was finally about to rest. Pierre sat in the chair beside her bed and called his father-in-law to let him know that his grandbabies were on their way. He even called Mekco but was surprised he didn't get an answer.

The only time Erica had seen Pierre cry was when his mother died the year before, so seeing Pierre cry again while she was delivering the twins touched her heart.

***

That night after visitor hours were over and Eric and Theresa left the hospital, Pierre knew that the twins were gonna be the most spoiled kids in the world.

"So, what you thinking about, baby?"

Erica smiled. "I'm just happy they are finally here and so precious."

Erica held her mini-me while Pierre held his junior. "So, we already know he's a junior, but what about my princess? How about we just name her Princess?"

"Oh no, I'm not having that, Pierre," Erica said seriously.

"Why not? She gonna be my princess."

"Girls with names like that be spoiled and get beat up in school. I don't wanna deal with all that."

"That's when Daddy gonna get the strap. Ain't nobody gonna bother my babies."

Erica thought back to their conversation about baby names. "Whatever happened to the name Paris?"

"Damn, I forgot about that name, but I like it. Can my baby name be Paris?"

"You lucky I like that name too. So here we have Pierre and Paris Miller."

Pierre placed a kiss on Erica's lips. She didn't know it, but she was in for a big surprise. Pierre thought about how he was gonna take her to Paris in a few months just because when he first saw her, her eyes lit up like the lights on the Eiffel Tower at night.

Mekco was pissed the fuck off. Nicole called the police on him and had him arrested. He was so hot about the situation that he started fighting the arresting officers. When it was all said and done, he had got his ass beat. The ho-ass police didn't even let him make his phone call. They threw his black ass in the cell, and that was it.

It was two weeks since he had been there before they finally let him make a call. He was sure they were breaking the rules somewhere down the line and had even threatened to sue their asses.

Making his first call, he dialed Nicole's number. He was surprised that she even had the nerve to answer his call.

"Hey, baby," she softly said into the phone.

Not giving a fuck if anyone was listening, Mekco yelled at her dumb ass. "Bitch, when I get out, I'm gonna kill your stupid ass."

He knew she got his point, so he quickly hung up. He wasn't sure how long he would be there, but he couldn't wait to strangle her ass.